EL DESCONOCIDO:
BUTCH CASSIDY

Also by Suzanne Lyon
in Large Print:

Bandit Invincible: Butch Cassidy
Lady Buckaroo

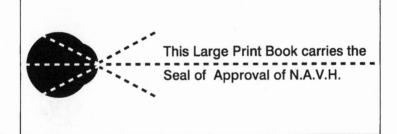

EL DESCONOCIDO: BUTCH CASSIDY

A WESTERN STORY

SUZANNE LYON

Thorndike Press • Waterville, Maine

Copyright © 2002 by Suzanne Lyon

Published in 2003 by arrangement with
Golden West Literary Agency.

Thorndike Press® Large Print Western Series.

The tree indicium is a trademark of Thorndike Press.

The text of this Large Print edition is unabridged.
Other aspects of the book may vary from the original edition.

Set in 16 pt. Plantin by Christina S. Huff.

Printed in the United States on permanent paper.

Library of Congress Cataloging-in-Publication Data

Lyon, Suzanne.
  El desconocido : Butch Cassidy : a western story /
Suzanne Lyon.
      p. cm.
    ISBN 0-7838-9118-0 (lg. print : hc : alk. paper)
    1. Cassidy, Butch, b. 1866 — Fiction. 2. Outlaws —
Fiction. 3. Large type books. I. Title.
PS3562.Y4459D47 2003
  813′.54—dc21   2003047362

For Tim, Michael, and Jay,
with all my love

I have been informed . . . that Boyd and a companion named Maxwell . . . were killed at San Vicente near Tupiza by natives and police and buried as "desconocidos" (unknowns).

Letter from Frank Aller, Chilean vice-consul in the American legation, to Alexander Bensen at the legation in La Paz, Bolivia, July 31, 1909, referring to Harry Longabaugh (the Sundance Kid) and Butch Cassidy.

PROLOGUE

1957

For the dozenth time the young reporter checked his directions, scribbled on the edge of a dog-eared map, as he steered his beat-up '49 Plymouth over the rutted country road. His abbreviated notes — *L on CR 34, R abt 1 mi. past crk, R at fork in rd, just past drainage ditch* — jerked in and out of his field of vision. What the hell kind of directions were these, anyway? Was that indentation with a trickle running through it a drainage ditch, for Christ's sake? But the clerk at the five and dime in town had made it sound as though any idiot, even a citified one like himself, could easily find his way around this blasted no-man's land.

"Oh, sure, not more'n five miles to Miz Harris's place, ya can't miss it," the clerk had assured him, ringing up his pack of Luckies. "She'll be there, all right, she don't have nowhere to go."

So here he was, somewhere smack dab in the middle of Wyoming, praying his undercarriage didn't get ripped out and wondering why in hell he was on this assignment in the first place. Well, in point of fact, there was no mystery to that. As the youngest staff reporter at the Spokane *Herald*, he routinely covered the least interesting, most mundane of happenings around town. The opening of the new barbershop, or the Rotary Club elections — those were the stories that carried Cal Weatherby's by-line. That's why he had jumped at his editor's offer of a chance to do some investigative reporting. Only to find out it involved hunting down some long-lost relative of some long-dead criminal.

"I don't get it, boss," he had argued. "Why would anyone in Spokane care about some dead outlaw from Wyoming?"

"Read the file," his editor had grumbled, tossing a thin folder across the desk. "This particular dead outlaw may have lived out his golden years right here in Spokane. There's a lot of folks might be interested to know they've been friends and neighbors with the notorious Butch Cassidy."

Weatherby had grudgingly opened the file. "He can't be all that notorious . . . I've never heard of him."

"That, kid, is either because you're young or ignorant or both. In his day, Butch

Cassidy was one of the most . . . well . . . respected, not to mention successful, bad guys there was. Made more friends than enemies, so they say. Just read the file and get your ass down to Wyoming to check it out. Supposedly the man had a long-lost girlfriend around there, maybe even a bastard kid or two."

Weatherby read the file. Intrigued, in spite of himself, he did some more digging and came away convinced of two things. First, Butch Cassidy had died forty years ago in some backwater South American village and had, therefore, never graced any of the front porches in Spokane, Washington. Second, if the outlaw had ever been with a woman long enough to call her a girlfriend, it had escaped the notice of every print reporter or historian who had ever written on the subject. Nonetheless, after a week of poking around Wyoming, he had turned up a couple of rumors that thoroughness required he check out. Hence this uncomfortable journey to the home of — he glanced at his notes again — Mrs. Mary Harris.

Pulling onto an overgrown side road just past the dubious-looking ditch, he inched slowly along, cresting a slight rise, and dropping down toward the river or creek or whatever passed for water in these parts. He braked in front of a ramshackle cottage, its paint peeling, its shingles drooping, but surrounded by pretty flowers and flanked by a well-tended vegetable garden. Squawking chickens loudly protested his arrival as he stepped from the car, brushing the dust from his pants and straightening the knot in his tie. He pocketed his pad and pen and knocked solidly on the frame of the screen door. The inner door stood ajar. Peering through the screen, he could see a woman emerge from a room at the back.

"Yes?" she asked pleasantly, pushing the door open a few inches.

The reporter smiled broadly, noting details of her appearance that he would later commit to paper. She was a handsome woman, in her mid-sixties probably, had most likely been quite attractive in her youth. Her iron gray hair was pulled back from a dark, square face that looked lived in, if not particularly aged. Her most striking feature was her eyes — ice blue beneath dark brows that showed no sign of gray.

"Who is it, Grandma?" A young girl skipped into the room and peered out from behind the older woman's back.

"Ma'am," he tipped his hat, "my name is

Cal Weatherby. I'm a reporter with the Spokane. . . ."

"A reporter?" She let the screen door fall shut.

"Yes, ma'am," he hurried on. "I'm doing a story for my paper on the outlaw Butch Cassidy. Have you heard of him?"

The woman folded her arms across her chest and stared at him a moment. "Ain't nobody around here hasn't heard of Butch Cassidy."

"Right. Well, see, I ran across some friends of yours, that is, assuming you're Missus Mary Harris . . . ?"

She continued to stare at him with no change in expression. He forged on. "Anyway, Missus Harris, some friends of yours told me that you might have a particular reason to know Butch Cassidy better than most, that you may indeed be related to him. Is that true?"

Her ice blue stare deepened. Still she said nothing. Finally she turned to the girl peeking out from behind her and asked her to remain inside the house. Closing the inner door firmly, she let the screen door slam shut and faced Cal Weatherby, hands on hips.

"Ain't no friends of mine told you that," she declared with narrowed eyes.

Weatherby cleared his throat. "Well, ma'am, friends or acquaintances, I'm not sure which, but more than one person hinted to me that you might be . . . Butch Cassidy's daughter."

"Nothing but rumors!" she said heatedly. "People are always spreadin' rumors about me!"

"Why is that?"

"None of your business!" She turned to go.

"Look, Missus Harris," he rushed on, "if you say the man wasn't your father, then that's that. Who, after all, would know better than you? But do you mind my asking who was your father?"

"I mind you asking anything. Now get on outta here, I got work to do."

"But if Butch Cassidy wasn't your father, why can't you tell me who was?"

She raised a shaking finger and pointed it at him angrily. "I don't have to tell you a damn thing! Now, you're on my property without an invitation, and in this part of the country, that's a shootin' offense. I was you, I'd hightail it real fast!" Yanking open the door, she slammed it behind her, rattling the windowpanes and kicking up dust on the front stoop.

Muttering to himself, Weatherby returned to his car, tossed his reporter's pad on the front seat, and backed down the road, leaving a trail of dust and flying feathers in his wake.

Peering from behind faded curtains, Mary Harris watched him leave. She put a hand over her racing heart. Turning on her heel, she pushed open the swinging door into the kitchen, snapped an apron over her housedress, and began pummeling the bread dough rising on the counter. The young girl, small and dark with the same cool blue eyes as her grandmother, eased into the room, taking in the older woman's thin, pursed lips and knitted brow.

"Grandma," she ventured, "is everything OK? Did that man upset you?"

Mary pounded the dough mercilessly. "Yes, sugar, he did. Lotta nerve comin' around here, askin' questions that ain't none of his business."

"What kind of questions?" the girl asked, although she had been listening at the window and knew very well what the man had said.

"Ain't none of your business, neither, sugar."

The girl slipped into a kitchen chair, nervously fingering the edge of a woven place mat. She knew better than to cross her grandmother, but if what she had heard was true. . . .

"Grandma," she tried again, "what that man said . . . about your father . . . some of the kids at school say the same thing. Rolly Grouse, he says your mama wasn't ever married. That's not right, I know it's not! I told him he was a lyin' little son-of-a . . . well, I told him off, all right!" Her blue eyes flared as she watched her grandmother's stiff back.

Mary gave the dough one last punch and turned to face her granddaughter, anchoring her floury hands on sturdy hips. "Sugar, people'll say all kinds of things just to get a rise out of ya. Best to just ignore talk like that."

"So it's not true, then," the girl pressed. "Great-grandpa Ole *was* your father?"

The older woman snorted and turned back to her bread dough. "He wasn't much of a father, but he's the only one I ever knew."

The girl shifted in her seat, unsatisfied with this response. "Grandma, please. I want to know."

Mary's shoulders sagged. She slapped the dough into a bread pan, slid it into the oven, wiped her hands on her apron, and came to

14

sit at the table. "Louisa," she looked lovingly at the pretty child, named after her own grandmother, "you're likely gonna hear all kinds of things growing up around here. Some of it's true, some of it ain't. Like I said, it's best to just ignore all of it. What I'm gonna tell you now, I tell you just so you know in your own mind what's true and what's not. But these are private things, you see, things that nobody outside of our family needs to know."

Louisa nodded solemnly, her eyes riveted on her grandmother's face.

Mary took a deep breath and exhaled it slowly. She had told this story once before, to her daughter, Louisa's mother, a troubled girl who had found not peace of mind, but shame and bitterness in its telling. Shortly after learning the truth, the young woman had gotten pregnant, given birth to Louisa, and gone off to the big city, leaving the baby with Mary to raise. But Louisa was different — stronger, more resilient, more like Mary's own mother.

Folding her hands on the place mat in front of her, Mary began calmly. "Sugar, you never knew my mother . . . she died long before you was born. Her name was Mary Boyd, and she was a remarkable woman. She was married, for over thirty years, to

Ole Rhodes, a feat in itself, seein' as that man must have been as difficult to live with as a bad itch. But she stuck with him, birthed two children by him, saw one of 'em die young. She was a good wife and a good mother, but I don't think I ever saw her truly happy a single day in her life." The old woman paused, lost in distant memories.

"Grandma," Louisa said after a while, "your mother had three children, didn't she? You, Aunt Hazel, and the boy who died young."

Nodding gently, Mary rose to stare out the window over the kitchen sink. "That's right, sugar. Ole Rhodes was not my daddy. He finally took me in, after Mama threatened to leave him if he didn't, but, for the first six years of my life, I lived with an old Indian woman. Mama would come to see me as often as she could, but Gray Hair raised me, took care of me."

"Then . . . who was your father?" Louisa whispered.

Mary turned and fixed her startling eyes on her granddaughter's tense face. "This is what my mother told me. Working in the general store one day, she met a man, a strong, kind man who had ridden all night in search of a doctor for a sick child. She fell in love with him, the kind of love that never dies no matter what life does to throw up obstacles or pull you apart. They had a brief time together, but he wasn't the kind of man who settled down. He was a roamer, a seeker, a free spirit . . . he was an outlaw."

Louisa swallowed hard. "Was he Butch Cassidy?"

"Mama never called him that. She called him George. And she never told him about me. He never knew he had a child." The older woman's eyes misted. This was the greatest of her sorrows — that her father had never even known she existed.

"What happened to them, Grandma?"

Mary shrugged, dabbing at her eyes with the end of her apron. "Mama married and went on with her life, and Butch . . . well, it's a long story."

PART I
1896–1897

CHAPTER ONE

"Dear Lord," intoned Herbert Bassett, his bristly gray beard vibrating on his dark suit coat, "we gather in Your name on this Thanksgiving day to praise You for the blessings You have bestowed upon us . . . our homes, our families, our friends, the abundance of nature that surrounds us with beauty and provides us with sustenance."

He raised his head and scanned the crowded dining room, his bespectacled eyes halting on two figures in the back. "Please hold in Your safekeeping all those sharing in this meal today, especially those who have chosen to dwell outside the boundaries of mankind's society but who have so graciously provided the feast we are about to enjoy."

The two men in back exchanged glances from beneath bowed heads. The shorter one smiled and winked.

"Finally, Lord," Bassett continued, his voice becoming husky, "help us to remember loved ones who are no longer with us, most especially my beloved wife, Elizabeth, who must surely inhabit the brightest star in Your firmament. Amen."

"Amen." Butch Cassidy turned to his tall companion and spoke under his breath. "The old guy really loved her, I reckon."

Elzy Lay shrugged, turning toward the kitchen. "So did every man in this room, at one time or another. There was a lot to love."

"Ain't that the truth," agreed Butch, thinking back to his own affair with the beautiful and refined Elizabeth Bassett. But that had been seven years ago, and Butch, now thirty, had no trouble chalking the episode up to youthful indulgence. Still, he had to smile as the memory of that summer washed over him. On the lam from the Telluride hold-up, his first bank robbery, he had come to Brown's Park and hired on at the Bassett ranch, only to find himself stuck in the middle of a tug of war between Elizabeth and her fifteen-year-old daughter, Josie. Although in the ensuing years he had evaded many a lawman's bullets, he often thought escaping intact from the Bassett Ranch had been his neatest trick.

Following Elzy into the kitchen, Butch removed his suit coat and tied a butcher's apron over his white shirt and vest. He rubbed his hands together enthusiastically. "OK, boys, what do we do first?"

Harry Longabaugh, more widely known as the Sundance Kid, stood at the stove, dishing up gravy. "I thought you was in charge of this operation, Butch."

"Hey, I had the idea . . . am I supposed to do everything?"

Harvey Logan, looking like he wanted to kill somebody, anybody, pulled at his starched collar. "Some idea," he winced. "I ain't never been so uncomfortable."

"Now boys," — Butch placed a placating hand on Logan's shoulder — "Elzy and I agreed that putting on this Thanksgiving dinner was the least we could do to thank all the folks here in the Park for . . . well . . . looking out for us all these years. Ain't that right, Elz?"

"Yeah, sure," Elzy replied distractedly. He stood before the huge roast turkey, a carving knife and fork held suspended in the air. "Should I start with the legs, you s'pose, or the breast?"

The three outlaws stared at the bird in puzzlement. "Tell you what," Butch suggested, "let's let old Herb carve it up. That's a job for the master of the house, ain't it? OK, Kid, you bring the mashed potatoes and gravy. Harvey, grab them cranberries, and I'll hand out these rolls."

With a flourish, the four, aproned outlaws marched into the dining room, Elzy leading the way, carrying the magnificent turkey. The guests, about thirty in all, erupted into laughter and applause, tickled that these rough fugitives from justice would act as their servers for the day. Butch grinned broadly. There was nothing he loved as much as a party. Unless it was sleeping under the stars in a high country meadow where the only sounds were the coyotes howling and the wind rustling the tall grass. This paradox had not escaped his notice. He just figured that's the way he was — he liked being on his own, unless it happened he felt like having some company.

The room hummed congenially as the quartet of waiters moved back and forth between the kitchen and the crowded tables. Butch grabbed the coffee pot off the stove and began filling cups. As he leaned toward Josie Bassett, she looked up and gave him a shy smile, her creamy complexion showing almost no sign of the freckles she had sported as a young girl. Butch smiled back and even gave her a little wink; safely married, Josie was no longer a threat.

Moving on down the table, he hefted the

heavy pot in the direction of Ann Bassett's cup. With a little gasp, Ann reached out and lightly slapped his hand. "My goodness, Mister Cassidy, what on earth do you think you're doing?"

"You don't want coffee?"

"Of course I do, but not served out of that old thing!" She pointed at the huge iron pot in his hand. "We do have a lovely silver service for special occasions. And while I'm offering hints on etiquette, I might mention that one does not reach all the way across a person's plate to fill a coffee cup. Leads to elbows in the face, don't you know?" Tossing her dark head, she tittered loud enough for the whole table to hear. "Really, Mister Cassidy, you can rob banks and hold up pay trains without the flicker of an eyelash, but when it comes to serving coffee at a grand party . . . well, that's a different story!"

Butch colored. Ann Bassett, Josie's younger sister, had been an eleven-year-old brat when he first met her, and nothing about her had changed. But there was no sense in letting her get to him. "That's true, Miss Ann," he admitted. "Good thing I picked outlawing over waitering, ain't it?"

Everybody laughed as Butch beat a hasty retreat. Slamming the offending coffee pot onto the top of the cook stove, he started opening cupboard doors, muttering to himself. "Silver service. What the hell's a silver service, and what the hell's it got to do with coffee?"

Harry Longabaugh entered the room, carrying empty serving dishes. Of the four bandits, he looked the most natural wearing fancy clothes, as he tended to pride himself on his sartorial taste. "What's that you say, Butch?" he asked, scraping more potatoes into a bowl.

Cassidy turned to his friend and leaned against the cupboard, his arms crossed over his chest. "Kid," he mused, "you grew up back East, in polite company, so to speak. What do you do with a silver service?"

"Jeez, Butch," Harry complained, balancing dishes as he pushed the door open with his hip, "I ain't got time to teach you the finer points of living."

"I ain't got time to teach you the finer points of living," Butch repeated to the swinging door as he turned to resume his search.

"Is this what you're looking for?" Josie Bassett McKnight stood before him, bearing an elegant silver tray and coffee service.

He smiled at her appreciatively. "Yes, ma'am, I reckon so."

Smiling back, she set the tray down and started to fill the sugar bowl from the canister.

"Hold on there!" Butch took the spoon from her hand. "You ain't supposed to be doing any work today. Just let me take care of this."

Josie dropped her eyes, her hand burning where he had touched it. "I don't mind. Truth to tell, I'd rather be in here." She laughed nervously. "Ann gets to be a little much. I hope she didn't embarrass you."

"Naw, I guess I'm used to her antics." He retrieved the old black coffee pot and began filling the elegant silver one. "She ain't changed much, even if she is all grown up into a real beauty . . . though she can't hold a candle to her sister."

Butch smiled at the young woman kindly, not meaning to do more than compliment an old friend. But Josie blushed bright red and threw a hand up to pat her strawberry blonde French twist. She had never gotten over her infatuation with Butch Cassidy, married and a mother although she might be.

She sighed. "Oh Butch, I wish you hadn't've left here that summer. Everything changed with you gone. There wasn't any more . . . I don't know . . . excitement once you left."

27

"No excitement in Brown's Park? That's hard to believe."

"Are you teasing me, Butch?" Josie pouted. "You of all people should know that for all its wild reputation, nothing much ever happens in Brown's Park, unless you count Val Hoy's barn burning down a few years back. But that summer you worked for us . . . I'll never forget it. You were racing horses for Mister Crouse, and you won big against that filly out of Green River, remember? Almost everybody in the Park turned out to watch, and, when you pulled it out at the end, we were all so proud of you!"

Butch set the pot back on the stove. He remembered quite well the day Josie spoke of, although what came to mind most vividly was the way her mother, Elizabeth, sitting tall and lady-like atop her fine Thoroughbred, had tipped her head to him as he passed by on his victory lap. That small gesture had meant more to him than all the hoots and hollers from the rest of the crowd.

"Maybe I shouldn't have left," he said quietly. "That was a good time, and Lord knows it ain't all been a bed of roses since then."

Josie gave him a troubled look. "I heard

about a lot of it. How you got arrested for horse thieving and spent some time in prison."

"That's true . . . the prison part, not the horse stealing part. I ain't saying I've always kept my hands clean, but that particular time they was pure as the driven snow. You know, Josie, I ain't done half the things people say I've done. Look at your sister . . . she accused me just now of robbing trains. I ain't ever robbed a train! It might not be a bad idea, but I ain't done it yet. Once you get a reputation of a certain kind, people'll believe anything about you."

Josie moved toward him. "I know what I believe about you," she said, her eyes shining.

"Josie. . . ."

"Hear me out, now. You know I'm not happy, Butch. Jim's not the man I thought he was when I married him. I've always cared for you since I was fifteen years old and you showed up on our doorstep, tired and dirty, but sporting that huge grin of yours. Please, Butch, I don't want to live this way any more. I want to go with you. . . ."

"Josie!" He grabbed her shoulders roughly. "Stop talking this nonsense. You got no idea what kind of life I lead. Believe me, it ain't fitting for a lady like you."

"Please don't say that. . . ."

The door swung open, admitting Elzy, Harry, and Harvey. "Dessert time!" Elzy announced, dumping a slew of dirty dishes on the table.

Ducking her head, Josie fled from the kitchen, tears brimming in her eyes.

"What the hell, Butch?" Harry teased. "Can't you never keep your hands off the women?"

Dessert was served, the tables cleared, and still nobody left the party. The men pushed the furniture against the walls; Sam Bassett brought out his fiddle; Joe Davenport his guitar; and Josie was prevailed upon to play the zither, although she looked a bit forlorn in the midst of such gaiety. Everybody danced, from the tiniest toddler to old Herb Bassett himself. Butch squired his share of partners, young and old, around the floor, laughing, joking, and cutting up in his inimitable way. Ann Bassett managed to place herself in the dashing outlaw's path more than a few times, flashing her dark eyes and tossing her curls as she made some smart remark or other.

Finally, as light was just beginning to tinge the eastern sky, the party drew to a close. Fellow Brown's Park residents said their good byes, and those from farther away retired to the bunkhouse. Butch wandered through the empty rooms, picking up stray cups and moving furniture back in place. He came upon Elzy and his new bride, Maude, snuggling together on a wine-red horsehair sofa in the parlor.

"Ain't you two got some place better to do that?" he growled. For some reason he didn't want to admit, it bothered him to see Elzy and Maude so happy together. He had always believed the outlaw life to be incompatible with love and marriage. Yet here was his best pal, smitten with the pretty Maude, and still his most reliable lieutenant in all their nefarious ventures. And Maude seemed not the least troubled by her husband's occupation or the type of life it required her to lead. Whether holed up in their cabin in Brown's Park or camped out in a remote cañon in Robbers Roost, Maude cheerfully followed her man. According to Elzy, Maude never even complained when he had to be gone for long periods of time. Well, there wasn't likely more than one woman in the world like that, and Elzy had found her first.

"Now, now, friend, don't be a poor sport." Elzy disentangled himself from his wife's embrace and unfolded his lanky frame.

"Seems to me there was plenty of young ladies giving you the eye tonight. Hell, that Ann Bassett was stuck to you like a burr to corduroy. If you're lacking for female companionship, there ain't nobody to blame but yourself! Come on, Maude, let's go home." He turned to his chastened partner. "You coming?" His expression told Butch that his company was not exactly desired.

"Naw. You two go on. I'll bunk here for a few hours. I ain't seen Logan or Longabaugh in a while. Guess they went hunting for a bottle with Charley Crouse. Reckon I'll look them up." Waving the newlyweds off, Butch ran a tired hand through his sandy hair. He had no intention of joining his friends for a late night tipple, but he needed to save face in front of Elzy who, he feared, viewed him as something of a pathetic case.

Back in the kitchen, he poured himself one final cup of coffee. It occurred to him that a little shot of red-eye might help induce sleep. Wondering if old Herb was the type to keep a secret stash, he started going through cupboards, pushing aside cans and boxes in search of a hidden bottle.

The kitchen door opened and in walked Ann Bassett, hands on hips. "What on earth are you looking for?" she inquired, her tone as nasal as a crow's caw.

"Nothing." He closed the cupboard door. "Just making sure everything's put away proper."

Ann arched a dark eyebrow and crooked her finger at him. "Follow me." Leading the way into the dining room, she reached into the buffet and extracted a bottle of Old Crow. "You may have some of this on one condition . . . that you let me join you."

It was Butch's turn to look skeptical. "I ain't interested in adding corrupting the morals of a young lady to my list of crimes."

"Don't be silly! I'm eighteen years old, and this would hardly be my first taste of whisky." Very decisively she uncorked the bottle and poured two generous tumblers. Carrying both glasses, she strode into the parlor and sat on the horsehair sofa most recently occupied by Elzy and Maude. Patting the seat next to her, she smiled saucily. "After all, not every girl has the opportunity to share a drink with the famous Butch Cassidy."

Sighing, Butch took a seat. It was late and he was tired, but good manners required that he spend at least a few minutes humoring the lady of the house, which, with Elizabeth dead and Josie married, was now Ann's position.

Clicking her glass against his, she took a

long sip, closing her eyes as the warm liquid slid down her throat. She was pretty, all right, with her thick dark hair and round face. A narrow black velvet ribbon tied around her neck held in place a gold locket that lay just at the hollow of her throat. Butch wondered, in a detached way, what it would feel like to kiss that soft, white skin. It would most likely be pleasant, but not worth the trouble.

Ann opened her eyes and caught him studying her. She smiled over the rim of her glass. "Penny for your thoughts."

"I was thinking that it's funny you should call me famous. I ain't all that well known, outside of my friends and whatever family still owns up to being kin to me. There might be a couple of sheriffs who've heard my name, but I wouldn't exactly call that being famous."

"But of course you're famous! Why, everybody in this part of the country knows about you. Around here, you're famous for being a good neighbor as much as anything else."

"Well, that's something then. That kind of fame I guess I can live with." He stared at his drink, running his finger around the rim of the glass. He had started to feel melancholy, and he did not like feeling melancholy. But something about the day — being back at the Bassett place, or seeing Maude and Elzy together — was dredging up old memories. Memories of Elizabeth and their brief spark of attraction. And, always and forever, memories of Mary. Mary Boyd was a flame that burned inside him yet, one he feared would never be extinguished.

Ann finished her drink in one swallow and set it down, leaning across Butch to reach the table. She pulled back only part way, letting her body stay in contact with his. "So, Mister Cassidy, where are you headed next? Or is it a secret?" She giggled.

Butch summoned a smile. "Me and the boys'll hole up somewhere for the winter."

"Just you and the boys?" she asked suggestively.

"Well, Maude'll be there, of course. Maybe she'll bring a lady friend with her so she don't have to be the only woman in camp."

Leaning closer, Ann murmured in his ear. "What if I came as Maude's lady friend? Would you like that?"

Butch fought the urge to laugh. She was just a kid, for Christ's sake; she didn't know what she was saying. But the thought of spending an entire winter with Ann Bassett was enough to make a man cringe. She might be easy on the eyes, but that mouth on her!

"Listen, Annie," — he patted her knee and rose tiredly — "you got better things to do than hang out with the likes of me. Some women have tried it before, and there seems to be general agreement . . . I'm a hopeless case."

He was expecting her to rant and rave, maybe throw a tantrum like she used to do as a bratty eleven-year-old. Instead, she sat back with a smug smile on her face. "We'll just see about that, Mister Cassidy."

CHAPTER TWO

Maude Lay sat on the verandah of the elegant Palmer House in Green River, Utah, sipping her tea. She did this every morning . . . sat and waited and watched for somebody — exactly whom, she did not know — to come fetch her. After two weeks of this idleness, she was beginning to lose patience, although she knew someone had to come soon; Elzy could not stand to be apart from her for long.

Gazing over the rim of her china cup, her eyes traveled down the length of the broad avenue. She caught sight of a rough-looking character heading her way, his shoulders bobbing in time with his crooked gait. Wearing a coarse cotton shirt, woolen coat and trousers, he looked no different from the scores of other men in this bustling railroad town, but somehow Maude knew he was the one. She turned to her companion, a dark-haired, hazel-eyed beauty, and said: "He's here."

The other woman followed Maude's gaze and nodded slowly.

Sure enough, the man clomped up the stairs to the verandah, paused to take his bearings, and then shuffled over to the two young ladies. "You're Maude Lay?" he said, his voice like scraping gravel.

"Yes," she replied, staring at his peculiar eyes, one blue, one brown.

He removed his hat, revealing a head full of long, stringy hair. "My name is Blue John. Elzy sent me for ya."

"Yes," she said again. "I've been waiting for somebody. Are you ready to take us now?"

Blue John's brow furrowed, and he looked in confusion at Maude's companion. "Us? Nobody told me there'd be two of ya."

"It was a surprise to me, too," Maude said. "A very pleasant one. Let me introduce Miss. . . ."

"Hold on now." The grimy outlaw rubbed his stubbled chin in consternation. "I don't know as I can take somebody back to camp who ain't expected. Butch'd have my head."

The two women shared an amused look. "Not in this case," said Maude. "I'm sure Butch will be very pleased to see my friend."

"Yes, Blue John," the other woman spoke for the first time. Rising gracefully, she turned a dazzling smile onto the grizzled

38

longrider. "Don't worry, everything will be fine."

"Well . . . all right then. Let's load up your stuff. We got to be on our way. It'll take two days to get where we're going."

The heavily laden wagon pulled up on a ridge overlooking a landscape of sandy swales and hidden depressions. "Roost Flats," Blue John announced, his strange eyes scanning the horizon.

Seated next to him, Maude breathed in the fresh desert air. "How much farther?" she asked.

"See that knob yonder?" He pointed far to the south. In the back of the wagon, the dark-haired woman rose from her seat on an ammunition box and followed Blue John's outstretched arm. "The pack train's gonna meet us there."

"Did you hear that?" Maude turned to her friend. "We're almost there."

The woman nodded and smiled, her eyes pinned on the distance.

Hours later, agonizingly long hours for the anxious Maude, the wagon drew up in a cedar-shaded park where several horses and mules grazed lazily. Two lanky figures reclined beneath a tree. One of them jumped up and met the creaking conveyance before it had lumbered to a stop. Swinging his bride down from her seat, Elzy twirled Maude in the air. "Hey, baby, didja miss me?" They shared a long kiss.

Awakened by the commotion, Butch raised his head off the ground and blinked out into the sunlit clearing. Coming slowly to his feet, he stepped out of the shadows, stifling a yawn. He paused in mid-stretch, his eyes riveted on the woman in the back of the wagon.

"Etta!" A huge smile broke over his square-jawed face.

The dark-haired woman's eyes lit up. "I'm here, Butch. Are you glad to see me?"

"Damn' right I am!" He helped her to the ground and then stepped back awkwardly, suddenly all too aware of Elzy and Maude, still clenched lip to lip. "How'd you find me? I must be getting sloppy in my old age if it's that easy to track me down."

"You told me how to locate Maude, remember? I sent a letter to her parents' house, and she wrote back, telling me to meet her in Green River." Etta paused, searching for something in the outlaw's pleased, yet guarded, expression. "You are happy to see me, aren't you Butch?"

"Absolutely." He surrendered to a smile that crinkled his pale blue eyes. "Winter

40

camp's starting to look a hell of a lot more inviting! Come on, Blue John, let's get this stuff loaded on the mules. Say, Elzy, think you could lay off there long enough to lend a hand?"

Sorting through the wagon's load, they picked out the women's things and a few immediately needed supplies and packed them onto their string of animals. Then the four of them set off down the trail, leaving Blue John to follow with the rest of the gear. By the time they reached camp on the eastern rim of Horseshoe Cañon, it was nearly dark. Etta could see two large tents and one smaller one in the cedar-lined clearing. Half a dozen men moved about the camp; as the newcomers neared, they looked up from their various chores and eyed the women closely. Etta felt a sudden thrill, knowing these were some of the most wanted thieves in the West.

While the men unloaded the pack string and tended to the animals, Etta and Maude offered their assistance to the camp cook, a tall, dark young man who spoke not a word as he went about his business. Maude took no notice of the taciturn cook, chattering on about their "invigorating" journey and assuring Etta that in the light of day she would see what an enchanting place they had come to.

41

Soon, with much talk and gruff camaraderie, the gang gathered around the campfire to eat. Elzy wolfed down his plate of venison and beans and grabbed Maude's hand, yanking her to her feet so quickly her coffee spurted onto her lap. Grinning lasciviously, he tipped his hat to his bachelor friends and escorted his wife to their private tent.

"That boy's never been much of an after dinner conversationalist," commented Butch, idly rubbing the ears of an ugly little black dog.

Etta, wrapped in a warm blanket and holding her own cup of coffee, dropped her eyes as the men laughed, a few casting suggestive looks her way. Sitting across the fire from her, Butch noticed her uneasiness. He got up to pull the coffee pot out of the hot coals and moved around the fire to refill her cup, and then his own. He lowered himself easily to sit next to her. *Staking his territory?* Etta wondered.

"These hardcases ain't much for manners, Etta," he said. "Has anyone bothered to introduce himself?"

She laughed. "Maude made a brief pass at introductions, but I'm not very good with names. It would certainly help to hear them again."

"This here's Joe Walker, a fine hand with the horses." He nodded at a man to his left who tipped his hat politely. She smiled a greeting. Butch continued around the circle. "Bub Meeks, an old cowpunching buddy of mine . . . Harvey Logan . . . the less you know about him, the better" — the men, except Logan, chuckled — "that tall cuss is Ben Kilpatrick, and the half-breed over there who calls himself a cook is Indian Ed Newcomb. This old bear on my right we call Silver Tip, which you'd know why would he take off his hat. Come on, Tipper, show the lady your pretty silver locks there!" Embarrassed, the thick-shouldered Silver Tip ducked his head, ignoring the taunts of his compatriots. "Well, he'll have to take his hat off someday. Maybe you'll be around to see it. The story goes he's the spitting image of his mama . . . that when he first caught sight of her when he was still a-squallin' in the crib, it scared him so bad his hair turned gray!" All the men chuckled, including Silver Tip who seemed not to mind the good-natured ribbing. "Blue John oughta be getting in with the wagon tomorrow," Butch went on, "and we're expecting one or two more to show up as time goes by, but, for now, this is it. What about it, sweetheart, think you

43

can stand to spend all winter with these plug-ugly varmints?"

Pulling the blanket tighter around her, Etta looked at each man in turn. "I'm looking forward to it," she said firmly, determined not to appear weak or frightened.

The conversation turned to manly things — horses, hunting, guns. Etta listened silently. Evidently the gang was preparing for another hold-up — where, they did not say — by graining and training a select group of horses. There was much debate over how many and which horses to use, each man promoting his favorite mount. Although left out of the conversation, Etta hung on every word, fascinated by the intricate planning such a venture required.

Suddenly it was very late, and the men, one by one, got up to go to their tents. Butch stayed put, drinking his coffee and staring thoughtfully into the fire. Soon there was just the two of them left. Shivering, Etta pulled the blanket close.

"This must seem mighty cold weather to a Texas gal," said Butch.

"I'm no Texas gal. That just happened to be where I was when you found me." Etta looked away. "Do you really mean it that you're happy to see me? I know you weren't expecting me, even though back at Fannie's you did ask if I wanted to spend the winter with you."

He reached over and gently tipped her chin so that she looked into his eyes. "I'm real glad you came. I've been feeling down-right lonely of late, and you're just what the doctor ordered."

Etta melted. "Oh, Butch, I'm so pleased you feel that way. Because I almost didn't come. I thought perhaps, when you left San Antonio, you'd return to that girl you ran away from . . . that maybe she would agree to meet you in Robbers Roost."

The outlaw stared at her with narrowed eyes. "What are you talking about?"

"I'm talking about the woman you're in love with," Etta said boldly. "You never mentioned her, but I know she exists. When you showed up at Fannie's door, you were the hurtingest man I'd ever seen. There's only one thing can make a man look like that . . . a lost love."

Butch rose abruptly and moved to the other side of the fire. "That's all over with," he rasped. "It don't matter now."

Etta was silent. It was obvious to her that this woman, whoever she was, did still matter to the stocky cowboy who stood be-fore her, his shoulders hunched protectively into his thick coat. But she did not want to argue the point. After all, she did not need to be loved by Butch Cassidy, just to be wanted by him.

An extraordinarily beautiful woman, Etta had been in the unique position, for a prostitute, of being able to choose which men would receive her favors. That, plus the fact that the madam of the house, Fannie Porter, viewed her more as a daughter than an employee had ensured Etta a relatively comfortable existence. But the dark-haired beauty did not crave comfort, or stability, or even money. She craved adventure. And when Butch Cassidy had walked in the door of Fannie Porter's San Antonio establishment, Etta knew adventure had come calling.

Butch walked over, pulled her to her feet, and resettled the blanket around her shoulders. "When you met the pack train earlier today," he said, brushing a stray hair from her cheek, "I thought at first you was someone else. Not . . . the woman you mentioned before, but a gal from Brown's Park who favors you some, leastways in the looks department. I sure was glad it turned out to be you."

Etta smiled happily.

"Come on," — he circled her waist with one strong arm — "let's go bunk down."

46

She held back. "With all the rest of the camp?"

"Now, Etta, give me a little credit. Elzy and me pitched another tent way over behind them rocks. We ain't going to be anywhere near the rest of the gang."

Snuggling into his embrace, Etta looked at him with wide eyes. "Oh, Butch, everything about you and this place and this night excites me! All that talk around the fire about pulling the next job . . . I just want you to know you can trust me. Maybe I could even help you somehow."

He laughed. "You want to join the gang?"

"Why not?" she breathed. "I can do everything they can."

He grinned, and then kissed her hard. "Everything they can and a lot more besides," he whispered.

CHAPTER THREE

As Maude had promised, Etta became entranced with their high desert hide-out. For the most part, left to their own devices, the women ventured beyond their camp on the eastern rim of Horseshoe Cañon to explore the labyrinthine gulches, ravines, and side cañons of the Roost. Etta marveled at the multicolored sandstone ledges and cliffs, leaking plum-stained streaks of desert varnish; at the juniper and piñon dotted meadows; at the wind-creased dunes, long since transformed to stone. Although the days were generally mild, the nights turned cold, and it was not unusual to wake to snow crusting the rocky hillsides and stunted brush. But by noon, the winter-slanting sun would lap up the snow in all but the most shaded areas.

"Look!" Etta cried one day as she and Maude walked across the bench lands on the western rim of the cañon. She pointed to a herd of wild horses prancing across the desert far in the distance, the dust kicked up by their flying hoofs rising to mingle with the purple outline of the snow-capped Henry Mountains. "What freedom," she murmured, transfixed by the awesome sight.

"They won't be free for long," Maude said. "Someone will catch them sooner or later."

"Probably," Etta agreed reluctantly. "I hope I won't be here when that day comes."

"Most likely not." Maude resumed walking, hands clasped behind her. "The men will send us away pretty soon, you know. Spring's just around the corner . . . that means all the training they've been doing will soon be put to good use."

"I'm well aware of that. I don't see why that means we have to leave, however."

Maude stopped and stared. "What on earth can you mean? When it's time to pull the job, they'll break camp . . . everyone will scatter. Elzy would never leave me here unprotected."

"No, no, dear, you misunderstand me. Of course, I realize we can't stay in the Roost indefinitely. But why should we be sent away, you to your parents and me to . . . wherever, as though we are playthings to be discarded once we've outlived our usefulness? Why shouldn't we be allowed to help, for heaven's sake? I, for one, am fully capable of holding a relay string of getaway horses."

Her companion shook her head in disbelief. "You've gone completely loco. Do you have any idea how dangerous it is to rob a bank? People don't just smile and hand over the money . . . 'Here, take it, it's yours.' No, they tend to get a tad upset and do nasty things like send out posses to track the robbers down and shoot at them. Outlawing's a crazy life to live, for a woman or a man. When I think of Elzy. . . ." She broke off, her voice choking.

Etta placed a comforting hand on her arm. "I didn't realize you felt that way. You've always seemed so carefree when it came to Elzy's outlawing."

Maude wiped a tear from her cheek. "That's how Elzy wants me to be. If I showed any worry, or nagged at him, it would be over between us. He loves his way of life more than he loves me."

"I don't believe that," Etta said firmly.

"Well, it's true. Until now, it hasn't really mattered. I've been willing to put up with the fear and worry because I love him enough for the both of us. But . . . well, things are about to change." She looked at

50

her friend with a mixture of apprehension and anticipation. "I'm pregnant, Etta."

"Maude! How wonderful!"

"Is it? I'm not so sure. It changes everything." Sighing, Maude clutched her elbows. "I want Elzy to quit the gang. I don't want to raise a fatherless child, and, if he keeps on this way, he'll wind up dead or in prison."

Etta shrugged. "Maybe not. Anyway, this is a young man's game. He'll probably give it up in a few years."

"And then what? Ride on the fringes of the gang, like Blue John or Silver Tip? Be an errand boy for the ones who call the shots? I can't see Elzy doing that. He and Butch are a lot alike. They're smart, and they like to be in control. No, if Elzy's going to change careers, he needs to do it now, while he's still young enough to build a new life."

They walked in silence for a spell. "Have you told him about the baby?" Etta asked.

"Yes. He seemed happy enough about it. I don't know, perhaps I shouldn't have saddled him with another worry right now. Who knows if he'll even be alive six months down the road."

"He will be." Etta linked her arm through Maude's and patted the young woman's

51

hand. "With all the planning and preparation they've been doing, it'll come off like
clockwork. Elzy will be home to take care of
you and the baby in no time."

Maude sighed again. "You're sweet to say
so. I'm sorry I jumped all over you about
wanting to help the gang. I'm just touchy
right now. In my condition, I couldn't consider doing such a thing, but I guess there's
no reason why you shouldn't. Have you
mentioned it to Butch?"

"Only in passing," Etta admitted. "I'm
waiting for just the right moment."

"Now that I think about it, I wouldn't be
at all surprised if Butch likes the idea . . . he
often does crazy things. Anyway, it would be
hard for him to turn you down, he's so sweet
on you."

"Go on with you," Etta scoffed. "I only
wish it were true."

"But it must be! Why, he treats you like a
queen!"

"Oh, I've no complaints about that. Butch
is as nice as they come. But sometimes, you
know, he has a way of looking at me . . . I'm
not sure I can describe it, but it's as though
he's not seeing me. His eyes look into mine,
but his thoughts are somewhere far away.
And when he holds me, he's gentle and
loving, but, in some odd way, he's not really

there. Oh, I don't know. . . ." Etta shook her head in exasperation.

"It's just men, honey. They've always got something on their minds besides you . . . food, horses, guns. It doesn't mean they don't love you in their own way."

"Hmm, maybe you're right." Sliding down a slickrock boulder on her rump, Etta held out a hand to help Maude. "But it looks to me like our fearless leader is carrying one gigantic torch, and it doesn't burn for me."

"So he's told you about Mary Boyd?"

Etta pulled Maude's hand through her elbow as they continued walking. "No, my dear, he has not. But I'm all ears. . . ."

While the women were exploring the western rim of the cañon, a lone rider approached the outlaw camp from the north. Covered in road dust, he sat his mount confidently, his small, narrow eyes endlessly scanning the horizon. Every now and then, he raised a gloved hand to stroke his thick, dark mustache. When he was close enough to make out the tents, he held up in a grove of cedars and rolled a smoke, watching carefully. Satisfied that all was in order, he moved on, hallooing his arrival. Butch and the others stepped out to greet him.

"You made good time, Kid. Any luck?" Elzy held the horse's bridal strap while the traveler dismounted.

"You could call it that," he answered, turning to spit.

Butch reached out to grab Longabaugh's shoulder. "Here, let the man rest a mite before giving him the third degree. Blue John, take care of his horse. Come on, Harry, grab you a drink of water and something to eat."

Longabaugh filled a plate and gathered with the rest of the crew around the ever-smoldering campfire. Normally a quiet man, at least when sober, he stared a bit uneasily at the circle of hard-bitten faces that stared back. Unlike Butch, and to a lesser extent, Elzy, Harry Longabaugh did not enjoy the spotlight. He ate slowly, and, when he was finished, he drew a clean handkerchief from his pocket and dabbed at his mouth.

"Indian Ed, bring this man some coffee," Cassidy directed. "OK, Kid, give us the lowdown!"

Longabaugh drew up his knees, his boot heels scrabbling over the rocky ground. "It's gonna be a bitch," he growled. "Don't even know where to start, there's so god-damned many problems."

Troubled looks passed around the fire.

Only Butch seemed unperturbed by this announcement. "Just start talking. Tell us everything you can think of. The more details we know, the easier it'll be to come up with a plan."

Longabaugh acknowledged this suggestion with a curt nod. "Like you told me, Butch, I went and got myself hired by the coal company. You figured that'd be the only way to scout the town without raising no suspicion, and you was right . . . Castle Gate's a company town through and through. Anybody who ain't employed by the Pleasant Valley Coal Company sticks out like a preacher in a whorehouse."

"That just means we'll have to make a quick strike," Harvey Logan broke in, mumbling through his thick, black beard. "Ain't no reason to hang around town ahead of time, is there?"

Longabaugh cast him an annoyed look. "Yeah, Harvey, as a matter of fact there is. If you'd shut up and let me talk, I'd be getting to it."

"Let him talk now, fellas." Butch nodded a go-ahead to his weary lieutenant.

"We can't just ride in on the day the payroll arrives 'cause no one in town knows exactly when that'll be," Harry went on grimly. "The money comes in from Salt Lake about every two weeks, but never on the same day or at the same time. Not even the paymaster knows for sure. When it does come in, they blow a certain blast on the mine whistle as a signal to the workers, and then the paymaster walks over to the station to get the money. Both times I watched him, he came back to the office, carrying a leather satchel and two or three bags of coins. By this time, most of the workers are milling around the office waiting for their money, which is another problem . . . there'll be a lot of witnesses, probably some toting guns."

Again the bandits exchanged dark looks.

"What's the office itself like?" Elzy queried. "Easy to get into and out of? Any chance of posing as a miner and stealing the loot once you get inside?"

Longabaugh shook his head. "Don't see how. The office is on the second floor, and the only way in or out is by an outdoor staircase. The workers line up on the stairs, go inside to collect their pay, and then go back down. There'd be such a crowd blocking the stairs, the only way to get away in a hurry would be to sprout wings and fly."

"So we take the money while the paymaster's coming back from the train," Butch said, thinking aloud. "What about the getaway route?"

"I was getting to that." Longabaugh stroked his mustache, refusing to be hurried. "Most likely, that's the biggest problem we got. See, there ain't hardly one god-damned horse in that entire town. It's set down in this narrow cañon where there ain't much room to get around. All the miners just walk everywhere. They's mostly bohunks who wouldn't know the back of a horse would they see it anyways. Some cowboy prancing into town is gonna attract a hell of a lot of attention. I've been racking my brain, trying to figure out how we steal a payroll and get away without no horses to ride, but damned if I can do it."

The scout's words were greeted with frowns and grumbles around the campfire. Maybe this heist was just too dangerous to pull off. Maybe Cassidy had, for once, bitten off more than he could chew.

Butch sat back, one strong hand rubbing his chin, oblivious to the mutterings of his colleagues. He pondered for a while, then checked back in with a confident smile. "This payroll's too big a haul to give up without a fight. I got me an idea or two, but I got to sleep on it. Anything else?"

"That's about it," Longabaugh shrugged.

"Good, 'cause all this talk about money's made me work up an appetite! Hey, Indian

Ed," he called, "get me some grub, will ya? Dang it, where's the women, Elz? That no good half-breed won't let us eat till the ladies show up."

"Women?" Harry's head shot up.

"Hell, yes, boy!" Grinning, Butch clapped him on the back. "Didja think we was roughing it?"

Just then, Maude and Etta emerged from the cedars, laughing, their dresses streaked with reddish dust, strands of hair falling about their flushed faces. Maude took one look at the group of men and clasped her hands in delight. "Etta! Look who's here . . . the Sundance Kid!"

CHAPTER FOUR

One hundred brush strokes a night. Fannie had told her it would keep her hair healthy and shiny, so Etta observed the ritual religiously. She found it to be a soothing way to end the day — brushing away stray cares and worries with each stroke. Sometimes Butch, watching her in the glow from the lantern, would playfully try to throw her off count, calling out wrong numbers until she lost track of the right one. Sometimes he would take the brush from her and finish the job himself, his rough hands snagging in her silky tresses, but his touch gentle and sure. "One hundred," he would whisper, and then lean forward to kiss the nape of her neck. Those were the nights when Etta felt most at peace.

Tonight she sat cross-legged atop the soft blankets and robes that made up their bed, applying the brush automatically, her thoughts racing like one of the wild mustangs she had seen that afternoon. For the first time since coming to the Roost, she felt unsettled, restless, as though she had made a wrong turn somewhere and gotten lost. It was not like her to feel this way, for Etta was usually sure-minded about what she wanted and how to get it. If she saw an opportunity, she would pick up and follow it, never regretting where the path led. But here she was, jumpy and nervous, completely confused as to the source of her discontent.

The tent flaps parted, and Cassidy entered, looking preoccupied. He dropped down next to her, pulled off his boots, and lay back, head propped in his hands, eyes narrowed in thought. For several minutes, the only sound was the rasp of Etta's brush.

She sighed deeply, wishing that her lover could be his usual carefree self tonight. Now, more than ever, she needed his quick smile and soft touch. Laying her brush aside, she nestled against his chest, her fingers toying with a button on his shirt. "What's on your mind?" she asked, resting her chin on his shoulder.

He draped an arm around her absentmindedly. "Thinking about the job. Based on what Harry said, it ain't gonna be as easy as I thought."

"Tell me about it."

So he did, recounting the various obstacles Longabaugh had reported. "Some of the others want to give it up . . . think it's too dangerous. But it'll work. I just need to come up with a plan. There ain't nothing can't be done if you got a plan."

"Well, that's your specialty, Butch," Etta murmured. For some reason, all his talk of plans and strategies failed to excite her tonight, although ordinarily she hung on every word. She shivered slightly, and he pulled at the heavy buffalo robe, covering them both.

"Who is this Harry Longabaugh?" she found herself asking. "Just another hard-case?"

"Harry? Nah, he's all right. Little rough around the edges when he's had a drink or two, but he's got class. Knows how to handle himself, and he's god-damned fearless, near as I can tell."

"Fearless?" Etta echoed.

"That's right. Ain't a-feared of nothing. He's a good man to have on your side in a pinch."

Etta shivered again, although she was toasty warm underneath the buffalo robe. "Why is he called the Sundance Kid?" she asked.

Sitting up, Cassidy removed his shirt and pants and slid back under the robe. He pulled Etta close, stroking her arm. "Guess he spent some time in jail in Sundance, Wyoming, for horse thieving. Way he tells it, he tried to bust out about every other day, but the governor still pardoned him for good behavior. He's one lucky son-of-a-gun."

Etta breathed into his chest, softly fingering the cross he always wore around his neck. She could feel Butch's muscles relax as he slipped into sleep. Tired from her outing with Maude, she wanted to follow him there, but she couldn't; her blood pounded, and her brain raced with jittery, unconnected thoughts. For the hundredth time, she wondered about Mary Boyd, the woman who, she guessed, had given him that cross. What had brought them together, and, more importantly, what had torn them apart? Was he just too much of a free spirit to stick with one woman for long? Maybe they were all like that, these men she had come to know around a winter campfire: outcasts and renegades who refused to live by the rules, who desired their dangerous freedom more than the love of a good woman, or even a bad one. Look at Elzy Lay. If his young wife was correct, he preferred outlawing to the married life.

But why did it have to be one or the other? Why did the woman always have to play the long-suffering role, alone with her worries

62

while her man risked everything for the thrill of it all? If she could find a man who wanted her by his side wherever he went, who would love her for the chances she took as much as for the refuge she offered, there was a man who could capture her heart.

Perhaps Butch was that man, if she put it to him just right. But, no, it should not be something she had to convince him of; it should just be something they both felt, deep in their bones. It should be something she could see in his eyes, something that would tell her this man was up to the challenge, something like she had seen tonight in Harry Longabaugh's somber gray eyes as he had stared at her across the flickering campfire.

Restlessly Etta turned in Butch's sleep-heavy arms and reached to douse the lantern.

He stirred. "Etta? You and Maude need to start packing your things tomorrow. Elzy and me decided it's time you girls headed back to town for a while."

Etta froze, disappointment swelling her breast. "Why so soon?" she said softly.

"We're gonna be training in earnest now. We may need to move at the drop of a hat. It's best if you and Maude go somewhere safe."

Etta waited, silent and still, until the sound of his deep, even breathing returned. "Oh, Butch," she whispered, "can't you see I don't want to be safe?"

The next day Cassidy had left by the time Etta woke, gone over to a neighboring outfit to trade some horses they told her. Maude had already begun packing, and the rest of the camp was down by the makeshift corral, watching Joe Walker break a wild stallion. Bored and unhappy, Etta wandered over to the campfire and poured a cup of thick, gooey coffee. Scrunching up her nose at the bitter brew, she drank it nonetheless, drawing in deep breaths of clean desert air in between sips. Sunday, Butch's little black dog, pressed his nose to her leg. She knelt and petted him, wondering why his master had gone off and left not only her, but his dog, too.

The sound of boots scraping on rocky soil made her start. Turning, she saw Harry Longabaugh leaning against the chuck wagon, one foot crooked in front of the other, watching her intently.

"Mister Longabaugh! I didn't see you there." She smiled, one hand at her brow to block the bright sun.

He touched two fingers to his hat in

greeting, a hat, Etta noticed, brushed clean of the dust that had settled on it during yesterday's journey. The rest of him appeared equally tidy — pressed trousers, clean shirt, shined boots. A remarkable feat for someone who had ridden across the desert for two days and slept in a tent the previous night.

He continued to stare at her with his dark, deep-set eyes. Etta felt herself calming, the anxiety of last night and this morning seeping away as she stood in the sun, a cool breeze rustling her skirts, smiling at this unusual stranger.

"No need for formality," he said finally, coming toward her. "Call me Harry."

"Very well. And you may call me Etta."

He nodded and looked as though he were about to say something, but thought better of it. Nervously he brushed his mustache, letting his gaze wander down to the men at the corral.

Etta raised the cup to her lips, pondering the difficulties of conversation with a man like the Sundance Kid. The normal rules of social discourse did not apply to people such as themselves — outlaws and prostitutes who couldn't talk about the past and wouldn't talk about the future. For them, there was only the here and now . . . only the moment that unfolded with each passing second. Still, there was a sense of freedom that came with living only for the present.

"It seems, Harry," she said, tossing away the remains of her coffee and giving him a tentative smile, "that I am to be sent away shortly. My presence is deemed to be a hindrance to the serious business at hand. Even now, I should be helping Maude with the packing. But I've always wanted to explore farther up the cañon, beyond where one can go on foot. Today would be a perfect day for a ride, don't you think? Would you mind accompanying me, that is, if you're not too busy doing other things?"

His eyes locked onto hers. "Just let me saddle the horses."

Within the hour, they were mounted up and headed north, following the dry creekbed that had carved out a jagged rent in the earth. Etta had packed meal provisions and told Maude of her plans. She had no idea what Longabaugh had said to the other men, and she did not care. What did it matter what any of them thought, even Butch, should he learn of their little escapade? He had no claim on her, especially not now, when he had told her she must leave. For all she knew, once Blue John had deposited her back in Green River, she would never again lay eyes on Cassidy or his gang. No promises had been made, no assurances received. No past, no future . . . just now.

They rode in silence, Longabaugh in the lead as their horses picked their way down the narrow sandstone ledges until they reached the floor of the cañon. Cattle trails wound throughout this level area choked with low bushes and grass. Etta came abreast of Harry and smiled again. The rocks echoed with numerous sounds — jays calling from high up in the cedar ridges, grasshoppers buzzing and clicking, the horses swishing through the stirrup-high sandgrass. They covered quite a distance before Longabaugh pulled up and looked her in the eye.

"I'm a plain-spoken man, Etta," he said. "I don't know no other way to be. So tell me . . . how is it you come to be here with Cassidy?"

She gave a small shrug. "Fate, I suppose. Do the details really matter?"

A rabbit skittered through the brush, startling his horse. Bringing it around expertly, his gaze never wavered. "What do you think fate has in store for you now?" he asked.

"I really couldn't say. You know, for a plain-spoken man, you're really rather mysterious. Are you trying to tell me something?"

"Damn' right. I want you to be my woman."

Etta caught her breath, shocked and not a little angry at the presumptuousness of this well-turned outlaw whom she had only just met. Yet crowding out the irritation was a palpable sense of excitement. It was as though he had thrown down the gauntlet, daring her to match his boldness. Stomach fluttering, cheeks burning, she spurred her mount, hoping to buy time.

They rode for another hour, sticking to the rocky creekbed whenever possible so as to avoid detouring into one of the many side cañons. The sun rose straight overhead, and the sky was an uninterrupted azure backdrop for the pink cliffs. Coming around a bend, the walls on either side opened up a bit, revealing a valley floor studded with sagebrush and catclaw bushes.

Suddenly Longabaugh reined up. "Jesus," he murmured, "what the hell is that?"

Etta squinted into the distance, at first not sure what it was he saw. Directly ahead of them was a huge sandstone cliff, its wavy striations varying in color from rust red to pink to ivory. At its base were some brown markings. She threw up a hand to shield her eyes, and then inhaled sharply. The wall was full of drawings — pictures and scenes created by some ancient peoples who had inhabited this beautiful cañon eons ago.

"Indian paintings," she whispered. "Let's go closer."

As they rode nearer, the drawings became larger and more distinct. There were human figures, some no more than inverted triangles with heads, some with arms and legs, carrying spears or bows and arrows. There were animals, horned or with elaborate antlers. There were flocks of sheep guarded by shepherds, hunters, and powerful-looking figures who might have been tribal leaders. The art was primitive, but breathtaking.

Dismounting, they climbed up the rocky embankment to get as close as they could, Longabaugh holding out his hand to assist Etta. Tentatively she fingered one of the ocher-colored markings. "Amazing. How many hundreds, maybe even thousands of years have these been here, I wonder? And what were the people like who made them?"

"Look at this." Harry had wandered down to the first set of drawings, which depicted a tall, ghostly figure with eerie, round eyes surrounded by half a dozen smaller, more solid shapes. "What do you make of this? Kind of gives me the shivers."

"Maybe it shows them worshipping their god."

Longabaugh cocked his head, perusing the scene. "Looks like a hell of a scary god, if that's what it is."

A smile tugged at Etta's lips. "I take it you believe in a more benevolent deity."

"I believe in two things . . . myself and Mister Colt," he said, resting his hand on the .45 at his hip. Then, with a sly look, he grabbed her arm and pulled her close, their faces no more than an inch apart. "I could believe in God, if He would let me have you."

Etta pushed away, her heart in her throat. "You shouldn't make fun of such things."

"I ain't never been more serious," he said levelly. "You know something's happening here, Etta. Don't try and deny it."

"I don't know anything," she replied, climbing back down toward the horses, "except that I'm hungry. Let's eat here, shall we? Maybe the holy ghost" — she nodded over her shoulder at the mystical figure on the wall — "will enlighten me."

Spreading a blanket, she set out their simple provisions — biscuits, some bacon left from breakfast, dried apples, and a precious chunk of cheese. Longabaugh picked some berries off a nearby bush and added them to the assortment.

"What are these?" Etta asked. "Are you sure they're edible?"

"Barberries. You can eat 'em raw, but they're even better made into jelly. We could take some back with us . . . maybe Indian Ed would put them up."

"Unfortunately I won't be around long enough to taste any of it. Maude and I leave in just a few days."

He said nothing, but reached out and drew one finger along the back of her hand where it rested on the blanket. Etta felt a chill and involuntarily glanced at the ghost-like figure looming above them, its huge eyes seeming to see everything. When she turned back, Harry was, as usual, staring at her.

"You're an odd man," she blurted out. "You have hardly anything to say other than to keep repeating how much you want me. You haven't even asked where I'll go when I leave here, which I'd think would concern you at least a little bit if you're as crazy about me as you say. I can hardly believe you mean any of it, but then I see the way you look at me, and it . . . well, it takes my breath away."

He leaned closer, his eyes like magnets drawing her to him. "Etta," he said, "like I told you, I'm a man of few words, and, when I do talk, I say exactly what I think. No beating around the bush. 'Course, that can be a problem when you're talking to women, 'cause they usually don't want to hear the plain truth. But you ain't just any woman. I could tell the minute I laid eyes on you that you and me was meant to be together. There's no need to ask where you're going, 'cause, wherever it is, I'll be right behind you." His gaze shifted to her mouth, mere inches from his. "This ain't something you or me can change, Etta. It's meant to be."

Close, so close now, their lips almost touching, Etta forced herself to pull back. "You presume too much, Mister Longabaugh. What makes you think I feel the same way as you?"

He laughed lightly and got to his feet, unfazed by her rejection. "Because it's fate, Etta, that's why. You were meant to meet Cassidy so he could bring you to Horseshoe Cañon so I could find you and we could be together from now on. I know you believe in fate, sweetheart."

Etta began gathering the remnants of their dinner, no longer certain what she believed. It was true she was attracted to him and strangely thrilled by his plain talk and lack of artifice. And when she looked into those gray eyes of his, she felt herself falling, mesmerized by the intensity she saw in them. But it was all too sudden. Other men had declared their undying love for her on similarly short notice and not a one of them was still around to vouch for it. Why should Harry Longabaugh be any different? Still, when he looked at her, there was something there she had never before seen in a man's eyes. Something that said his desire was not just for her, but for what they could be together.

"It's time to head back," she said, busying herself with repacking the saddlebags.

He watched her for a minute, then grabbed his canteen and gave it a shake. "Better fill this up or we'll run out before we get back."

She looked at him in surprise. "Where will you find water? The creek's dry as a bone."

"Come with me, I'll show you."

They walked back down the creekbed a hundred yards or so until they came to a tiny, crack-like cave Etta had not noticed on their way in. Water seeped from its sides, not the alkaline stuff one found up on the bench lands, but clear, clean rainwater. Squatting on his boot heels, Harry scooped aside sand from a narrow depression in the rock floor and waited for the water to gather. Cupping his hand, he took a sip, then looked up at Etta. She knelt beside him and drank. It tasted sweet and was so cold it hurt her teeth. Letting the water gather again, he immersed the canteen, watching the air bubbles surface and break.

"You're a very smart man," Etta said, wondering how he could bear to keep his hand in the icy water. "How did you know there'd be water in this cave? You can't tell from the outside."

"Oh, I ain't so smart," he said softly, "not smart like Butch is anyways. But I've lived in this country ever since I was a boy, mostly having to fend for myself, and you can't hardly do that without learning a trick or two. I'd've been dead twenty times over if I hadn't figured out how to find water in the desert."

Etta turned toward him, studying his profile. He was handsome, but not remarkably so. His nose sported a prominent bump, and she guessed his voluminous mustache had been grown to camouflage a weak upper lip. But, at this moment, he seemed quite remarkable, and more intriguing for having shared a bit of his past with her. She found herself wanting to know more.

Rising, he held out his hand. She grasped it and, coming to her feet, slipped on a wet stone, falling against his chest. His arms came around her, and he stared down at her flushed face. "This is how to find water in the desert," he whispered.

A jolting sensation rocked her to the base of her spine. Pressing close, she pulled his head down, desperately seeking his mouth. Too late, she remembered a first kiss should be a gentle, testing sort of thing, not this wild tasting of lips and tongue, but she couldn't help herself — she was lost.

His response was immediate — fire meeting fire — and she forgot any embarrassment she might have felt over her own wanton behavior when she realized that he possessed no more control than herself.

Quickly now he picked her up and carried her back to the horses, laying her down on the blanket they had spread before the magical ancient drawings. Covering her body with his own, he murmured over and over again: "I love you, I love you, Etta." Hardly believing her own ears, she repeated the words back to him, allowing herself the luxury of thinking that, at last, she had found her fate.

Later, under the watchful eye of the holy ghost, they talked about what to say to Butch. "We can't carry on behind his back," Harry insisted. "It wouldn't be right. We got to tell him first thing and let the chips fall."

Etta smiled and brushed the hair out of his eyes. "I hardly think Butch is going to fight you over me. It's not as though he has to defend my honor."

"Still, I could tell by the way he treated you last night he feels something for you."

"I think what Butch feels toward me is gratitude for having made him a little less lonely this winter. He's in love with someone else, you know. Maude told me all about her. He'll never admit it, but this woman hurt him terribly. I would never do anything to add to his pain, but, quite frankly, I don't think it's in my power to hurt him. We had our little interlude this winter, and it was pleasing to both of us, but it's time to move on. Butch is all wrapped up in planning the next job, and as for me" — she leaned over and kissed him lightly on the lips — "well, let's just say I've got other things on my mind now, too."

Despite Etta's assurances, Harry insisted that they confront Cassidy immediately, but, on their return to camp, his plan was thwarted.

"He ain't back yet," Elzy informed them. "Said he might be gone two or three days. Listen, Etta, I know you probably don't want to leave without seeing him, but I got to ask you a favor. Maude ain't feeling too good, seeing as she's in the family way and everything" — he blushed bright red — "and I'm real anxious to get her back to her folks' house. Blue John's willing to take her out tomorrow, and I'd be grateful if you'd go with them. It'd ease my mind considerable if she had another woman with her."

Etta's heart sank, but what could she say? Promising Elzy she would be ready to leave in the morning, she went back to her tent and penned a note to Butch, explaining what had happened between her and his trusted friend, and assuring him he would always hold a special place in her heart.

Very late, after the rest of the camp had long been asleep, Harry came to her tent. They made love and held each other close until dawn, making each other promises that vanished in the air like a frosty breath.

CHAPTER FIVE

Wednesday, the 21st of April. Blustery winds scooted cotton-puff clouds across the sky, whipping up dust devils that careened against the carbon-rich walls of Price Cañon. Deep within those walls, the Pleasant Valley Coal Company sent its miners to extract from the earth the fuel of industry. All manner of men, many speaking the guttural language of their Eastern European home- lands, had come to the tiny town of Castle Gate, Utah, to work the mines. Many were family men who diligently sent their pay checks to wives and mothers struggling to feed hungry mouths. For most, the greatest excitement they knew was spending fifty cents at Caffey's Saloon on Saturday night. Until the 21st of April.

Bolstering the saloon's outside wall, Butch Cassidy and Elzy Lay held their reins loosely, surreptitiously keeping an eye on Castle Gate's comings and goings. Despite Harry Longabaugh's accurate report of the rarity of horses in the town, not a single passer-by gave the pair more than a mildly curious glance. Butch had theorized that while a cowpuncher sitting astride a typical cowboy's saddle might arouse suspicion, even the inhabitants of this narrow cañon would be accustomed to the sight of a couple of jockeys riding in and out of town, working out their mounts. As a result, Butch's mare, Babe, and Elzy's big gray, Kid, were saddleless, sporting only racing surcingles.

Butch gazed idly in the direction of the train station, his slouch hat disguising sharp eyes that searched for any sign of commotion indicating the impending arrival of the noon train. Elzy sighed and spat the toothpick he'd been working over into the dust. "I'm thinking, if it don't come today, the jig's up."

"Why's that?" replied Butch, still eyeing the station.

"This is the third day we've been riding into town on our 'race horses'. People are going to start wondering what we're up to. Case in point . . . yesterday some local started admiring Kid and asking all sorts of questions. I told him we was getting ready for some matches up in Salt Lake City, and that shut him up, but, I'm telling ya, we're starting to attract attention."

His words were punctuated by a sharp whistle that reverberated off the cañon walls. It repeated in a series of blasts that was an obvious code. The two men looked at each other.

"Your worries are over, pal," Butch said, "she's on her way."

The pair swung calmly onto their bareback mounts and moseyed over to the coal company's headquarters. Amid a gathering crowd, Butch dismounted and handed the reins to Elzy. Yawning broadly, he sank down on a box at the foot of the wooden steps, crossed his legs and tipped his hat forward, looking for all the world like a man trying to catch forty winks.

A few blocks away, the train rumbled into the station. At the top of the stairs, a door slammed. Two pairs of feet descended rapidly, one producing the familiar *clomp* of boots, the other a soft, flapping sound. As the pair came into Butch's field of vision, he was amused to see that Carpenter, the paymaster, had not bothered to change out of his bedroom slippers. The man shuffled along with his clerk, Lewis, at his heels. Cassidy pulled back his own booted foot to let them pass unhindered.

"It would be the noon train, just when I've sat down to dinner," Carpenter complained, removing a napkin from the front of his shirt and stuffing it in his coat pocket. "I've got a mind to send you by yourself next time, Lewis, but you'd probably make a mess of it."

From beneath his lowered hat, Cassidy caught Elzy's eye and grinned. "Like taking candy from a baby," he murmured, and leaned back comfortably against the wall. For a brief second, he imagined what tomorrow's headlines would look like: *DARING BANDITS GET THOUSANDS IN GOLD! BOLD STRIKE BEARS MARK OF BUTCH CASSIDY AND HIS INTREPID GANG OF THIEVES.* He loved that word — intrepid. Etta had called him that once, and, when he asked her what it meant, she told him it meant fearless, very brave. Of course, he was not fearless. It was stupid to be fearless because if you were not afraid of anything, that's when you'd start to make careless mistakes. But he was brave, and smart, and careful, and that's why he was a free man while so many others of his ilk sat behind bars.

In a matter of minutes, Butch could hear Carpenter and his clerk returning. "Stand back now, out of the way," grumbled the paymaster. "What's the rush, boys? Nobody gets a penny until Lewis has had a chance to enter this payroll in the books."

Grudgingly the miners gave way, some disappearing into the general store that occupied the first floor of the coal company offices, others retreating across the street to Caffey's. Only a handful remained, eager to be the first to collect their pay.

Butch stole a glance at the approaching duo. Carpenter toted a large leather satchel and two sacks of coins. Lewis carried one bulging sack. Behind them, Elzy, still atop Kid, quietly moved in closer, blocking their path in case they tried to run. The paymaster set one slippered foot on the bottom step and froze, a six-shooter pressed to his temple.

"Drop them bags," came the whispered order.

Carpenter complied immediately, but his young clerk stood in stunned disbelief, his mouth agape.

"You, too!" Butch demanded. "Hand it over!"

With a strangled cry, Lewis bolted for the front door of the store, knocking into Babe as he scrambled past. Already skittish, the mare backed and snorted nervously. Elzy held onto her reins firmly and threw his partner a warning glance. With no time to spare, Butch scooped up the bags and tossed them to Lay. Surprised, Elzy caught them but lost his grip on Babe's reins. A rifle shot pierced the air. Babe reared and bolted down the street. Spurring his mount, Elzy cornered Babe against the railroad trestle and managed to grab her reins with one hand, juggling the moneybags in his other.

"Get on! Get on!" he yelled, ducking low on Kid's neck as more shots split the air. Cassidy came running, leaping aboard the terrified Babe. The two flew down the narrow cañon, pursued by a volley of gunfire.

A mile or so downcañon, they pulled up behind a section house where they had cached their gear. "Damn, I hate getting shot at," Butch complained, hurriedly throwing his saddle across Babe's back.

"You're in the wrong line of business then," panted Elzy, yanking on his cinch strap.

Tearing open the leather satchel, Butch upended it. Out poured hundreds of shiny twenty-dollar gold pieces. "Well, I ain't gonna look for a new career just yet!" he chortled. He checked the other sacks, which were equally stuffed with silver and currency, and transferred everything to a canvas bag.

"Hey, what's that?" Elzy cocked his head, listening.

Butch peered around the corner of the section shack and pulled back sharply, pressing his back to the wall. "It's the engine, coming back down the line!" As he spoke, the locomotive shot by with Carpenter, the paymaster, hanging out the engineer's cab. Safely hidden, the two outlaws watched it speed toward Price, some nine miles away.

"Well, at least we know Walker did his job and cut the telegraph wires," Butch said, tying the loot behind his saddle. "Bad luck that ninny Carpenter figured out another way to get word to the sheriff in Price."

"As fast as that engine's going, the sheriff's gonna have heard the news before we get there."

"Maybe. But it'll take him a while to get up a posse. Meantime, we'll swing west of town and pick up our relay. By then, we're out of the cañon and can split up if we need to."

Breathing heavily, the men put the spurs to their mounts, following the path of the locomotive that had just passed them by. Back on the flats, they circled west, by-passing Price where by now the sheriff had most likely heard the news. At Gordon Creek, they switched horses. Their new mounts were not as fast as Babe and Kid; Butch had not planned on needing speed at this point in the getaway, but rather staying power to get them the forty miles to Mexican Bend on the San Rafael River. He had not counted on word getting to Price so soon, and he wondered whether the new horses could outdistance a posse. But their only choice was to push forward and try to lose their pursuers in the desolate country south of the Reef.

They had just skirted Desert Lake when Elzy pulled up, pointing to a trail of dust cutting in from the side. "Rider coming!" he shouted.

Butch scanned the barren landscape. "Nowhere to hide! Split up! We'll meet back at the Roost."

"Wait!" Elzy held up a hand. "Looks like Walker."

As the outlaws stilled their winded horses, Joe Walker rode up, concern evident on his crusty features. "You boys is too dang' popular! There's a posse called out already. I cut the wires, but some genius rode the engine all the way to Price to notify Sheriff Donant. Came screeching into the station, hanging on the whistle so everybody knew something was up!"

"We know," Elzy said. "It passed us while we was still in the cañon. How many's riding?"

"Plenty. Donant got word out to Huntington and Castle Gate so there's three groups heading this way. Can't be more'n a few miles back. You got the horseflesh to get out of this pickle, Butch?"

"We got a fresh relay stashed at Mexican Bend. Ain't but a few more miles. Still, I don't like it. There's too damn' many of them." Cassidy trotted out. Lay and Walker hung back, exchanging worried looks. Cassidy motioned them forward. "Here's what we do, boys. At Mexican Bend, we'll transfer the money to you, Joe. You take the fastest horse . . . barefoot . . . turn around, and head back north. Odds are they won't be able to track you, especially seeing as it's coming on dark. Elzy and me'll keep on towards the Roost . . . that's where they'll be expecting us to head. If we can make it to the Flat Tops ahead of them, we'll be fine. Ain't no posse in their right mind gonna follow us into the Roost. And if they do catch up with us, well, they'll have a hard time convicting us of anything if we ain't got the money!"

"I like the way you think, pardner." Elzy grinned.

At Mexican Bend, the switch was made. Walker pulled the shoes off the sleek mare Butch had been slated to ride and tied the bagful of money behind his saddle.

"After we leave a trail into the Roost, we'll follow you up north," Butch said. "Meet you in a day or two at Florence Creek. If we ain't there, head for Brown's Park. Now take care of my gold, y'hear!"

"You can count on me, Butch." With a nod of his head, Walker was off, tracking a deer trail that led away from the river.

Butch had left his dog, Sunday, with the fresh horses, assuming that by this point they would be setting a leisurely pace that the little animal could easily follow. As they pressed their horses into a brisk trot, Butch glanced back, hoping Sunday would be able to keep up.

"Reckon you can carry him across your saddle if need be," said Elzy, stifling a grin.

Butch shrugged, affecting an unconcerned air. "Dog ain't good for much anyway," he muttered.

Darkness fell, but the twosome pressed on, their only goal to put miles between themselves and the posse. They rode silently, letting the horses navigate the rocky terrain by moonlight. The April night was chilly, but neither man felt the cold. Elzy was lost in a reverie of Maude, remembering the tastiness of her luscious kisses, and hoping the money he had stolen today would keep them until the baby was born.

Cassidy refused to indulge in any such personal thoughts. At the moment, Etta's betrayal, if one could call it that, seemed of little import. Etta was a beautiful, smart, and plucky woman, but she had not touched him in that deepest part of his heart — the part reserved for Mary Boyd. When Harry had confronted him — nervous, defensive, primed to fight for his woman — Butch had almost laughed. Out of respect for Harry, he had managed to contain himself. Soberly he agreed that, if the Sundance Kid were truly Etta's heart's desire, he would not stand in the way. A little nonplused, Harry had extended his hand, and they shook, as though sealing a deal. Etta would probably have been horrified at the ease with which her transfer was made, but she would never hear of it from the lips of either man.

Riding through the moonlight, Butch kept his mind focused on the task at hand. Stay ahead of the posse, but leave a clear trail for it to follow — a trail that led away from the Castle Gate payroll money. But staying ahead of their pursuers was becoming a ticklish proposition. Cassidy's mount, which he had been aboard since their first relay at Gordon Creek, was tiring rapidly. Not daring to push the animal beyond an easy trot, the outlaw knew that even that pace could not be maintained for long. Finally, in the early hours of the morning, he signaled to Elzy to pull over behind an outcropping of rock.

"This old bay's got a hell of a lot of bottom to her, but she ain't gonna go no farther without a rest. Reckon we're gonna have to hole up for a couple of hours."

Wordlessly Elzy dismounted and climbed to the top of the outcropping. Crouching low, he studied their back trail, watching and listening. After a few minutes, he rejoined Cassidy. "Can't hear nothing. Don't see no lanterns or nothing, either. Maybe they figured they can't track us in the dark, so they're holding up till morning."

"Maybe. But they gotta be blind not to be able to follow the trail we've left. Hell, we might as well have erected signs . . . this way to the robbers."

Just then, Sunday limped into view, his tongue lolling in exhaustion. Butch grinned and squatted to rub the dog's ears. "Hey, boy, how ya doin'? Good dog, I knew you could keep up. Bet you're thirsty, eh?" Grabbing his canteen, he filled his hat with water and set it before the parched animal.

"Better be saving some of that for yourself," Elzy warned, stretching out on the ground and folding his slicker into some semblance of a pillow.

"Aw, there's plenty. Besides, we're almost to Roost Springs. What's the matter, anyway? Ain't you glad he showed up? He'll hear anything coming long before we do."

Sunday chose that moment to slurp up the last drop of water, circle twice, and plop down with his nose buried in his paws.

"Some watchdog you got there, pard." Settling back, Elzy tipped his hat over his eyes.

Butch surveyed the sleeping man and dog. "OK then, guess I'll take the first watch."

Two hours later, he roused Elzy. "Sun's up. We better get moving."

They did not have far to go now, but as the sun rose hotly over the open desert, Butch could tell that, despite their brief rest, his horse had no push left. Its head hung low, and it could not be urged to go faster than a labored walk. Elzy, whose mount was relatively fresh, suggested leaving the spent horse and doubling up on his. Butch was about to agree when something made him glance over his shoulder.

"Damn! They's within spittin' distance!"

Elzy turned to look. Sure enough, a tell-tale plume of dust signaled riders on their tail, maybe a half mile behind them.

Suddenly Butch pivoted in his saddle, looking this way and that. "Where's Sunday? God dammit, I thought he was right behind us."

Elzy squinted through binoculars at the approaching riders and at a small black dot that brought up their rear. "Jesus, Butch, that gimp dog of yours is all the way behind the posse!"

With a stricken look, Butch reined his horse to the right and down into a deep gully. Elzy followed. "Listen, Elz, that dog's been more loyal to me than most of the men I've known. I can't leave him."

Lay stared in disbelief. "Friend, in case you hadn't noticed, there's a bunch of law-men with guns breathing down our necks. It ain't the time to be worrying about your dog."

"I'm gonna go get him."

"You're gonna do what?"

"You climb atop that ridge and serenade our friends there with a little rifle music. I'll take your horse and double back to pick up

91

Sunday. If I stay down in this draw, I think I can get by without them seeing me."

Elzy shook his head in exasperation. "I made out maybe seven or eight of them. How'm I gonna hold off that many?"

"Once I get behind them, I'll start shooting at their rear. That'll confuse them, for sure. You game?"

"Do I have a choice?" Grabbing his gun, Elzy scrambled up the rocky hill and found cover. Butch headed back down the draw and circled around a small knoll, keeping out of sight, although he could hear the posse pass by. A few minutes later, shots rang out — Elzy holding the pursuers at bay. Cassidy whistled, and Sunday limped out from behind a cactus bush, shaking all over in excitement at seeing his master.

"Up you go, buddy." The outlaw reached for his dog and held him over the front of his saddle. "OK, now, you and me gotta chime in to help our pard. Hold still." Sliding his Winchester from the saddle scabbard, he pointed it in the air and squeezed off a shot. The distant gunfire momentarily ceased; no doubt the posse was wondering who the hell was shooting at their rear. Retracing his steps, he came up to the backside of the ridge where Elzy was stationed. The gunfire had resumed, but it seemed more sporadic now. Hobbling Elzy's horse, he leashed Sunday to the saddle horn, warning the little dog to keep quiet.

Joining Lay at the top of the hill, he looked down on the scene below and grinned. Scattered across a hundred yards or so, the seven or eight men, including Carpenter, still in his bedroom slippers, had sought cover behind stray rocks and brush. Their frightened horses had run off, taking all the spare ammunition with them.

"Looks like we got them right where we want them," chuckled Butch.

"Damned if your going back for that dog didn't set up the whole thing," marveled Elzy.

"It always pays to be loyal to them who's loyal to you," Butch opined. "Come on, let's get outta here."

Riding double, they continued on toward the Roost. After a few miles, they came upon a middling-size ranch and persuaded the friendly owner, to the tune of a fifty dollar gold piece, to sell them his two best horses. Circling back north, Sunday perched proudly on his master's saddle, they rendezvoused with Joe Walker at Florence Creek. Walker told them the good news: the Castle Gate heist had netted them seven thousand dollars in gold.

CHAPTER SIX

Following their usual practice, after pulling a big job, Cassidy's gang split up, each finding some out-of-the-way place to lay low until the furor died down. Butch took his share of the Castle Gate money and headed up to Wyoming, alighting at the ranch of the unsuspecting Hilman family near Sheridan. Although some of the boys, flush from their criminal successes, found it hard to settle back into a humdrum routine, Butch enjoyed the change of pace. It was satisfying to put in a hard day's work and then fall into your bunk at night, too tired to worry. It gave him pleasure to be around a typical, industrious rancher like Dan Hilman and his family. Butch performed whatever tasks were assigned to him without complaint, and in his spare time often took thirteen-year-old Fred Hilman out for target practice.

One morning in early June, a tall, dark-haired man rode into the yard. Soon after, Butch, who called himself Leroy Parker, came by to request a few days' leave. It was grudgingly granted, and the duo rode off.

"Looks like a good set-up," commented Elzy, surveying the neat-looking buildings and newly repaired fence of the Hilman Ranch.

Butch nodded. "Work's hard but the missus serves pretty decent chow. Gotta admit it's kinda nice being around a young 'un again. Their boy reminds me a little of myself at that age. How's your situation?"

"Can't complain," Lay replied tersely. Lately he'd had very little to say, and, although he wasn't talking, Butch surmised there was trouble between him and Maude. At Florence Creek, when they had divided the money and split up, Elzy had indicated he was headed for Vernal where his wife was staying with her parents. A few weeks later, he had shown up in northeastern Wyoming, alone. It could be that Maude had simply decided to stay with her parents for the duration of her pregnancy, but Elzy's grim demeanor hinted at deeper problems. Butch felt for his friend, but it was not the kind of thing he could ask him about. Anyway, who was he to offer advice to the lovelorn?

The next day they reached Hole-in-the-Wall, an inviting valley, tucked between sandstone cliffs on one side and the Big

Horns on the other that belied the starkness of its name. Butch had summered there a few years back, and had briefly considered making it a permanent residence until he was chased away by the Johnson County sheriff on a bogus rustling charge. Well, maybe the charge had not been completely unfounded, but Butch was convinced he never would have been singled out were it not for his double-crossing partner, Al Hainer. But that was all in the past, and Butch put it behind him as he and Elzy rode through the well-hidden rent in the cliffs and down the rocky face toward a tiny cabin on Blue Creek.

Inside were several members of the gang, discussing plans for their next job. Cassidy had not called this meeting, but he had gotten wind of it and decided he and Elzy must put in their two cents. He was not particularly surprised or put out that some of his men would attempt a robbery on their own. The gang was more a loose-knit collection of individuals than a tightly woven fraternity with a strict hierarchy. Any one of them was free to operate on his own, with or without the approval of their leader. But, in this case, the job being contemplated was risky and premature, and Butch hoped to talk them out of it. Looking over the five men, hardened criminals all, he knew he had his work cut out for him.

"So boys, whatta ya got planned?"

Flat Nose George Currie stepped forward. "The bank in Belle Fourche, South Dakota, a week from today. It'll be the end of their big veterans' reunion, and the bank oughta be stuffed with loot." He looked to his compatriots for approval. All but Harry Longabaugh nodded their agreement. Cassidy wondered if Harry shared his reservations.

"A week from today? That ain't much time."

"Gotta strike while the iron's hot," growled Harvey Logan, brows drawn low over mean-looking eyes.

"That's true," Butch conceded. "Who you got scouting it?"

The men exchanged uneasy glances. A little frown played on Longabaugh's mustachioed lips.

"Don't need no scout," declared Walt Punteney, a big, blond kid who knew Butch from his Johnson County rustling days. "There ain't nothin' to it. This ain't like Castle Gate where you had to plan special 'cause of the horses and the timing of the payroll and everything. Belle Fourche is wide open . . . we ride in, take the money, and run."

Hooking his thumbs in his braces, Cassidy lowered himself into the nearest chair and tipped it back on two legs. "I was just thinking . . . being that there's a veterans' reunion in town, there might be a bunch of extra lawmen around. Then, too, I was wondering about the horses. There ain't been a lot of time since Castle Gate to train your relays for a quick getaway."

"We didn't figure on needin' no relays," said Flat Nose, his jaw set. "It's only ten miles to the state line, and, once we get into Wyoming we'll be free and clear."

"Then you plan to cut the telegraph lines so the sheriff won't wire ahead to the law in Wyoming?"

Flat Nose hesitated. "Well . . . yeah, that's what we're gonna do."

"Well, then, boys." Butch slapped his thighs and rose. "Sounds like you got it all worked out. Good luck!"

Elzy nodded to the gang and followed Cassidy out the door.

Flat Nose watched them go, a look of resentment on his ugly face. "Aw, hell, he's just sorry he didn't think of doing this job himself. What does he think? That he's the only one around here who can rob a bank?"

"I don't know," muttered Tom O'Day, taking a slug from his ever-present flask.

"You never thought of cutting the telegraph wires."

"Shut up, you lousy drunk!"

"Wait a minute, Flat Nose, he's got a point," chimed in Punteney. "Maybe we should talk it over with Butch some more."

"Aw, who needs him?"

Harry Longabaugh went out in the yard where Butch and Elzy were mounting up. "You got them all riled up in there. They thought they knew just what they was doing, and now they ain't so sure."

"Well, that's what I aimed to do," Cassidy chuckled. "What about you, Kid? You gonna ride with them?"

Longabaugh shrugged. "Reckon so. I know they sound a mite disorganized, but Walt's right, it should be a pretty easy job. Anyway, I could use the dough."

Butch heard the unspoken words: *to keep Etta in style.* Swinging into the saddle, he looked down at his friend. "Keep those jaspers in line for me, now. I'm planning something big, and I can't afford to lose five of my men."

Longabaugh nodded and watched the pair ride off.

After a few miles of ambling through the tall grass, green from early summer rain, Butch pulled up and sat his horse, gazing south toward the Big Horns. Elzy recognized the look on his partner's face, indicating he was cogitating on something, and kept quiet, rolling a smoke while he waited. By the time he tossed the butt away, Cassidy was ready to talk.

"Where to?"

Elzy masked his surprise. He had assumed they would head back north, Butch to the Hilman Ranch and he to his own temporary hide-out. "Whatta ya got in mind?"

"Thought I'd head over the mountains, look up some folks over toward the Wind Rivers," Butch said vaguely. But he did not need to spell out his intentions to Elzy. The Wind River Mountains were home to the Indian reservation and Mary Boyd. Mary Boyd *Rhodes,* now that she was a married woman.

Elzy shook his head sorrowfully, knowing something of the heartache his friend must feel. His own Maude, sweet, luscious Maude, had become a stranger to him, pushing him away where she had once welcomed him gladly. He could tell Butch that it wasn't any good . . . that by the time a woman had decided she was through with you it was too late to change her mind. But it was the kind of thing a man did not want to hear, not from his best friend or his worst enemy.

"Well, then," Elzy said, looking away, "guess we'll meet up later."

"Sure. Baggs . . . Fourth of July." Cassidy's steady tone reassured Elzy, and for a moment the two men looked at each other frankly, each sensing the other's troubles, each grateful those troubles would never be voiced. "We'll set off fireworks like they ain't never seen!"

In truth, Butch could not have said what prompted his return to the Wind River region. Maybe it was just because he was by nature a nomad, never content unless he was on the move. Maybe it really was a desire to see old friends, like Emery and Alice Burnaugh who had often sheltered him at their road ranch. But it surely was not due to any yearning for Mary Boyd. No, that act in his life had been played out and the curtain rung down. He wanted nothing to do with that two-timing half-breed. She had promised to wait for him while he was in prison, but, instead, had married another man, some no-account farmer named Ole Rhodes. Butch had given her the chance to leave Rhodes and come with him, and she had refused. All right then. He knew when he was beat, and he had no intention of letting himself in for more misery. Still, as he rode into the pretty town of Lander on the banks of the Popo Agie River, he found himself taking second looks at every woman on the street with dark skin and long, black hair.

A couple of hours in Lannigan's Saloon, surrounded by friends and admirers, returned the swagger to his step. As the late afternoon sun beat down on the dusty town, he ambled contentedly along the wooden sidewalk. The door to the general store swung open, and a little girl, no more than five or six years old, stepped in front of him. Smiling, he reached in his shirt pocket for a piece of hard candy to give the child, as was his custom. But then the little girl turned to look at him, and his hand stayed, his smile frozen as he stared at the most beautiful child he had ever seen.

Jet black hair framed a perfectly shaped, mocha-colored face. Pretty pink lips turned down into a slight pout that, years hence he had no doubt, would coax the strongest of men to do her bidding. But most remarkable were the pale blue eyes that stared into his own, mirror-like.

Recovering himself, he offered her the piece of candy.

"Thank you," she said politely, and stuck it in the pocket of her pinafore.

"How about a peppermint, too?" he asked, proffering another sweet.

The little girl hesitated. "I'll have to ask my mother." She turned to go back inside the store.

"No, wait a minute!" Butch put a hand on her arm, suddenly uneasy. For some reason, he did not want to let the girl out of his sight, nor did he want to meet her mother or father or anyone else who might connect her to the real world. He just wanted to look at her, memorize every lovely, childish feature of her budding face, and store the memory away for the rest of his life.

"Go ahead, take it," he said a bit roughly. "Ask your mother later if you can keep it."

She looked at him, seeming to assess his trustworthiness, and then took the mint from his hand, slipping it in her pocket with the other piece. "Thank you," she murmured again.

He stepped off the sidewalk into the bright sun and tipped his hat to her. "Good bye now, sweetheart. Be a good girl."

She smiled at him, showing a row of little, white teeth with one missing on the bottom. He smiled back and strode off with his cowboy's rolling gait. He had just mounted up and turned his horse when the girl's mother came out of the store, accompanied by an old Indian woman with sunken cheeks and creased skin. Following her daughter's gaze, the mother caught sight of Cassidy as he turned the corner. Her eyes widened, and her breath caught in her throat. "Who was that man, honey?" she asked, keeping her voice calm.

The little girl shrugged. "Somebody nice who gave me candy. Can I keep it, Mama?"

The mother turned to look at the old Indian woman, grief and remembrance in her eyes. The old woman gazed back evenly and placed a comforting hand on her arm.

Sighing, the pretty young mother stroked her daughter's dark head. "Yes, honey, of course. Do keep it. Keep it forever."

CHAPTER SEVEN

Harry Longabaugh had been in tough spots before, and he was not about to panic, but if he did not find shelter soon, he might well be enjoying the hospitality of the Butte County jail. Clutching his injured arm to his side, he dropped down behind an outcropping of rock, studying what appeared to be lights in the distance. Must be Newcastle. An opportunity to find food and rest, but risky, too, especially since it was a county seat and thus home to a sheriff and his deputies, all of whom would without doubt be on guard tonight.

Still, he had no choice. He was on foot, had no money or food, and was just barely ahead of the posse that had shot his horse out from under him and nicked his forearm with a bullet. He could go no farther.

Cursing under his breath, he hauled himself to his feet and started toward the distant lights, staying in the cover of trees whenever possible. He should have known better than to get involved with the Belle Fourche job. Butch had been able to foresee a ruinous outcome — why hadn't he? Yes, he needed the money, but what good would money do him if he were rotting in jail? Not that there was any money to be had, even if he got out of this jam. Flat Nose and the others had so thoroughly botched the robbery that they had made off with only ninety-seven dollars. Ninety-seven fucking dollars! That came out to less than twenty-five dollars per man, not including Tom O'Day who had managed to get himself caught before he even made it out of town.

There was a lesson in this that Harry intended never to forget — no more thieving with people who did not take their thieving seriously. Butch had tried to warn him, but he had not listened. Hell, there'd been no reason to worry. Flat Nose and Logan had been around the block a time or two — they should have known what they were doing. True, Punteney was a mite green and O'Day was a drunk, but still, like Punteney had said, they should have been able to waltz right in, take the money, and run.

But no one had predicted that the bank cashier would pull a gun on them. Flat Nose had panicked, shooting into the air as a warning to the look-outs on the street. And then all hell had broken loose. Every Civil War veteran in town had heard the call to arms, and, before they knew it, it was the Battle of Gettysburg all over again. Four of the bandits had managed to flee with the ninety-seven dollars Logan had grabbed from one of the bank customers, but O'Day, drunk as a brick, had gotten nabbed right there on the street.

"Amateurs," Longabaugh muttered as he lurched into the outskirts of Newcastle. "No more amateurs."

Leaning against the livery stable wall, he considered what to do. On his feet for two days now, he was dead tired and sorely tempted to curl up in a doorway to sleep. But that would invite sure discovery. Besides, he needed food and a dressing on his arm. The hour was late; most lights were extinguished. Yet down the block he could see a lamp shining in the window of someone's house. It was his only chance — if he did this right, he could avoid a ruckus.

Keeping to the shadows, he sneaked noiselessly to the back of the house. Six-shooter in hand, he rapped twice on the door. Inside, a chair scraped, then footsteps approached. The door swung wide.

" 'Evenin', mister." Harry quickly pushed his way into the kitchen, softly closing the door behind him. "Sorry to barge in like this, but I need a favor."

Blinking unfocussed eyes at the intruder, the young man stood speechless. On the table beside him lay several papers and a pair of wire-rimmed glasses. The smell of freshly brewed coffee permeated the room, making Harry almost dizzy.

"Get me some of that brew," he ordered.

The man rushed to obey, pouring the bedraggled outlaw a steaming mug. Harry reached for it with his wounded arm, grimacing as pain shot through it. The man's eyes widened at the sight of the bloody coat sleeve.

"That's right, I'm hurt," Harry rasped, "but I ain't done nothing wrong, leastways nothing that should concern you." It was a far cry from the truth, but somehow he had to reassure the frightened man. Taking a chance, Harry put his gun down on the table. "See, I ain't gonna harm ya. I just need your help. A place to rest, something to clean up this arm with. That's all I'm askin', mister."

"Why should I help you?" the man blurted, backing away clumsily.

Sighing with weariness, Harry sank into a chair, resting his injured arm on the table within easy reach of his gun. "Like I said, mister, I don't aim to hurt ya. But I got friends out there who don't want to see me come to no harm. I can't account for what might happen to you and your family if you see fit to throw me out, or tell the sheriff about my little visit tonight. Put me up for a couple of days, just until this arm starts to heal, and I'll be on my way, never bother you again."

"What about these so-called friends of yours? How can I be sure they won't come for me after you've left?"

"They won't never know a thing about you, 'less'n I tell 'em." Harry's hand inched closer toward the gun. He was getting a tad impatient with his reluctant host, and, if the silly fellow did not give in soon, he'd wish he had.

"I guess I have no choice but to believe you. I'll take you upstairs to the attic. You'll be safe there."

"You're smarter'n you look, friend. Whatta ya got in the way of grub?"

Longabaugh awoke several hours later, the sun stealing through the shuttered attic window heating the tiny room to an almost unbearable temperature. Still, it was better than being out in the open, a sitting duck until his arm was better and he could rustle up a horse.

Shirtless, he swung his legs over the side of the cot and checked his bandaged wound. His benefactor had put some kind of salve on it and bound it tightly, and it felt much better. Crossing to the window, he tipped the shutter slightly open and peered out. The street was quiet, showing no more than ordinary daytime activity. Below him, a door slammed, and a girl of about eight or nine skipped down the walk and out to the street, a book bag slung over her shoulder. So the man did have a family. Good. All the more reason for him to keep quiet about the outlaw in his attic.

Sinking down on the cot, Harry leaned his head back and closed his eyes. He was still tired from his ordeal, but now, after a few hours of deep, almost drugged, sleep, his thoughts had the power to keep him awake.

And who did he think of, day and night, almost without cease? Etta. Beautiful, smart, playful, brave Etta. There was not another woman on the face of the earth like her, and she was his. Waiting for him in Denver. With any luck, he would be out of this jam and in her soft, sweet arms in a few short days. Not much richer, unfortunately, but she would not care.

Oh, how his life had changed since meeting her. All of a sudden, he had found himself thinking about things he would never have thought about before, things like jobs, and houses, and children, and respectability, things that only a couple of months ago would have made his blood run cold. But the more he thought about these things, the more he realized they were not things he really wanted. He wanted Etta, and, if she had required them, he would have crawled through fire to get them for her. But, of course, she did not. She had made it clear she wanted only a promise that she would be his partner in life, going with him wherever the winds blew. The only reason they were apart now was that she had had some business to wrap up in Denver. While she was thus occupied, he had planned to come by some quick cash via the Belle Fourche job. Then they would be together, forever, living life as no man and woman ever had before or would again.

Harry's lips parted in a smile as he pictured Etta's lovely face, her enticing figure, her beguiling laugh, her sensuous eyes. Did other men feel about their women the way he felt about Etta? Elzy and Maude Lay had always seemed a happy couple, but Elzy had nevertheless been willing to spend weeks, even months, away from his wife. And Butch? Harry wasn't sure Butch had ever loved any woman, although Etta told him his heart had been broken by a little Indian gal. But that was just female talk. Butch was not the type to fall in love, seriously in love. God knows if he hadn't fallen prey to Etta's charms, he must be made of stone.

Just as well. Butch was their leader. It would not do for him to go all soft over some woman. Thank God, he, the Sundance Kid, had found a woman who only made him stronger.

PART II
1898–1900

CHAPTER EIGHT

"Mister French, got a minute?"

"I was just going into town." William French rose from his desk and headed for the door, nodding to his new foreman, Perry Tucker, to accompany him. "What's on your mind?" he inquired in clipped British tones. "I'm in a bit of a rush. Got to finish in town and then get back and see to that dam we're trying to build."

Tucker hurried to keep up. "Got a couple of boys for you to meet, sir. Think they'd be real good hires. You don't come across their kind every day."

"What makes them so special?" French strode across the yard, eyeing the two dust-covered cowboys, waiting near the stable door.

"Well, sir, they're damned smart, and they know their way around horses and cows like no one I've ever seen." Tucker and French halted in front of the two men. "Sir, this is Jim Lowe and William McGinnis. Boys, this here's the WS manager, Mister French."

Lowe, a broad-shouldered man with sandy hair, a square jaw, and piercing blue eyes, held out his hand. McGinnis, taller and darker than his partner, did likewise. French shook sturdily, perusing them with a practiced eye. He was always on the look-out for good employees, and these two did have an air of competence about them.

"What brings you men to southwestern New Mexico?" he asked.

Lowe met his gaze directly and gave him a friendly grin. "Mac and me got kinda tired of them cold winters in Wyoming and Colorado. Thought we'd try it down south for a spell."

"Your timing isn't the best then, is it? If you stay on, you'll have to endure a hot desert summer first."

"That's fine by us. We're used to the heat, ain't we, Mac?" Lowe winked at his partner, who smiled back cagily.

"I see," said French, not missing the *double entendre*. "Well, boys, Tucker here seems to think you'd be excellent additions to our crew. What exactly did you have in mind for them?"

"Sir, I thought Jim could be my assistant and handle the trail drives. And Mac's a hell of a bronc' buster."

"Very well, we'll give you a try." French nodded to his two new cowboys. "But if there's trouble of any sort, you'll be sent packing. The WS is a law-abiding operation . . . nonetheless, we don't want to give the sheriff any reason to come visiting. All right, welcome aboard, boys."

Lowe and McGinnis expressed their thanks and moved on toward the bunkhouse with Tucker.

"I think he's on to us," muttered McGinnis.

"Not a chance," said Tucker. "French ain't no dummy, but he don't know Butch Cassidy and Elzy Lay from Lewis and Clark. We're just enough out of the way down here that we don't get much news from up north. Speaking of which, what is the news? Must not be all good if you boys are feeling the need to hide out in this god-forsaken place."

"That's the trouble with you, Tucker," commented Butch, halting by the bunkhouse door. "You just never could appreciate your surroundings. Now me, I think this is one pretty place."

In truth, the WS ranch, running several miles along the San Francisco River, enjoyed a beautiful setting, particularly now, in spring, when the river ran higher than a trickle and the cacti were all in bloom. Perry

Tucker, whom Butch and Elzy had known as a sometime rustler and good hand back in Wyoming, smiled his agreement. "It'll do at that. But seriously, boys, what brings you down here?"

Butch glanced toward the bunkhouse and moved away from the door. "We wasn't kidding about feeling the heat," he said, his voice low. "Things was starting to close in. Last summer, Bub Meeks got arrested for the Montpelier job. Then, in September, Punteney and Logan was hauled in for Belle Fourche. Logan got shot in the ambush . . . hear tell his arm got ripped up pretty bad. Anyways, they threw them into the can in Deadwood with O'Day. We sprung them later that fall. Logan made it into Canada, but Punteney and O'Day got caught again. They're coming to trial any day now. We got them damn' good lawyers, but, hell, the bank cashier's identified both of them. They'll need a miracle to get out of this one."

Butch paused to roll a smoke, pondering the irony of the situation. Here he was forking over thousands of dollars in lawyer's fees for the defense of two screw-ups who got captured not once, but twice, for a robbery he warned them not to undertake and which netted all of ninety-seven dollars. Not that there was ever any question that he would stand by them — as members of the gang, that's what he owed them.

"The big cattle ranchers are getting all het up over rustlers these days, too," Butch continued. "They're pestering the local sheriffs to do something about it . . . even hiring their own stock detectives. Last month, the governors of Utah, Colorado, and Wyoming met to try to figure out how to break up all us so-called outlaw gangs, but nothing ever come of it. Everybody's thinking about fighting Spain now, so they ain't got time to worry about a little rustling here and there. That war's the best thing ever happened to us."

"I heard a bunch of hardcases was thinking about enlisting," Tucker said.

"Damn' right!" Elzy saluted sharply. "I'd be proud to fight for the good old U.S. of A. . . . was it willing to offer me full amnesty, that is!"

Butch chuckled. "Yeah, we met in Steamboat and talked it over. Decided asking for amnesty might be a little dicey, so Uncle Sam's gonna have to do without our services. But even with the war occupying everybody's mind, Elzy and me thought it'd be a good time to lay low . . . wait till the goddamn' stockmen and all their politician toadies cool down."

"Well, you couldn't have picked a better place to disappear for a while," Tucker said. "There ain't much law to speak of around here. The sheriff's way the hell over in Socorro, and he don't worry too much about what goes on in this part of the county."

"Music to my ears!" Butch smiled. "Yeah, me and Elz, or should I say Mac, just want to drive some cattle and bust some bronc's for a while. Strictly legit, ain't that right, Mac?"

"Strictly legit, Jim."

Their resolve lasted about a year.

In the early morning hours of June 2nd, 1899, Union Pacific Engineer W. R. Jones peered through the rainy darkness at what seemed to be a lantern swinging in the distance. Leaning out the side of his cab, he squinted at the light, which moved steadily back and forth.

"What do you see?" called his fireman, Dietrick.

"Light up ahead. Looks like a signal of some kind." Jones rapidly took stock. The Overland Flyer No. 1 had just passed the section house at Rock Creek, Wyoming, and was not scheduled to stop again until Medicine Bow, fifteen miles away. Making an unplanned stop in the middle of the night was almost too dangerous even to consider, what with all the gangs that were roaming around these parts. Still, what if someone was trying to warn them that the rain had washed out the bridge just ahead?

Making a split second decision he would later regret, Jones yanked on the brake lever, bringing his massive locomotive to a screeching halt. As they pulled abreast of two shadowy figures next to the rails, the light he had seen was suddenly doused. Then, before the train's huge wheels had come to a full stop, a man swung up into the cab, brandishing a six-shooter. Behind him, a second man, similarly armed, climbed halfway up, keeping a look-out down the length of the train. Both men wore dark clothing and masks. Their hats, dripping rainwater, were tugged down low, almost meeting the tops of their masks.

Jones backed away slowly, his throat dry with fear. "Listen," he croaked, his eyes darting to the man on look-out. "There's a second section right behind us . . . coming up right behind us, I'm telling ya."

"I see the headlight," confirmed the look-out.

"Yeah, and there's a carload of soldiers on board," Jones said. "They'll be coming right up on us!"

The first outlaw snorted. "Pull up just

over the bridge," he commanded in a raspy voice.

"There . . . there ain't enough time," Jones protested. "That second section'll be right here."

With a swing of his arm so fast Jones didn't see it coming, the outlaw brought the barrel of his gun down on the engineer's forehead. "Shut up and do what you're told! Be quick about it!"

"Better do what he says," advised Dietrick, opening the boiler door to shovel in more coal.

Jones felt a trickle of blood slide down his cheek. Outside, the rain beat tinnily on the engine's cab. In this weather the engineer of the section behind them might not see their train stopped on the tracks until it was too late. Whatever these goons had planned could not be as bad as getting rammed by a speeding locomotive.

Returning to the controls, Jones edged the train forward slowly.

"Faster!" came the order.

The engineer felt the barrel of a gun dig into his ribs. Finally they cleared the small, wooden bridge. Jones was instructed to stop again. Several other figures emerged from the shadows. One of them walked up to the cab and said something to the look-out.

"We're clear," the look-out relayed to the man holding Jones at gunpoint. "It's gonna blow."

No sooner were the words out of his mouth than an explosion rumbled the floor of the cab. Jones and Dietrick exchanged shocked looks. The bandits had blown up the bridge. Now there was no way the second section could reach them. They were on their own.

The one in charge moved to the side and gestured with his gun. "All right, now. Take it slow and easy. Climb down outta the cab."

Jones moved to obey, but Dietrick stepped back to close the boiler door. As he raised his arm, his sleeve brushed the bandit's face, pulling askew the mask that covered it. For an instant, he caught sight of a dark beard and long, straight nose.

"Shit!" the outlaw grunted, hastily readjusting the mask. Dietrick saw the gunman's hand come up and thought he was about to be struck, as Jones had been. Flashing black eyes, the thief grabbed the fireman's arm and shoved him toward the ladder. "Try that again and you'll be a dead man!"

Slipping in the mud, the two trainmen were ordered to uncouple the passenger cars. That accomplished, they were led back to the cab and once again told to pull ahead, this time about two miles. The robbers had now cut them off from not only the second section, but from most of their own train. The locomotive was attached only to the tender car, baggage car, express car, and two mail cars.

Jones's mind raced, grudgingly admiring, even through his fear, the precise planning exhibited by the robbers. Although he could not positively identify them, even the one whose mask had been dislodged, he had more than a hunch who they were. This crime had all the hallmarks of a Wild Bunch hold-up. If that were true, he'd best do exactly what they told him — those boys were not to be trifled with.

Moving back to the mail cars, the robbers, now numbering six by Jones's count, shouted to the clerks to open up. They were met with silence. The leader turned to Jones. "Tell them to open up or we'll blow the door."

Jones nodded quickly. "Burt, it's Jones. Do what he says . . . they've got dynamite."

Nothing happened, although they could hear soft voices coming from inside the car.

"Goddammit!" yelled the leader. "There ain't no time to be discussing things! Just open the fucking door!"

He punctuated his remark with two gunshots into the car. The door immediately slid open. Two of the robbers hopped aboard and began dumping out mail sacks, warning the cringing clerks to stay out of the way. Momentarily one of the masked men returned to the door and spoke to the leader. "We ain't finding much. So far about fifty bucks in cash."

"It's taking too much time. Let's try the express car."

Herding Jones, Dietrick, and the two mail clerks ahead of them, the outlaws banged on the express car door. "Open up!"

No answer.

"Open up, I said!"

Silence.

The leader turned to Jones, an angry glint in his dark eyes. "I'm getting fucking tired of these assholes trying to be heroes. Tell him to open up!"

The engineer stepped close to the door of the car, the better to be heard over the drumbeat of rain. "Woodcock, this is Jones. Open up! They've got guns and dynamite and ain't afraid to use either!"

"I won't do it!" came the muffled reply.

"Don't be a fool!" yelled Jones. "They blew up the bridge and shot their way into the mail car. They mean business!"

Even as he spoke, the leader was motioning to his men to set a charge under the door. They worked quickly and efficiently, one strapping the dynamite in place while the other used one of the mail sacks to shield the charge from the rain.

"You've got five seconds to open that door, Woodcock!" called the leader. "Then we blast it open!"

They waited in silence. Hearing no response, the leader nodded to his men who lit the charge and retreated with the others to a safe distance. The door blew, rocking the car on the tracks. Leaping inside, the bandits glanced at Woodcock, lying dazed in a corner. But their focus was on two huge Pacific Express Company safes, the repositories of the treasure they sought.

Kneeling by the fallen clerk, the leader asked him for the combination to the safes. Woodcock gazed at him with unfocussed eyes. "The combination, dammit! Give me the fucking combination!" Woodcock's eyes rolled back in his head, and he fainted.

"Shit," the robber growled. "We're gonna have to blow them safes, boys. How long we been stopped?"

" 'Bout an hour, little more, maybe," someone answered.

"We're running out of time. Make sure you do it right 'cause we ain't got time to do it again. You there" — he pointed to the mail clerks — "haul Woodcock outside if you don't want him blown to pieces."

As the trainmen and four of the outlaws sought cover, the other two packed dynamite around the safes. Finished, they lit the charge and sprinted through the shredded door. Seconds later, a huge explosion ripped apart the car, blowing out the sides and lifting the roof into a crazy angle.

"Jesus!" the leader exclaimed. "You blew up the whole fucking car!"

"You said to make sure we got it done the first time," mumbled the man who had set the explosives.

"Come on, let's see what we got."

The dynamite had succeeded in not only destroying the express car, but in blowing the doors off the two safes. Scooping up the contents, including a stack of cash with a burned corner, the robbers filled their bags and took off on foot, headed for the open prairie.

Jones and Dietrick, feeling lucky to be alive, noted the direction of their escape. "Why ain't they on horses?" Dietrick wondered aloud. "They ain't gonna get far afoot."

Jones shook his head at the caginess of the brazen outlaws. "Reckon they don't want no

127

one to be able to track 'em. My guess is they've got horses stashed nearby."

"Even so," said Dietrick, "in this rain, it'll be easy enough to track their footprints to wherever they left their horses."

"Just their bad luck. You can't predict what Mother Nature'll do."

But Butch Cassidy had, indeed, planned for whatever Mother Nature might decide to do. On a bluff not too far away, Cassidy and Elzy Lay waited with six unshod getaway horses and about twenty range and wild horses they had rounded up. Scrambling to the top of the bluff, the train robbers swung onto the saddled mounts and headed out in different directions, while Cassidy and Lay rode amongst the herd, shouting and waving their hats until the spooked animals scattered to the four winds. As the sky lightened on a dreary, gray morning, all that could be seen were a jumble of hoof prints in the slimy, red mud. No one would ever know which ones belonged to the Wilcox train robbers.

CHAPTER NINE

William French steered his buggy along the road from Springer to Cimarron. Above him, a turquoise sky framed the landscape while, on every side, creeks and arroyos threaded their way to sage-dotted mesas that stair-stepped up to the blood red Sangre de Cristos. At this altitude, the air was crisp, even in the midst of summertime heat. But the unsurpassed beauty of northern New Mexico was lost on the WS manager. His mind was hundreds of miles away, on the ranch and all its problems.

Lowe and McGinnis had been gone for over a month now, and their absence was having its effect. The pair of veteran cowboys, only nominally under Perry Tucker's direction, had together cleaned up his entire operation, getting rid of dead weight and bringing in top hands from across the West. Strangely, many of these new hands only stayed a week or two, but there always seemed to be more where they came from.

And with the arrival of Lowe and McGinnis, the rustling of WS cattle had practically come to a halt. Furthermore, as trail boss, Lowe had performed the unheard of feat of keeping his crew under control when they reached town at the end of a drive. Several of the merchants in Magdalena had complimented French on his well-behaved outfit.

All of this brought great satisfaction to the sturdy Englishman, and, if it also raised certain suspicions, it was easy enough to discount them. As long as things were going so well, what business was it of his to inquire into the background of his men? Besides, he'd been too busy overseeing the construction of a dam in the river to pay close attention to the day-to-day operations.

But now they were gone, and his cowboys were returning to their lazy ways, the rustlers were becoming emboldened, and the orderly and efficient operation of the WS was threatened. Lowe and McGinnis had said they would be back, and French knew them as men of their word. He just wished they'd hurry up about it.

Suddenly, over the sound of creaking buggy wheels and jingling harness, French became aware of a different noise. Narrowing his eyes against the desert glare, he searched the distance, finally making out a figure, well off the road, shouting and desperately waving to him. Reining in, he waited for the stranger to gain the road.

"Thank God you stopped! I thought you'd drive right by." The weather-beaten man stumbled forward and collapsed by the buggy's wheel, stretching his worn-through boots out in front of him. French quickly hopped down and offered him a sip from his canteen. The man gratefully accepted, spitting a couple of times into the dust before taking a long pull. As he drank, the WS manager took his measure. He was a middle-aged man, clothes well cut although they were torn and dirty at the moment. He did not appear to be armed. French wondered what on earth he had been doing, wandering around the desert. When the stranger was revived enough, he put the question to him.

"Name's Reno," croaked the exhausted man, leaning his head against the wheel spoke. "I'm with the Colorado Southern Railroad."

"This must have to do with the hold-up," French speculated. Springer had been bursting with the news of the daring robbery a few days earlier of an express car near Folsom.

Reno closed his eyes and nodded. "I was riding with the posse put together by Sheriff Farr. We trailed them to Turkey Cañon, but they set up an ambush. The sheriff got knocked off his horse . . . I think he must've been shot. His horse spooked and ran, so I went after it."

"You left the fight to chase the sheriff's horse?"

"It was still carrying Farr's rifle," Reno explained, coloring with embarrassment. "I figured he'd need it."

French shook his head. "Go on."

"That's all there is, really. I lost the horse in a maze of cañons and couldn't find my way out. Decided my best bet was to head back towards town. But it was a lot farther than I thought. Damned glad you came by."

French did not bother to ask why the man had decided to cross the desert in midsummer, risking its deadly heat, instead of returning to the aid of his fellow posse men. He guessed Reno had figured his chances of survival were better in the desert. "How many outlaws were there?" he asked.

"Four, I guess. We didn't get a real close look at them. I saw one of them go down, so maybe there's only three now."

"The posse shot one of the outlaws?"

"Yeah, the one named McGinnis, I'm pretty sure."

French's head snapped up. "One of them was named McGinnis?"

"I'm pretty sure that's what Farr said just before they winged him."

French uttered a curse and stalked away, hands jammed at his hips. He had not wanted his suspicions about his hired men confirmed. Still, unlikely as it seemed, perhaps the McGinnis who had been shot in Turkey Cañon was not the McGinnis he knew. Helping the railroad man into the buggy, he reined around. "I'll take you back to Springer so you can contact the authorities."

A month later, French sat at his desk, chewing an unlit cigar and staring pensively out the window. Since his return from up north he had been debating what to do about Jim Lowe and the other WS hands he employed. It had been confirmed that the man shot in Turkey Cañon and later apprehended was William McGinnis, his former bronc' buster. Mac was currently recovering from his wounds in a Santa Fé prison, charged with the murder of Sheriff Farr. French knew it would be naïve to believe that Jim Lowe, who had been, well, thick as thieves with McGinnis, was not also of the outlaw persuasion. And what about all the men Lowe had brought on, who came and went so mysteriously? How many hardcases was the WS Ranch sheltering?

Still, what was he to do about it? Lowe and the others continued to work diligently, and he had no solid proof of their crimes. Besides, if he let them all go, the WS would once again be the target of rustlers.

A knock on the door jarred him out of his reverie. "Yes," he called, tossing the mangled cigar into the trash can.

Jim Lowe entered, followed by a dark-haired man with close-set eyes and a thick mustache. "This here's Tom Capehart," Lowe said by way of introduction. "We wondered if we might steal a minute of your time."

"As long as that's all you're here to steal," replied French pointedly.

Lowe paused for a minute, then chuckled. Pulling up a chair, he sat, crossing an ankle on his knee. Capehart wandered over to stare out the office's big bay window. "We're here to talk to you about Mac McGinnis," announced Lowe.

French raised an eyebrow. Several times he had come close to asking his hired hand what he knew about his friend's involvement in the Folsom robbery, but then thought better of it. Now here was Lowe broaching the subject. "Go on," he said.

"Capehart just rode in from up north. He's got news of how it all went down. Tell him, Tom."

Capehart hesitated.

"Go ahead," Lowe urged.

Deliberately Capehart drew his coat back and rested his hand on his hip just above a mother-of-pearl-handled Smith & Wesson. French met the man's narrow eyes, wondering if the gesture was meant to intimidate him.

"There was three of them," Capehart began, his voice surprisingly soft. "Mac, Sam Ketchum, and a fella named Franks."

"Ketchum!" French exclaimed. "I'm not at all surprised to hear he was involved. You know he worked here for a while until he stole my favorite horse. Bastard! I never did get that horse back."

"I had heard about that," Lowe said, nodding his commiseration. "It takes a low man to steal from his boss. But I guess you could say he got his just reward. He got shot in the gunfight and later died of blood poisoning."

"I see," said French, momentarily taken

135

aback. "And what about Mac? I heard he was shot as well."

"That's right," said Capehart. "Took one bullet to the shoulder and one in the back. Should've killed him but he's tough. Anyway, in spite of the fact the posse had wounded two of the three men they was after, they pulled back when night fell . . . gave the boys a chance to get away. Mac made it to Lincoln County and holed up on a ranch. The people there was nice enough to tend to him. Bad luck for him, though, another posse came by. He fired off a couple of shots and tried to sneak out the back, but they caught him. Turns out, they wasn't even looking for him, they was after some horse thieves. If he'd just kept quiet, they'd never have suspected him."

Lowe turned to French, a somber look on his face. "You probably know the rest. Mac's in Santa Fé being held on a murder charge."

"Did he kill Sheriff Farr?" French asked.

Capehart crossed his arms over his chest. "Nobody knows for sure. There was a lot of gunfire. The bullet could have come from any one of their weapons."

"What happened to the third man, Franks, I believe you said?"

Capehart paused and shot Lowe a quick

glance. "He got away. Trail's dead, they say."

French had a sneaking suspicion the trail led directly to this room. Capehart, if that was indeed the man's name, seemed remarkably well informed.

"Jim" — French leaned forward in his chair and placed his elbows on the desk — "why are you telling me all this?"

"Me and some of the boys is trying to raise Mac's bail money. Until we get enough together, we was wondering if you'd post a bond. You know Mac's a straight shooter . . . he'll be there to stand trial. But he ain't fully recovered from getting shot, and it'd be damned hard on him to have to sit in jail for the next six months."

Startled, French sat back, stroking his chin as he pondered the implications of what Lowe was asking him to do. If he secured McGinnis's bail, would the WS gain a reputation as a haven for outlaws? Perhaps it was already known as such in criminal circles, and he had been too busy, or too dense, to notice. Yet, if he refused, would he be bringing trouble down on himself and the operation? Glancing at Lowe, who sat quietly, respectfully waiting for an answer, he found it hard to believe this man was the type to seek retribution. On the other hand, there was obviously a great deal he did not know about Lowe and the other men in his employ.

Sighing, he came to a decision, one based more on what his gut told him than his head. "I'll post the bond, though I'm not sure that will even be possible. If I'm not mistaken, train robbery in the Territory of New Mexico is a capital offense and, therefore, not bailable. In any event, if it would help, I'll testify to Mac's good character . . . that is, while he worked here, of course."

Lowe came to his feet, grinning, and stuck his hand out across the desk. "Much obliged, sir. You won't be sorry."

The WS manager gave him a dour look. "I do hope not."

"If you ain't got any objection," said Lowe, "I could use Tom here out at the horse camp. He's a mighty fine hand."

Yes, thought French, *undoubtedly a most capable man. One who wouldn't mind hiding out for a few weeks at a remote camp twenty miles into the backcountry.*

He sighed. "Very well. Will you take him out there?"

"Thought I would," replied Lowe.

The two men turned to leave. French hesitated, but then decided he had a right to ask the question foremost on his mind. "Jim . . .

why did Mac rob that train? If he needed money, why didn't he come to me? I'd have given him an advance . . . surely he knew that. Why did he do it?"

The man called Lowe dropped his head, a rare look of frustration crossing his broad, open face. "I wish I knew," he said softly. "I could've told him not to get mixed up with any of them Ketchums . . . they're a sorry bunch of no-good losers. But Mac's his own man. He goes his own way."

"So you knew nothing about it?"

French found himself staring into a pair of ice blue eyes, suddenly gone dark and wary.

"Thank you again for your help," said Lowe, planting his hat on his head. "It won't be forgotten."

Outside the ranch house, the two renegades swung onto their mounts and, leading a couple of well-supplied pack horses, headed for the hills. Now was a good time to drop out of sight for a while, and the WS horse camp, deep in the wilderness of the Mogollan Mountains, was the perfect place to do that.

They had barely cleared the gate before the mustachioed man turned to his companion, a worried look drawing his brows together. "He knows everything, don't he? He's got it all figgered out."

Butch shrugged. "Most likely. He ain't no fool. 'Course, it would help some, Harry, if you could work on that poker face of yours a bit."

"Shit, I thought I was cool as clay. You might've told me you was going to ask me to give it to him straight. If I'd've had time to think about it, I would've left out a few details, you know, the stuff that only someone who was there would know." Leaning over, the Sundance Kid spat in disgust.

"Well, that's just the point now. I didn't want you thinking about it too much or you might've come up with some far-fetched tale as flimsy as Etta's underdrawers." At the mention of his sweetheart's intimate apparel Harry appeared annoyed, but Cassidy took no notice. "French would've seen the lie for what it was and would never have agreed to post Elzy's bond. The way it is now, he respects us for being up front with him. I'm betting he'll cover for us someday if he has to, leastways within the bounds of the law."

"Maybe he'd cover for you. He don't owe me nothing."

"You're my friend. That's good enough to keep his mouth shut, long as he don't have no solid proof you committed any crime. Don't worry, Harry, French has got plenty of suspicions but no proof. And far as I know, he ain't connected any of us to our real names."

"What happens when he does?" Harry grumbled.

"We move on," said Butch, his smile fading. "We just keep moving."

For the next couple of months, Cassidy and Longabaugh stayed hidden at their remote camp in the mountains. But their isolation did not prevent them from getting news from the outside world. They were informed that, true to his word, William French had attempted to post bond for the man he knew as Mac McGinnis, but that it had been refused. They heard that the trial had been moved to Raton, and that it was scheduled to begin in early October. Elzy, from all accounts, was recovering from his wounds, but had lost much of his strength. Butch could do nothing to help him, aside from continuing to funnel money to his attorneys.

Then they got word — Elzy Lay, still known to the authorities as William McGinnis, had been found guilty of murdering Sheriff Farr and sentenced to life in prison. Butch heard the news stoically, threw his bedroll behind his saddle, and rode out on his own. Through the long, cold night, black and starless, he cursed the circumstances that had led to the locking up of his friend and partner. From their first meeting years ago on Diamond Mountain in Brown's Park they had shared a bond that had remained unbroken through many separations. But now it was entirely possible that Butch would never see Elzy Lay again. He was beset with the kind of thoughts he rarely sanctioned. Was the cost for the kind of life he and his accomplices wanted to live too dear? Was the life he had rejected, one that was beholden to rules and responsibilities, nonetheless one that offered rewards for a man approaching middle age? Did he have the fortitude to do as he had advised Harry Longabaugh and keep moving, covering his tracks as best he could, and continuing to seek out places where his name and face were not known?

Nothing seemed certain any more, except that, if he were to continue down the path he had chosen, he must do so with ever increasing care and watchfulness. He had survived as long as he had in this business by being well prepared, and daring only when he knew he could bring it off. Those who were caught or killed, he always said, had simply not planned well enough. Why, then, had Elzy Lay, a man whom he considered to be his equal in shrewdness and ability, been taken prisoner? Undoubtedly Elzy's error had been in joining forces with the hot-headed Sam Ketchum. He should have known better, but ever since his break-up with Maude he had seemed not to care what happened. Another example of how dangerous it was to get tangled up with a woman. Was it even possible to have both freedom and love?

He returned to camp in a variable mood, by turns angry, sad, or resigned, to find Harry Longabaugh squatting by the smoldering fire, mooning over a letter from Etta. The same messenger who had delivered the news about Elzy had dropped off a bag of mail, including this note addressed to Harry Alonzo Place in Etta's strong, well-formed hand. The alias was not one Butch had heard before, but someone had evidently connected it to the man presently going by the name of Tom Capehart. Although the letter had only arrived the previous day, its edges were already dog-eared. Harry had obviously read and re-read his lover's words until they were committed to memory.

As he stared at the flowing script, Harry pictured the way she must have looked as she penned the missive — perhaps sitting at her dressing table, her long, dark hair loose about her shoulders, a tear brimming on the edge of her deep, liquid eyes. Of course, tears were not exactly Etta's style, but, at the very least, her brow must have been furrowed with worry and with the misery of missing him.

Butch pulled the coffee pot from the glowing ashes of the fire and poured himself a steaming cup. "What's Etta's news?" he asked.

Sighing, Longabaugh folded the note carefully and placed it in his jacket pocket. "She's worried. Wonders where I am and when I'll be back."

Butch made a face. "Shit, Harry, I never figgered you to go all moony over a piece of pussy."

Harry was too depressed to rise to the bait. "It wasn't supposed to happen like it did," he said with a long face.

"What wasn't? You going moony, or the train robbery getting fucked up?"

"Either, I reckon," Harry admitted. "I ain't got no regrets about Etta, but I sure as hell wish I hadn't've got mixed up with that Ketchum bastard."

"Most likely, you ain't the only one feels that way," said Butch, thinking of Elzy spending the rest of his days behind bars.

"I was just going to be gone a couple of weeks. Long enough to pull the job and circle back around to Denver when I was sure the coast was clear. Then when the thing went south, with the sheriff getting killed and Elzy locked up, I figgered I better stay hidden for a good long while. I managed to get word to Etta that I was OK, but I didn't dare tell her where I was. Can't really blame her for being upset."

Butch threw a disdainful look across the campfire. "I can't believe what I'm hearing. You're a god-damned outlaw, Kid, not some pasty-faced pencil pusher. When you rob a train, odds are you're going to attract a posse. When you got a posse shooting at you, the possibility exists that someone'll get hurt. Etta ain't stupid. If I know that gal, she ain't busting your chops over a job gone bad."

"No, no, that ain't it," said Harry, shaking his head. "She ain't mad at me 'cause the job went bad. She's mad at me 'cause she wanted to be part of it and I wouldn't let her."

Butch stared at his friend for a moment, and then gave an amazed chuckle. "By God, she meant it. Etta told me once she wanted to be part of the gang, and I brushed her off, didn't think she was serious. I'll be damned, that's one spunky woman."

Jealous of any private conversations Butch and his beloved may have shared, Harry's head sank into his collar. "Well, now that she's mine, I don't much fancy the idea of her riding with us. Like you said, outlawing's a dangerous activity. Ain't no place for a woman."

Butch watched the fire, mulling things over. "Not for just any woman," he said, after a while. "But for Etta? I don't know, it might work. Nobody'd be expecting a female robber. Say she was to walk into a bank, all gussied up, looking high class like she does, with you on her arm in one of them fancy suits you got. Mister and Missus Respectability. Hell, you two could sweet talk the cashier into handing over every last dollar without even pulling a gun!" He smiled, remembering his oft-stated resolve never to get entangled with a member of the fairer sex. Romantically, that still made sense. But, professionally, it was perhaps time to reëvaluate.

Harry was staring at him with a perplexed look on his face. "You're the idea man, Butch, but that's gotta be the craziest thing I ever heard."

Cassidy grinned. "Yeah? Well, let's ask your girlfriend what she thinks!"

CHAPTER TEN

"Brilliant!" Etta's hazel eyes shone with excitement as she reached across the table to clasp Butch's hand. "I always wanted to be part of the action, but to actually pull the hold-up myself, with your help, of course . . . why, that's the cleverest thing I've ever heard of! Don't you think so, lover?"

Seated next to her in the dimly lit saloon, Harry was having difficulty concentrating. He and Cassidy had only ridden in to Denver that afternoon, and, if he didn't get Etta into bed soon, odds were he'd expire from pent-up desire. "What say we carry on this conversation somewhere more private?" he said thickly, leaning over to kiss her neck. "Like back at the room."

"But we haven't eaten yet, darling. I don't know about you, but I always . . . think . . . better on a full stomach. And Butch here has given me a lot to think about." She winked across the table.

Groaning, Harry sat back. "OK," he

sighed. "You two do all the talking you want. I'm gonna go get us another round."

Cassidy smiled sheepishly as his partner pushed away from the table. If he had an ounce of sensitivity, he ought to make himself scarce right about now. But the truth was, he, too, had missed Etta, and the prospect of enjoying a civilized evening with her, sharing a meal, a few drinks, and lively conversation, was too good to pass up. Nevertheless, if she wanted him gone, too. . . .

"Maybe I should leave you two alone," he ventured.

"Nonsense. The only thing better than being out with a handsome man is being out with two handsome men. Besides, you've intrigued me with your idea for a new *modus operandi*. I want all the details."

He studied his fingers wrapped around the whisky glass in front of him. He had cleaned up when he hit town, gotten a shave and haircut, had his nails trimmed and buffed. All to no purpose, he mused, seeing as it would not be him going home with the beautiful woman seated across the table. It was not that he coveted Etta, it was just that after months of hiding out it would be nice to have a woman to come home to.

"Butch, are you all right?" Etta gave him a concerned look.

"Yeah, sure. I was just thinking." He looked up as Longabaugh pushed his way through the noisy crowd, balancing three full glasses. "Maybe the only m.o. I ought to be coming up with is one for going straight."

Harry set the glasses on the table and squeezed in next to Etta. "What's that you say?"

"Maybe it's time to turn over a new leaf . . . think about going legit." Butch sipped his drink.

Harry and Etta exchanged looks. "You're joking, ain't ya?" Harry laughed uneasily.

His partner glanced around, making sure no one was listening. "You know as well as I do how it's going down. Elzy and Bub in prison, Flat Nose gunned down, our recent run-in with Murray. Life is getting too damned dangerous."

"Wait a minute," Etta broke in. "What are you talking about? What happened to Flat Nose? And who's Murray?"

"Flat Nose bought it back in April . . . posse gunned him down."

Etta inhaled sharply, blinking back sudden moistness in her eyes. Her tears were not so much in grief over Flat Nose Currie's fate, for she had never met the man, but because it could just as easily have been Butch or Harry run down by a posse. They were all living on the edge, a dangerous, if thrilling, place to be.

"Murray's a Pinkerton detective, tracked us down in New Mexico," Harry went on.

"My God!" Etta paled. "What happened?"

Harry shook his head. "The less you know, the better, sweetheart."

"Go ahead, tell her," prompted Butch.

Etta smiled at him gratefully.

Stroking his mustache, Longabaugh eyed his partner across the table. He had, of course, intended to tell Etta everything in private because he had assumed Butch would object to him sharing confidences with his girlfriend. Now his partner had made him look bad, like he was the one who did not trust Etta. Scowling, he turned to explain.

"Some of the money from the Wilcox job got one edge burned off when the safes blew. This Murray fella was assigned to track it down. When some of it turned up around the WS, Murray appeared and started asking questions. He showed French, the WS manager, a picture of Butch and asked if he knew him."

"So the Pinkertons have connected you to the Wilcox robbery?" Etta turned a worried face to Cassidy.

He shrugged. "According to French,

Murray didn't come out and say as much. But it appears they've put two and two together."

"Did French identify you?"

"Well, he couldn't very well risk being accused of aiding and abetting a known outlaw, now could he? He told Murray he knew me as Jim Lowe, but that I wasn't at the ranch right then."

"Which was true," Longabaugh said. "We was both in Alma. Butch was tending bar."

Etta raised a sculptured eyebrow. "So now we can add saloonkeeper to your list of accomplishments?"

"Hey, it ain't bad work, long as you don't drink up your profits." Butch grinned. "Actually, I was just filling in for a friend. But it turned out to be kinda handy 'cause Murray walked into the place, not realizing it was me behind the bar. He didn't recognize me right off the bat, so he starts asking questions, and pretty soon I've got it figgered out who he is."

"Did you escape before he recognized you?"

"Hell, I wasn't gonna run from that weasel! Harry was all for making the problem disappear permanently, but, instead, we just talked some sense into him."

"How did you manage that?"

151

Butch smiled and downed his drink. "Convinced him it was not to his benefit to mess with the Wild Bunch. You know, your lover boy there can be mighty convincing when he needs to be."

"I ain't doing so hot tonight," complained Harry, running his hand over Etta's velvet-covered thigh beneath the table. Smiling, she laced her fingers through his, halting his exploration. He let loose a frustrated sigh.

Etta frowned, thinking. "So you've evidently been connected to Wilcox. Is that the reason for all this talk of going straight? Maybe you should rethink it, Butch. I mean going straight poses its own set of problems, doesn't it? You can't just all of a sudden reform your ways and expect the law to forgive and forget."

"Nah, that ain't how it works. I'd have to ask for a pardon."

At that, Longabaugh's ears perked up. "Hold on there, bud. What about the rest of us? You getting pardoned don't do me or Harvey or any of the other fellas any good."

"Oh hush, Harry." Etta gave his hand a schoolmarmish pat. "Butch is only thinking out loud. He'd never leave the gang hanging out to dry."

Harry said nothing, but the stubborn look

on his face made it clear he did not at all cotton to the direction of his partner's thinking.

Butch sighed, sorry that he had broached the subject. In truth, contrary to Etta's assumption, he had done a lot more than just think about going straight. A few weeks ago, he had made contact with his long-time friend and attorney, Douglas Preston, to ask his advice on the matter. Although he was wanted in a number of states, Preston had counseled him to begin his application for amnesty in Utah, where Cassidy's family still resided. The Parkers were honorable folks, and, if Butch were to try to rehabilitate himself, it made sense to do it in his home state. Consequently, after resting up in Denver for a few days, he intended to head to Salt Lake City to see if it were possible to begin a new life. But thinking about it made him jittery, made his gut quiver like barbed wire strung too tightly.

He looked to Etta, wanting to talk it out with her. Of all the women he knew, she was the one with the best head on her shoulders, able to look at a problem from all sides and not get all emotional about it. Sort of like a man would, but even better, because with her, there was no out-size ego to get in the way. But Etta had finally succumbed to

Harry's entreaties, whispering into his ear and letting his hands encircle her waist and pull her close.

Rising, Butch dropped some coins on the table and ambled off, idly scanning the room to see if any of the female flesh caught his fancy. Etta pulled away long enough to watch him go.

"Poor Butch."

"Poor Butch!" Harry turned her chin back in his direction. "I'm the one's been pining away for the last six months. Don't you feel sorry for me?"

"Of course not! At least you've got me to pine for. Poor Butch doesn't have anyone. He must be so lonely."

"Lonely, my foot. That jasper must have a thousand friends, all the way from Canada down to Mexico."

Etta rested her head softly against her man's shoulder. "Perhaps he'd trade a thousand friends for just one lover."

CHAPTER ELEVEN

The banks of the Grand were just starting to green up with spring run-off, but the river still ran low enough to make for an easy crossing. Butch sat his tall bay, thinking back to the day sixteen years ago when he had first crossed this river, on the run from the law in his home county and headed for the bawdy mining town of Telluride. Eighteen years old and already an outlaw. His mother had pleaded with him not to leave, tried to make him see that he would be better off staying and facing his accusers. He could see now that she had been right. He should have turned himself in, accepted his punishment, and been done with it. But the boy he had been back then couldn't see beyond the dreams of his youth, dreams of independence and adventure, of wide-open spaces and the freedom of the road.

Now the man looked back over the years and wondered if he'd really changed. Was he any more willing, now, to turn himself in and face the music? Were his dreams different now? A wry smile played on his lips. No, his dreams had not changed any, only the means of achieving them.

He urged the bay into the chilly water and crossed easily, barely wetting the soles of his boots. The warm spring sun soon dried his horse's coat to a sleek finish. He pointed the animal northwest, toward the town of Green River where he planned to put up for the night.

How well he knew this desolate country, perhaps even better than the handful of ranchers who scratched out a living on these arid flats. His own family's homestead in Circle Valley was downright lush compared to this desert, yet it had never provided more than the most basic subsistence for the Parkers. Whether that was due to his father's pitiful farming skills, or the fact that with thirteen mouths to feed the family's needs were simply too great, Butch didn't care to ponder. All he knew was that he ought to fall on his knees and thank God, or whoever might be listening up there, for delivering him from that particular hell.

In fact, the more he thought about it, the happier he was that that brash young teenager had high-tailed it away from home. Surely the life he had forged since then had been far superior to the life of a dirt-poor sodbuster, married to a woman who was stove-up by the age of thirty from having birthed too many god-damned babies.

He winced inwardly as a vision of his mother's lined face and prematurely gray hair came to mind. He had always wondered if his leaving had made her life harder, and hoped that his younger brothers had been able to take up the slack for him. But, although he loved his family and occasionally missed his mother, he had no intention of returning to the Parker fold. Nor was he above trading on their good name, if that's what it took to make this pardon thing work.

As always when thoughts of home and family crossed his mind, he remembered the one woman he might have loved, if she had let him. Mary Boyd had taken more from him than he thought he had to give. There had even been a time, right after he got out of prison, when he had contemplated settling down with her. But she had been weak, had not been able to wait for him, and now she belonged to another man. What would she do, he wondered, if his petition for amnesty were successful and he came to her an unencumbered man? Before it even had a chance to take hold, he pushed the thought away from him. Still, something made him dig in his spurs to pick up the pace.

★ ★ ★

It had been many years since Butch's last visit to Salt Lake City, and in that time the little town at the base of the Wasatch Mountains had changed. No longer merely a commercial center for farmers and ranchers and the headquarters of the Mormon Church, it had grown into a mining and industrial powerhouse and, with Utah's recent entrance into the Union, the seat of state government. Butch was amazed at the hustle and bustle on its wide avenues, the maze of telephone and electric wires that crisscrossed over his head, and the grandiose buildings that cast shadows on the brick-paved streets.

After stabling his horse and finding lodging, he decided to get right to his reason for being there. Preston had told him to present his case to an influential lawyer by the name of Orlando Powers. It was a name Butch was familiar with; a few years back, he had raised money to pay Powers's legal fees for representing Butch's good friend, Matt Warner. Whether Powers knew that the money to pay him had come from a bank hold-up, Butch wasn't sure. But the money had been funneled through Douglas Preston, whose association with Cassidy was widely known, so Powers likely had some inkling who was behind it all. That was why, despite having no appointment, the outlaw was fairly certain he would be civilly received.

Butch had been in such a hurry to see Powers he had not bothered to clean up first. When he stepped into the well-appointed office, the girl at the desk gave him a frightened look.

Removing his sweat-stained hat, he smiled engagingly. "Afternoon, miss. Was wondering would it be possible for me to see Judge Powers."

The girl hesitated, mindful of her employer's reluctance to see drop-ins, especially ones as scruffy-looking as this. "Who should I say is calling?" she asked, rising from her chair.

"Just tell him it's a friend of Matt Warner's and that Preston sent me."

She nodded and invited him to take a seat. Instead, he strolled over to the window to look down on the busy street four stories below. Out of habit, he assessed the various routes of escape before remembering that he was here on a perfectly legitimate call. Furthermore, if his business today were successful, he would never again have to look over his shoulder.

The door to the inner office opened, and

Orlando Powers strode over to greet him, hand extended. "Good day to you, sir," he boomed, his eyes alive with interest as he finally beheld the notorious outlaw of whom he had heard so much. "Won't you come in?"

Powers ushered him into his office, instructing the wide-eyed receptionist not to let anyone disturb them. Propping himself against his large mahogany desk, the lawyer crossed his arms over his chest and silently inspected his visitor. Butch stared back, trying to glean from Powers's demeanor whether the man could be trusted. He had received him immediately and had had the good sense not to greet him by name in front of the office girl. All of that showed a sense of discretion, at the very least.

"Reckon you know who I am," Butch began.

Powers nodded his big head slowly and deliberately. "Oh yes. Butch Cassidy, if I'm not mistaken. You appear to have been on the road for a while. Would you care for a drink?"

"That'd suit me fine."

Powers crossed to the sideboard and poured two shots of whisky. "Your health," he toasted, raising his glass.

Butch nodded his appreciation. "You

might say it's my health I'm here about."

Powers downed his drink and moved behind his desk. "Have a seat," he said, pointing to a chair opposite him.

Butch sat, running his hands over the smooth grain of the leather upholstery. Everything in this room was designed to put one at ease, but as he contemplated what he would say next, he found himself far from comfortable.

"Is what I say to you here considered confidential?"

Powers leaned back in his chair and regarded him over tented fingers. "If you're asking me do I consider this to be a privileged communication between a lawyer and his client, the answer is yes."

"Well, then" — Cassidy nervously drummed his fingers on the arms of the chair — "here's the gist of things. I'm thirty-four years old. I've been running from the law since I was eighteen. Some of what they say I did, reckon I might have done. But I'm also getting a lot of the credit, or blame is more like it, for things I never did. You might say I'm playing a losing game. Most of the fellas I've rode with are either dead or locked up. I can't see much future in continuing the way I've been going, so I'm looking for another way."

Powers's piercing gaze never wavered. "What way is that?"

Butch came to his feet and began to pace in front of the lawyer's desk. "Far as I know, there ain't no charges against me in Utah, leastways nothing they can pin on me for sure. My family lives here, and they're fine, hard-working people. Well, except for maybe my brother, Dan, but he ain't done nothing too terrible. So, I was thinking . . ." — he halted and looked directly at Powers — "maybe the governor would issue me a pardon. I'd give my word never to cause no more trouble if he'd just give me a chance to go straight."

Powers cleared his throat, casting about for a way to respond. He did not doubt the outlaw's sincerity, but it was an impossible request. Rising to pour more whisky, he attempted to formulate an explanation.

"Mister Cassidy. . . ."

"Butch."

"Butch . . ." — he handed him his drink — "I wish it were in my power to help you. But what you've suggested is tactically and legally impossible."

"Why?"

"No one can pardon you for crimes for which you've not yet been convicted. Furthermore, the governor has no power to grant you amnesty for any past or future crimes. For example, you say there aren't any charges against you in Utah, but what about the Castle Gate robbery? The governor cannot give you immunity from prosecution in that case. If you were to stand trial and be convicted, he could issue a pardon, but, as soon as you walked out the courthouse door, I can guarantee you the Wyoming and Colorado sheriffs would be waiting to arrest you for what you've done in their states."

"I ain't afraid to stand trial for Castle Gate or any other job!" Butch declared boldly. "There ain't no one who can identify me."

"Are you forgetting Carpenter?"

"Who?"

"The payroll clerk you robbed at Castle Gate. He got a good look at you. He's been quoted in the papers, saying he's sure he can positively identify you."

"Shit!" Butch slammed down his still full glass of whisky, spilling a few drops on the gleaming desk. "That won't stand up. Any lawyer worth his salt could tear holes a mile wide in that story."

"I wouldn't bet the farm on it. Besides, even if Carpenter could be discredited, you've got too many enemies, Butch. Somebody else is bound to turn up."

"I've got a damned sight more friends than enemies. The people in this state don't want to see me behind bars."

Shaking his head with the futility of it all, Powers spoke in a quiet voice. "Butch, which people are you referring to, exactly? The small shop owners and business men who are afraid to put their money in a bank because it might get robbed by the Wild Bunch? The poor miner who watched his payroll ride down the cañon with you at Castle Gate? The young railroad clerk, guarding the express car, who shakes in his shoes for fear he's next on your list? I've no doubt you've plenty of friends who like and admire you, but to most people you're a very dangerous criminal."

"Listen here," Cassidy took a threatening step forward, "I ain't never taken money from a poor man . . . only from banks and railroads who never yet did a poor man a favor."

"I know that's how you see it, Butch. But I think you'd have a tough time bringing Governor Wells around to that point of view, not to mention the governors of all the other states where you're wanted. Here's my advice . . . lie low for a while. Stay out of trouble for a few years, and then see about petitioning for amnesty."

"A few years!" Butch raked his hand through his hair. "You've got no idea what it's like living on the dodge, Judge. My luck won't last forever."

"Then perhaps you should think about leaving the country. Start over in a new place where no one knows your name. Who knows, if you keep out of the limelight for a while, perhaps someday you could return with the slate wiped clean."

Cassidy thought for a moment, rubbing his chin with a rough, chapped hand. "Is that all you got to offer me in the way of advice?"

"I'm afraid so."

Tiredly Butch settled his hat on his head and made for the door. "Thanks for your time, Judge. I wish it could be some other way, but . . . well, reckon I got no one to blame but myself."

He let himself out and crossed the front office, nodding to the receptionist as he passed. Powers called to him from the doorway. "Sir . . . take care of yourself."

Turning, Butch tried for a smile. "That's what I aim to do."

CHAPTER TWELVE

Butch's first inclination, following his disappointing meeting with Powers, was to flee the city. Always before, he had regrouped from a misstep by getting lost for a spell — setting out for the wide-open country and letting the stars and coyotes be his companions until he conjured up a new plan. But the afternoon had worn on, and he had paid for his lodging for the night, so he figured on staying at least until the next morning.

With time to kill and much on his mind, he picked a direction and started walking. The day that had started out warm and sunny had turned cold, and a brisk breeze hinted of oncoming weather. The surrounding mountains had disappeared in a shroud of clouds. Butch turned up the collar of his coat and jammed his hands in his pockets, thinking that a sane man would repair to his hotel for a hot bath, a meal, and a warm bed — comforts that should never be taken for granted, especially for one in his line of work.

He continued walking, unmindful of the passers-by, replaying his meeting with Powers over and over in his head. *No immunity from prosecution, too many enemies, lie low for a while, think about leaving the country.* Christ! He had counted so much on this working, it had never occurred to him that he would be turned down flat. For one thing, Preston had seemed so sure the mighty Powers could help him.

That god-damned Preston! Why the hell hadn't he known it would be no good? He probably just wanted to share a good laugh with Powers. He could picture them, sipping their expensive whisky in their exclusive men's club, keeping their voices low as they bandied about stories of their infamous client, lording it over lesser members of their profession because Butch Cassidy, the greatest rogue in the West, had put himself in their hands. Hell, what was in it for them if he went straight? They'd lose their most prominent client, the one that would get them written up in the history books.

He pounded the pavement, his anger and resentment increasing with each step, until suddenly, with no warning, he was left with nothing but emptiness, a feeling like falling through space with no idea of where the ground was. He stopped abruptly and closed his eyes. The sensation of losing himself was terrifying, and, if he had not been dimly aware of standing on a public street, he would have reached out a hand in search of an anchor. He took a deep breath, hoping no one had noted his odd behavior. The people on the street moved around and past him, paying him no mind, armed with their purposes in life. Did he envy them? At that moment, he could not say.

Shrugging back into his collar, he retraced his steps, eager to leave behind the remnants of his fear. He made his mind go blank, acknowledging only a desire to eat and sleep.

Next to his hotel, he spied a mercantile. In need of some shaving articles, he ducked inside. The aisles were full of people just off work. He found what he needed and took it to the counter where there was a long line of customers waiting to pay. Conversations swirled around him — people chattering about the sudden change in weather, their various ailments, last Sunday's testimony at Temple. Butch stood silently, a trespasser among small people discussing the small details of normal, everyday life, a life that, it seemed, would never be his.

He felt a tug on his arm. Turning, he recognized the receptionist from Orlando

Powers's office, looking at him from beneath light-colored lashes.

"Good afternoon," she said, her voice small and tinkly, like a chime made of seashells. "You probably don't remember me."

"Sure I do." It came out sounding gruff, as though he were angry with her for having drawn him back to the moment. He started over in a friendlier manner. "I remember thinking how lucky Judge Powers is to have a pretty gal like you working for him." He had actually thought no such thing, having barely noticed the girl in his preoccupation with other matters. But, he saw now, she was a cute little thing.

She blushed. "I confess when you first walked in, just off the street and all, I doubted the judge would see you. Forgive me if I acted rudely towards you."

"Why, you treated me better than I had a right to expect," he admitted. "Reckon Judge Powers don't get too many visitors right in off the range."

"Not too many. But you're a special case, aren't you? I could tell by the way he greeted you." She looked at him with frank curiosity.

Butch's guard went up. Small and cute this girl might be, but he would do well to be wary. They moved up a place in line as he sought to redirect the conversation. "You from around here?"

"I grew up in Rawlins, but, since my mother died, I've lived with my cousin just a few blocks over. She, my cousin that is, suffers from the catarrh, so I told her I'd bring her a remedy." She held up a bottle of cherry-colored syrup. "My name is Doris, by the way. Doris Byrd." She stuck out a tiny-boned hand.

Butch took it reluctantly, feeling awkward at making the acquaintance of a proper young lady. His experience had been almost exclusively with women of another bent. "Pleasure," he mumbled.

She waited, and he realized she expected him to reciprocate introductions. "I'm Jim. . . ." His mind raced. Should he use the name Jim Lowe? Probably not, since the Pinkertons were onto that alias. After all, she worked in a law office and might run across a flyer on him. His gaze settled on the shelf behind her where containers of Dr. Ryan's Invigorating Elixir were stacked. "Jim Ryan," he declared.

"Nice to meet you, Mister Ryan." She smiled, revealing two charming dimples. "Will you be stopping in town long?"

" 'Fraid not. My business here is done."

"What a shame." Her face fell. "The city

has so many new attractions, one could easily keep oneself entertained for several days."

A teasing look came into his eye. "If I was to stick around, would you show me all the attractions, Miss Byrd?"

"Why, I'd be delighted!" she exclaimed, innocently missing the hidden meaning in his question. "We could take in the show at the theater tonight, and tomorrow there's a band concert at Saltair, although if this weather keeps up, perhaps we'd want to reconsider. . . ."

She broke off, suddenly noticing Butch's guarded expression. They reached the front of the line and paid for their purchases. Doris kept her head down, mortified that she had appeared too forward in her enthusiasm. In truth, it was unlike her to take the initiative with men, but something about Mr. Ryan had attracted her from the moment she laid eyes on him. Now, fate had thrown him in her path again, and it seemed foolish not to take advantage of the coincidence.

They walked together to the front of the store where Butch took her elbow and guided her behind a rack displaying colored postcards. He fixed her with a kind look, noting again her delicate features and youthful innocence. There was a time in his life when he would not have hesitated to take advantage of a pretty girl's fascination with him. But caution was now his watchword, and it was clear he did not need the distraction of a Miss Byrd.

"Listen," he said, "a girl like you ain't got no business sharing the company of a man like me. I'm a stranger, just passing through. You don't know nothing about me, except I've been riding the trail for days on end to see if my lawyer can get me out of trouble. Pardon my saying so, miss, but you'd be a dang' fool to take up with someone like that."

Doris dropped her eyes, her cheeks flaming. "Judge Powers obviously thinks a lot of you. That's good enough for me. And, besides, I assume that, when you call for me, we'll sit down with my cousin and talk a little bit about your background. Abigail insists on meeting any man who keeps company with me."

"When I call for you?"

"Yes. Here's the address. . . ." She wrote quickly on the back of her receipt and pressed it into his hand. "I'm sure you're tired from your journey, so we won't expect you this evening. But tomorrow evening perhaps . . . ?"

He was half tempted to give into her persistence, which he found admirable. But the fact of the matter was he was too tired to make the effort, too dispirited to allow himself this small, human connection. "Miss Byrd . . . I'm leaving tomorrow morning."

Tears of embarrassment came to her pale eyes. "I see. My deepest apologies, Mister Ryan, for having foisted myself upon you. It was most unlady-like of me." She turned on her heel and pushed out the door.

Butch followed her onto the sidewalk. She paused at the corner, joining a group of people waiting for the next street car. Her posture, stiff with wounded pride, made him feel like a heel of the first order. Deciding to give her something pleasant to remember him by, he came up behind her, placed his hand on the small of her back, leaned over her shoulder, and whispered in her ear. "Lady-like behavior ain't all it's cracked up to be, Miss Byrd. Maybe someday down the road I'll be back and show you just what I mean by that."

Her eyes widened in shock, but she couldn't help smiling back, so handsome a picture did the rakish Jim Ryan make.

"My hotel's right there." He nodded across the street. "Can you get home all right?"

"Of course. My car comes right by here."
She drew up her shoulders and smiled
bravely. "It was a pleasure to make your acquaintance, Mister Ryan. Have a safe
journey, wherever you're headed."

"Good bye, Miss Byrd." He tipped his hat
and crossed the street, feeling her gaze on
his back. Silly young thing, to fall for a man
almost twice her age and a renegade to boot.
Not that she knew who he really was — if
she did, he doubted she would ever have had
the courage to speak to him. But still, she
must have known there was a shady side to
him. Some women were attracted to that in
a man, he reckoned, and you would not find
him complaining about that!

The next morning, Butch slept longer
than was his custom, and by the time he
rose, ate breakfast, and settled his hotel
bill, it was nigh on to mid-morning. After a
restless night spent pondering Orlando
Powers's advice regarding his future, he
had decided to return to Brown's Park
where he figured on hooking up with Harry
and Etta and the rest of the gang. He knew
Harry had been disturbed by his flirtation
with amnesty and would doubtless be relieved to hear it was not in the cards, after
all. But they needed to have a serious dis-

cussion of what came next. Should the Wild Bunch continue its reign of lawlessness, salting away booty for the inevitable day when that reign would end? Or had their day already passed so that, as Powers had suggested, their best course would be to leave the country before it all came crashing down around them?

Slinging his war bag over his shoulder, he caught sight of Orlando Powers crossing the hotel lobby, a look of relief on his expansive face.

"Glad I caught you," he said, clapping Butch on the shoulder as he steered him to a quiet corner of the large room. "I feared I'd be too late."

"Too late for what?" Butch said cautiously.

"Let's sit." Powers parked himself in an over-size, plush chair and motioned for Butch to do the same.

Butch sighed, annoyed at this delay. Now that he had come to terms with what Powers had told him yesterday, he was ready to move on. But he dropped his bag and sat. The chair wings enveloped them, affording complete privacy.

"How'd you find me?" Butch asked, worried that he'd been far too easy to track down.

Powers's eyes sparkled. "Through my office girl, Miss Byrd, who evidently was quite impressed with you. She made an off-hand comment this morning that she had enjoyed a chance meeting with Mister Ryan yesterday afternoon. I was not aware of your new moniker, so this meant nothing to me, but, when I inquired further, she revealed she meant the rather unkempt, albeit attractive, gentleman who had dropped in unannounced the previous day. I realized then, of course, that she was referring to you, sir, which was most gratifying as I had spent an almost entirely sleepless night coming up with a new plan for your rehabilitation and was not sure how to advise you of this. Luckily Miss Byrd knew where you were staying, and, as you can see, I have been able to intercept you before you departed."

Butch cocked his head impatiently. If lawyers charged by the word, they'd all be richer than John D. Rockefeller. "I'm still aiming to haul off pretty damned quick. Speak your piece."

Powers folded his hands, refusing to be put off by the outlaw's abruptness. "As I told you yesterday, Butch, amnesty from the government is not likely to occur in your case. But who else has a stake in the cessation of your criminal activities?"

"I ain't in the mood for a god-damned quiz," Butch grumbled.

"The railroads," Powers continued, unperturbed. "There can be no dispute that in the past decade the railroads have been the target of groups of longriders such as yourself and your colleagues, as much as, if not more than, the banks. Now, I happen to have numerous contacts within the railroad industry, particularly with Union Pacific, one of the more aggrieved lines, and I can tell you that U.P. officials are quite fed up with law enforcement's inability to protect their trains. They are desperate to halt these violent assaults against their personnel and property. Forgive my bluntness, Butch, for I am well aware that you yourself do not condone violence inflicted upon your victims. There are others, however, who are not so reluctant to use force. But that's neither here nor there. The point is the railroads want these attacks stopped."

"There's a headline for ya . . . 'railroads want robbers stopped'. Got any other news hot off the presses?"

Powers chuckled. "Naturally I'm not telling you anything you don't already know. But I want to make it clear that, in my view, the railroads are desperate enough to consider making a deal."

Butch's eyes narrowed. "I'm listening."

"I propose that myself and Douglas Preston, as your representatives, go to Union Pacific and ask them to grant you their own amnesty, in other words, agree not to press charges against you. In return, you would agree to leave them alone . . . forever."

Butch thought a minute. "What about the cases where they've already pressed charges? I thought you said the government couldn't grant me immunity from prosecution for any of those."

"Quite right." Powers leaned forward, elbows on knees. "But I'm sure it will come as no surprise to you that U.P. exercises a good deal of influence over various government officials. I believe it's quite likely they could convince them to delay prosecution indefinitely. It's perhaps a bit of a risk, but one should never underestimate the power of E. H. Harriman."

"I got to tell you, Powers, it'd stick in my craw to ask any favors from that bastard." Butch scowled, only too familiar with the flamboyant railroad magnate.

"No favors. A straightforward deal. You get what you want, Harriman gets what he wants, and everybody's happy."

"Not everybody. What about the rest of

the boys? Would they get amnesty, too?"

"I doubt they'd be willing to go that far. But without your leadership, Butch, how long could your gang survive? Look at Belle Fourche. Everybody knows the gang botched that job because you weren't in charge. Take away the brains of the operation and the brawn starts to look pretty puny."

Startled that the lawyer knew so much about his gang's activities, Butch mulled things over. If Powers knew so many details, then the law did, too. It meant the circle was closing, time running out. He must act now.

"Reckon there's no harm in seeing what they have to say. But I ain't gonna take just any deal. It'll have to be on my terms . . . and I want it in writing with E. H. Harriman's signature on the line."

CHAPTER THIRTEEN

With surprising alacrity, Union Pacific officials agreed to the deal, or, at least, agreed to meet with their nemesis to discuss it. A time and place, dictated by Cassidy, were set for the rendezvous. He chose Lost Soldier Pass, a former stop on the stage route to Lander, for its isolation and proximity to the rugged Green Mountains. Not fully trusting the railroad men, or even his own lawyers, he wanted every advantage should he need to make a quick escape.

He arrived well before the appointed time, circling the area cautiously before dismounting. It was a cold day, the air raw with the promise of moist, spring snow. A fire would have been nice, but he did not want to advertise his presence. He would stay well hidden until the others arrived, just in case they had double-crossed him and invited the law to come along.

Pounding his arms to stay warm, he staked his horse behind some brush and crouched down behind a large boulder. His breath in the cold air was visible. Not for the first time, he wondered if he was doing the right thing. This consorting with the enemy felt like betrayal, not just of his gang, who knew nothing of this meeting, but of himself. He despised these people and all they represented — the concentration of money and power in the hands of a few while regular folks struggled to survive. He had never felt the least bit guilty for stealing from them; in his view, he was just taking back what they had stolen in the first place. And hadn't he often used his ill-gotten gains to help out some desperate widow, or destitute farmer? He could hardly see why he was called a crook and hunted by the law while the real criminals freely plundered their defenseless victims.

Rising, he checked the perimeter one more time, mostly to warm himself with the movement. Satisfied no one could sneak up on him, he returned to his hiding place and ran a hand over his horse's nose.

"Reckon no one promised there'd be anything fair about any of this, eh, boy?" He continued to stroke the animal gently. "The system says I'm the bad guy, so either I got to stay real lucky and not get caught, or I got to work a deal. My luck's been mostly good up to now, but what if it runs out?"

The horse flicked its ears as though commiserating with its master. Butch leaned his arm on the saddle and continued to muse out loud. "What'll the two of us do if this deal goes through, boy? Stay out of sight for a while, I reckon, till we're sure it's gonna work. Probably oughta go somewheres where my name ain't so well known. Though I'd hate to leave this country . . . there ain't nothing like it."

He took a deep, bracing breath. Even on this cold, gray day, with the sky closing in around him, he felt the space that could no longer be seen, space stretching to the horizon.

" 'Course, we wouldn't necessarily have to leave," he told his horse. "Most likely we could settle some place where nobody'd bother us. I'd raise horses, just like before . . ."

He stopped short, remembering his previous ill-fated ranching venture with a partner who wound up betraying him. That misplaced friendship had cost him two years of his life, two years wasting away in the pen, and that had not been the worst of it. The worst thing was that he had lost Mary.

Damn this cold! He crammed his hands

under his armpits and shifted back and forth on his feet, trying to get the blood moving. Snow was coming down now, melting as it landed on his horse's warm hide, but starting to collect on the saddle's cold surface. He dug in his pocket for his watch and snapped it open. They were late. Hunching down behind the boulder, he blew on his hands.

Minutes passed. He kept his ears tuned for any sound of their coming, but all he heard was the creak of tall pine trees, swaying in the breeze, and the occasional movement of his horse. He waited. Soon the wind picked up, sending wet, pebble-like snow skittering across the ground. It blew against his cheek, forcing him to tuck his head into his shoulder. He checked his watch again. They were now very late. Something was wrong.

Removing the blanket from behind his saddle, he draped it around his head and shoulders and stood on the leeward side of his horse. The sleet-like snow came down harder, bouncing off the ground, the rocks, his horse, his own body, like tiny BBs. Where the hell were they? Something had gone wrong, and it could not be just this storm. They should have been here long ago, before the bad weather had moved in.

"Fuck this," he growled. Scrabbling in his bags for paper and pencil, he hastily scrawled a note, stuck it under a rock in the center of the clearing, and built a cairn over it. Still cursing, he swung onto his horse and trotted away, his trail disappearing in the fast falling snow.

Several hours later, a beleaguered party of four rode into the clearing, wet to the skin despite their shiny new Fish Brand slickers. They had started out of Rawlins that morning, only to be turned back by the severity of the storm, which had blown up from the south and immediately turned the trail into a nearly impassable sheet of slick mud. The two railroad officials, who had been dispatched from headquarters in Omaha, lacked the proper gear for such weather and had insisted on returning to town until the blizzard abated. Reluctantly Preston and Powers had agreed. While waiting for the skies to clear, the U.P. men got themselves properly outfitted.

The skies had never completely cleared, although the snow finally let up enough to allow them to proceed. But they were late, very late, and the two lawyers knew that did not bode well for the success of their mission.

Preston spotted the cairn immediately.

"He's been here," he said, furrowing his bushy eyebrows. Sliding from his horse, he kicked at the pile of rocks, uncovering the note Butch had left. Glancing at the others, he picked it up and read it, his face turning dark. Wordlessly he passed the note to Powers and stalked off.

"What's it say?" asked one of the railroad men.

Powers stretched his arm out as far as it would go and squinted at the smudged writing. "It says . . . 'Damn you Preston, you have double-crossed me. I waited all day but you didn't show up. Tell the U.P. to go to hell. And you can go with them'."

The August sun was stifling, the high desert heat oppressive at midday, although the night would be forty degrees cooler. Matt Warner pulled his handkerchief from his pocket and wiped his sweating face. He stared out the window of the train car, only half aware of the dry, brown landscape tumbling by. The other half of his brain was busy recalling his friend and former partner, Butch Cassidy.

Eleven years ago, he and Butch had held up the bank in Telluride, launching Butch's outlaw career. They had been close back then, sharing a love of fast horses and wild times. But their partnership had foundered, in part, Warner could now admit, because of his fondness for the bottle. Nevertheless, Cassidy had remained loyal, paying for attorneys when Warner got into trouble and making sure his family was provided for while he served his time. A man was lucky to have a friend like that. It would be wrong to turn your back on such a friend.

That was why, when Orlando Powers and Governor Wells had come to him and asked his help in getting a message to Butch, he could not say no, that, and the two hundred dollars Powers had pressed into his hand. Still, Warner would never have agreed to hunt up his friend if he weren't convinced he'd be doing him a favor. Seems that Butch had been thinking of going straight, just like Warner intended to do now that he was out of prison. But there'd been some mix-up with the U.P. men sent to negotiate with Butch, and the meeting had never taken place. Knowing Cassidy suspected a double-cross, Powers had sought out a trusted friend to bring him the message that the deal with Union Pacific was still on, if Cassidy wanted to reconsider.

Wiping his face again, Warner wondered how his old comrade would receive this news. If Warner were a betting man, which, in fact, he was, he would bet that Cassidy would reject the offer. As loyal and forgiving as Butch was with those who had earned his trust, once that trust was broken, there was no repairing it. No, if Butch Cassidy wanted to leave behind the outlaw life, he'd most likely do it without the assistance of the Union Pacific Railroad. Still, Warner would bring him the message — maybe they'd get a good laugh out of it. And he'd be two hundred dollars richer.

The rhythm of the train wheels kicked down a notch or two as they neared the Bridger station. Matt planned on getting off at Rock Springs and heading south from there, hoping to find the gang ensconced at Brown's Park.

Reaching into his bag, he pulled out a peach and started munching. In a matter of minutes, the train started up again. As he tossed the peach pit out the window and reached for his handkerchief, the conductor trotted down the aisle and handed him a telegram.

"It's from Governor Wells, sir," the man said, impressed with the import of such a message.

Surprised, Matt unfolded the note. *All agreements are off,* he read. *Cassidy just held up a train at Tipton.*

PART III
1902–1908

CHAPTER FOURTEEN

The Cordillera was as beautiful as its name. Rising abruptly from the sandy Patagonian plain, the chain of rugged peaks reminded Butch of his beloved Rocky Mountains. Just as the sprawling ranch he and Harry and Etta were homesteading on the pampas put him in mind of Hole-in-the-Wall. In many ways, this treeless prairie was a sight better than any ranch in Wyoming. No god-damned snakes, for one thing. Not many people, either, although he supposed no one would accuse Wyoming of being overpopulated. But it, along with everywhere else in the West, was getting too damned civilized, too . . . connected.

Not so here. This was wide-open country, untrammeled and largely unclaimed, and, although there were a few other ranchers around and a few Indians here and there, a man could ride for days without seeing another soul.

A frightened bleating rose above the gen-

eral noise of the herd. Turning his horse toward the distressed sound, he saw that a
young ewe had stepped into a rodent hole
and gotten her leg stuck.

"Stupid bitch," he muttered, her plaintive
cries leaving him unmoved. "Look where
you're going, why don'tcha." Dismounting,
he straddled the animal, grasped her leg,
and pulled it free. The ewe bounded away.
He stood and kicked dust into the hole.

The idea of being a sheep rancher had
never appealed to him, sheep being such
dirty, stupid animals. But it made sense
down here. He and Harry planned to lay
claim to twenty-five thousand acres, and
with that much grazing land they could
easily run both cattle and sheep. The market
lay to the west, over the mountains to the
coast of Chile. Luckily the Chilean government had cut a road through the pass last
summer, making the trip considerably
faster. That had been one of the consider-
ations when they chose this piece of property, that, and its remote location.

Butch climbed back into the saddle and
headed toward the four-room log cabin the
three of them called home. He smiled when
it came into view, a fine-looking structure
made of hand-hewn cypress he and Harry
had hauled down from the mountains. They

had gone the extra mile to erect a comfortable, sturdy cabin, hoping to make Etta feel it was a home worthy of her. She had risen to the challenge, decorating the walls with magazine pictures and setting out mementos of their travels. It was the first home that had ever been truly hers, and she seemed quite happy with it.

All except for the windows. Etta was insisting on real windows from the States that would have to be ordered next time they were in town. The local variety seemed fine to Butch, but if Etta wanted four-pane, double-hung windows, by God, she'd get them.

As he pulled up in the yard, he could see a rider slowly approaching. Automatically his hand went to his gun belt in a cautionary move that a year in the pampas still had not weaned out of him. Recognizing the oncoming mount as belonging to neighboring rancher Jock Gardiner, he relaxed.

" 'Mornin', Jim." Gardiner nodded a friendly greeting to the man he knew as Jim Ryan. "I'm pleased to find ya here today."

"Just caught me, too. Thought I'd mosey into town, do me some window-shopping, maybe take in one of the titty shows. Want to come along?"

Gardiner looked momentarily confused, then lapsed into a sheepish grin. "Jim, always joshin' ya are," he said in his thick Scottish brogue. "Ya know there's no such things in Cholila."

"Do I ever." Butch loosened the cinch on his saddle. "Just wishful thinking, I reckon."

"Now why would ya be wantin' to see the burlesque when ya've got such a lovely vision of womankind in your own home?" Gardiner glanced wistfully toward the cabin.

"She's purty to look at, all right, but after a while a man wants to do more'n just look. And with Etta, looking's all you're ever gonna get." Butch winked at the younger man.

It was no secret that Jock Gardiner had fallen under Etta's spell from the moment they had met on the boat coming up the Chubut River. The three Westerners had been scouting for a place to settle, and Gardiner, an educated man who had homesteaded a ranch in the province of Chubut, had helped them find their own place and sold them their first livestock.

Butch liked the young Scotsman and appreciated his savvy in dealing with the locals, but Harry, probably jealous of the man's attentions to Etta, treated him poorly. The chilly reception he received from Etta's "husband," however, failed to keep Gardiner from making frequent visits on some excuse or other.

Blushing, Jock hopped down and pulled a volume from his bags. "This just came to me in the mail . . . a book of poems by Mister Whitman. I thought to share it with Missus Place, knowin' how she appreciates such things."

"Well, now, that's mighty thoughtful of you, son." Butch clapped him on the back. "Let's go in and see what's cooking for dinner."

Etta turned from the cook stove as they entered and gave Jock a brilliant smile. The young man turned an even brighter shade of red. "Hello there, Jock, have you brought me something to read?"

"Indeed, ma'am, a book of poems."

"Wonderful. Perhaps you and I can read them together after dinner."

"Poems," scoffed Harry, who sat at the table cleaning his fingernails with his pocket knife. "How the hell do you get any work done when you spend half your time over here reading poetry?"

Etta set dishes on the table. "Poetry's one of life's rare pleasures, Harry. You'd do well to read some yourself."

"That right? Funny thing is, I'm so god-damn' busy running a ranch, I don't have time to do much reading." He flicked his knife closed and jammed his hands deeply into his pockets.

A little smile played on Etta's lips. She came around behind him and encircled him with her arms. "In that case, I'll take it upon myself to edify you. 'How do I love thee? Let me count the ways. I love thee to the depth and breadth and height my soul can reach. . . .'" She kissed Harry on the ear, simultaneously shooting a sly glance at the two men across the room.

As she started to move away, Harry caught her and pulled her onto his lap. "What the hell was that?" he asked, his voice gruff.

"Poetry. It does have its good points, you see." Taking his face in her hands, she gave him a quick kiss, and then hopped up. "Sit down, you two. You'll have to tell me what you think of this mutton stew. I threw everything into it but the kitchen sink."

After dinner Butch and Harry left to work on the storehouse they were building while Gardiner stayed behind to help Etta clean up.

"You ain't worried leaving them two alone?" asked Butch.

"Hell, no," sniffed Harry. "If Etta's gonna cheat on me, it ain't gonna be with that lily-livered priss."

Butch swung a hammer. "Who is it gonna be with?"

Harry narrowed his eyes. "What's that supposed to mean?"

"Don't mean nuthin'." Butch reached for another nail. "Just seems to me Etta ain't the cheating kind, that's all."

"Funny thing for you to say, of all people."

Butch halted in mid-swing. He turned to look at his partner, who stared back with red-rimmed eyes. "Guess it's my turn to ask what the hell you mean."

"You know damn' well what I mean. When Etta took up with me, she was still your woman. She cheated on you."

"Showed mighty good sense on her part, wouldn't you say?"

Harry relaxed, allowing himself a small chuckle. It caught in his throat and turned into a hacking cough. Grabbing his hand-kerchief, he wiped his streaming nose.

Butch picked up his toolbox and moved to the other side of the half built storehouse. Most days, he felt perfectly content with their little threesome, a *ménage à trois*, as Etta called it. There were times when he felt like the odd man out, and times, like now, when Harry became moody and was diffi-cult to live with. But Etta was an unexpected joy, like a bloom in the desert, brightening their days and making him almost forget they lived on the edge of nowhere.

He should have paid closer attention to her when she was his girl, that winter at the Roost. Maybe, if he'd tried harder to please her, she would not have had a roving eye. But he had been too busy planning the Castle Gate job and, might as well face it, still smarting over Mary Boyd.

He grimaced, remembering how, when he had first decided to take Orlando Powers up on his advice and leave the country, he had actually considered tracking down Mary and asking her to come with him. Thank God, he had come to his senses before making a fool of himself again over that woman. But the ache was still there, mostly buried now, only breaking out at certain moments — coming across an Indian woman on the road whose long, midnight black hair was like hers, or rolling over in his warm blankets first thing in the morning and thinking, for a split second, that he would wake up next to her.

Harry came around the corner, still wiping at his nose. His eyes looked red and watery. "Listen, Butch," he said, "Etta and me are thinking of going back."

Butch looked up in surprise.

"Not for good," Harry said. "Just for a

little while. Etta's been pining to see my sister, Samanna. They hit if off real good when they met last year, you know, on our way to New York, and they've been writing each other pretty regular. She thought now'd be a good time to go, before the rain sets in. 'Sides, I got to do something about this catarrh 'fore it kills me. Samanna knows some doctor specializes in sinus treatments."

"Gardiner says the native women can cure whatever ails you."

Harry snorted. "Maybe some herbal shit's good enough for him, but I ain't gonna let no witch doctor practice on me."

With a sigh, Butch tossed the hammer into the toolbox. Bracing himself against the storehouse wall, he gazed past Harry at the waving grass where his cattle grazed peacefully. A thrush tittered somewhere out in the meadow. Pretty purple flowers — he had not yet learned what they were called — dotted the yard.

How could Harry and Etta leave now, just when they were getting started?

"There's doctors in Buenos Aires," he said, although he could see Harry had already made up his mind.

"I know that." Harry dabbed at his eyes. "It ain't just for that, Butch. It's Etta. She wants to go back. You know how miserable it gets around here in the winter. It's been hard on her . . . no other white women nearby, no civilization to speak of. She's living on memories of that trip to New York."

Bullshit, Butch thought. *Etta's doing just fine.* Aloud, he said: "Don't know if I can run this place by myself. It's more work than one man can handle."

"That's why we thought we'd leave now, with winter coming on. Ain't as much to do when it rains all day long. Anyway, we was planning on hiring them two native boys to help out. You'll get by OK, Butch. We'll only be gone three or four months."

"It might not be safe to go back. We've only been gone a year. They ain't gonna give up looking for us that fast. Not after Tipton and Winnemucca."

Across the yard, the cabin door opened, and Etta emerged followed by Jock Gardiner. They exchanged a few words, and then Gardiner mounted up and rode away, touching a finger to his hat as he passed Butch and Harry. Etta spotted them and walked over, picking up her skirts to keep them from snagging on the prickly grass.

"Quick visit," Harry said. "Most times we can't get rid of the bastard."

Etta feigned a frown. "Now, now, Mister Place, try to be a bit more charitable. Jock's a lonely young man with no family of his own. You can't blame him for wanting some company now and then." She paused, sensing tension in the air. "You two having a heart-to-heart?"

"I told him you was wanting to go back to the States for a while," Harry said.

Etta's gaze quickly shifted to Butch. "Oh, dear. I had hoped we could bring this up all together. I'm sure Harry just sprung it on you without a full explanation."

"He explained, all right," Butch said, meeting her worried hazel eyes. "Said you wanted to visit with his family and he needs a doctor. Said you didn't want to stay for the rainy season. I can understand that, I guess. But you know, Etta, the rain's gonna come every year. It's a fact of life down here. You can't always be running away from it."

"I'm not running away from the rain," she said, standing tall, "and I'm not running away from you, Butch. This is my home now, and you and Harry are my family. When Harry told me about your plan to come to Argentina, I knew immediately that I wanted to come with you. This is an adventure of a lifetime, and I'm not giving up on it!"

Butch shook his head. "Then why are you going back?"

"When we left the States, I had no idea where we'd end up, or what we'd be living in." She turned to look at the cabin her men had built for her. "Now that we have a home, I want to make it perfect for us. A quick trip to New York and I can find everything we need . . . rugs, wallpaper, curtains . . . and double-hung windows, of course! We'll ship it all back and turn this place into our own private oasis. We'll never have to leave again."

The smile she turned on them was so full of hope and confidence, Butch knew he wouldn't stand in her way. She was still young. Too young to realize that "never" or "always" were concepts with no meaning for people like them.

"All right, then," he said. "Give me a couple of weeks to get things squared away. I'll go with you to Buenos Aires. I've been meaning to file our claim on this place with the land department there. I'll see you off."

Etta wrapped her arms around the two men and drew them close. "I love you both," she whispered.

Above her head, Harry and Butch locked eyes, knowing it wasn't that simple.

CHAPTER FIFTEEN

A month later, the threesome checked into the Hotel Europa in Buenos Aires, registering as Mr. and Mrs. Harry Place and James Ryan, Mrs. Place's brother. Two days after that, Harry and Etta sailed for New York.

Butch stayed on in Buenos Aires for another month, taking his fill of the city before returning to solitary life on the ranch. He worked his way through the brothels and drank far more than he was used to, aiming for a constant haze that would quiet all the nagging questions. Despite Etta's assurances, he was not at all certain she and Harry would come back. Harry's family ties were strong, much stronger than his own, and, if he decided to stay, Etta would stay as well. If they did not come back, then what? He could run the ranch by himself, with hired help, but he was no hermit. How long could he live all alone without going crazy?

His doubts kept him from filing their

claim with the land registry until the day he had planned to leave. But in the end, he did file it, deciding he would just have to take his closest friends at their word. Then he withdrew some money from the bank where they had deposited their share of the take from the Tipton and Winnemucca hold-ups, and headed for home.

The ranch had survived in his absence. The two *gauchos* he had hired to look after the livestock had done their job, and Jock Gardiner had come over a few times to supervise matters.

Upon his return, he settled into the daily routine of ranch life — tending the horses, feeding the chickens, making repairs, keeping himself fed and his clothes clean, although he was less particular about that than Etta would have been. The *gauchos* continued to help him with his livestock; he was glad they did not need much direction as he had not yet mastered even rudimentary Spanish. Now that Etta was gone, Gardiner was a less frequent visitor, but when he did come, he tried to help Butch learn a few key phrases in the native tongue. Normally a quick learner, Butch struggled with the lessons, usually giving up in frustration.

Around the first of May, the rains came.

Although Butch could often fool himself that he was back in the Rocky Mountain West, the deception came to a quick end with the onset of the rains. Unlike the quick cloudbursts at home, this was drenching rain, all day, every day, rain that mired his cattle and turned the roads into impassable rivers of mud, rain that molded his flour and wilted his blankets. He was glad he and Harry had laid in an ample supply of wood and that they had completed the storehouse so that the wood stayed dry. Some days were shrouded in a fog so dense he could not see the storehouse from the cabin door. Those were the worst days, when he felt trapped in a cage of his own making.

When he wasn't tending to the ranch, he spent his time reading the books Etta had left behind. It had been a long time since he had read anything besides a newspaper or magazine picked up in a barbershop. Some of what he read amused him, some of it, especially the poetry, he didn't really understand, but he liked the images it brought to mind. He smiled to himself when he came across Whitman's "trickling sap," "milky streams," "sweaty brooks," and "winds like soft-tickling genitals," picturing the besotted Gardiner reading these lines with Etta.

He closed the book and got up to stir the fire. The soft shifting of logs and *whoosh* of rejuvenated flame sounded thunderous in the quiet room. He stared at the fire, seeing Etta in his mind's eye.

Still holding the book of poems, he walked over to the room Etta and Harry shared, opened the door, and stepped in. He had only been in here two or three times since they left. A slight sheen of dust covered the crude dresser and bedside table. He would clean in here before they came home, although he had no way of knowing when that might be. They had not written at all, but that was to be expected. He had warned them it could be dangerous to write in the event someone was tailing them. But he had expected some kind of message, letting him know the date of their return. They had been gone five months now.

He came around the edge of the bed and sat down on the Wedding Ring quilt Harry's sister Samanna had sent with them. Etta always joked that it was the closest she would ever come to the real thing. On top of the dresser, in an ornate mahogany frame, sat the picture they had sat for in New York: Harry in bowtie and tails, top hat held at his side, shoes shined, hair slicked back, Etta wearing a beautiful velvet gown, a ruffled petticoat peeking out from the hem of her skirt, on her breast the gold lapel watch Butch had bought for her at Tiffany's.

He thought back to that day in New York, a cold day with the wind whipping in off the river. They had eaten in a fancy restaurant, and then walked, arm in arm, through the streets of lower Manhattan, stopping in shops and taverns every so often to warm themselves. Etta had been so happy, laughing and pointing things out to them in the shop windows — a silk scarf here, a beaded handbag there. He remembered telling her to buy whatever she liked, they were rich! But she had just shaken her head and said — "Not yet, not yet." — squeezing his arm in rising excitement.

Then they came to Tiffany's. Without a word, Etta led them inside the five-story edifice, into a gleaming space lined with glass-enclosed display cases, each containing cascades of jewels that sparkled like rays of sunlight on an alpine lake. Hanging back, Butch had grabbed Harry's elbow and playfully nodded at the two guards flanking the entrance. "I'll take the one on the right, you get the other one." Harry had smiled and winked.

A clerk in tails and white gloves had begun waiting on them, but when it became clear that they were serious buyers with serious money, Mr. Charles Tiffany himself appeared. After much deliberation, Etta had settled on the gold lapel watch, Harry on a diamond stickpin. Butch chose nothing for himself, since the only jewelry he ever wore was the cross necklace given to him by Mary Boyd.

The next day, Harry and Etta had gone to DeYoung's Studio to have their portrait taken. Etta had wanted to take a second photograph with all three of them, but Butch had declined. He was wary of getting his picture taken. Word had it that photo of him and Harry and three of their outlaw buddies they had foolishly sat for in Fort Worth had come to the attention of the authorities and was now decorating sheriffs' offices across the country.

He picked up the beautifully framed picture and stared at it closely, trying to divine what the two people in it, the two people closest to him in the world, had been thinking at the moment the shutter clicked. They both gazed directly at the camera, Harry looking solemn, even stern. Likewise, Etta's expression was sober, but with a touch of wistfulness, as though she knew this was the wedding portrait she would never have. Her long, thick hair was piled high on her head, except for a stray tendril that grazed the top of her collar. Closing his eyes, he remembered what she looked like with her hair down, what it felt like to run his hands through those luxurious tresses. He remembered how she would brush it, a hundred strokes every night.

God, how he missed her! Harry, too, but Etta most of all. He missed the sight of her, the smell of her, the sound of her. When she was here, he could handle his feelings; after all, she was his best friend's woman, and just being near her was usually enough. When the pressure built up too high, he would go to town where relief could be found with one of the local girls. But when she was gone, when he had only his memory of her to keep him company, he could hardly bear it. Not even a visit to town could satisfy his longing.

It wasn't love he felt for Etta, it couldn't be. He didn't think he was capable of love. All he knew was that he wanted her to come back . . . and Harry, too, of course.

The following morning dawned sunny with a welcome warmth to the air. To celebrate making it through the rainy season, he decided to ride to Leleque for some dealing with the local livestock company.

Before leaving, he grabbed up a letter he had written the night before, when he had been feeling so low. It was addressed to Mathilda Davis, Elzy Lay's mother-in-law, a woman who had always treated him like a son. Scanning the letter, he wondered if it sounded too pathetic — *I am still living in single cussedness, and I sometimes feel very lonely, for I am alone all day, and my neighbors don't amount to anything, besides, the only language spoken in this country is Spanish, and I don't speak it well enough yet to converse. . . .*

"You sad son-of-a-bitch," he muttered, but folded the letter and placed it in an envelope to mail anyway.

Leleque was bustling as many of the area ranchers had, like Butch, taken advantage of the sunny weather to come do some trading. People were in a holiday mood, and the bargaining became spirited, fueled, no doubt, by the jugs of red wine that passed back and forth. Butch was hampered by his inability to speak the language, so he was glad to see Jock Gardiner ride into the village square. With Gardiner translating, he purchased some cattle and sold a couple of horses. Buoyed by their success, the two men repaired to the local *cantina*.

"Any news of Mister and Missus Place?"

210

asked Gardiner, his brogue thickening under the influence of too much wine.

"For God's sake, Jock, call 'em Harry and Etta. We ain't Noo Yawk society, you know," drawled Butch. He pounded his empty cup on the table, signaling the serving girl for a refill.

"Harry and Etta," repeated Jock, smiling up at the girl as she poured more wine. "What have ya heard?"

"Not a damn' thing," grumbled Butch. "Etta must be on one hell of a shopping spree."

"Don't worry, she'll be back," said Jock confidently.

Butch eyed him over the top of his drink. "How do you know?"

Gardiner swirled the liquid in his cup, watching it with glazed eyes. "I haven't known Etta long, but she dunna seem like the quittin' sort to me. Also . . ." — he looked up — "she wouldna leave you for good, Jim. I've seen the way she looks at ya. It may be Harry she loves like a lover, but she feels somethin' deep and true for you, too, my friend."

Butch laughed him off. "You've had one too many . . . you don't know what you're talking about."

"I do," Gardiner insisted. "Sometimes

when we're readin' together, Etta'll laugh at somethin' and say . . . 'Jim would like that' or 'That's just like Jim'. I'm tellin' ya, man, you're on her mind and in her heart." An envious sigh escaped the young man's lips.

Butch felt his heart pounding in his chest. *What did this kid know about anything? Still, Etta had always liked the young Scotsman . . . maybe she had told him things. . . .*

"Gardiner, lad, how goes things?"

Butch looked up to see a hawk-nosed man, wearing expensive riding clothes, standing at their table. He spoke with an American accent.

"Mister Newbery!" Jock leaped to his feet. "What a surprise! Aren't ya usually in Buenos Aires this time of year?"

"Decided it was no good having an *estancia* in the country if I never saw it. Made a resolution to visit more often." He paused and glanced at Butch who was still seated.

"Have a drink with us." Jock gestured to an empty chair at the table. "This is my neighbor, James Ryan. He and his friends are workin' a ranch just outside of Cholila. Jim, George Newbery."

"Believe I've heard of you," Newbery said, shaking hands as he sat. "You've got a woman with you, isn't that right?" He

212

pulled off a pair of gloves, revealing well-manicured, delicate hands.

"That's right," said Butch. "How'd you know?" He did not care for the idea that news of their presence had gotten around, especially not to someone who spent a lot of time in Buenos Aires.

"Not too many white women in these parts," said Newbery jovially. "It's a bit of an event when we get a new one. You're American, too, I've heard. That gives me a reason for an official interest."

Alarm bells went off in Butch's head. He waited for Newbery to explain.

"I'm U.S. vice-consul, you see. Make it my business to keep track of any Americans living in the country. I was particularly interested in you and your friends, seeing as we're almost close enough to be neighbors." He smiled, showing a gold-capped eyetooth.

Butch's mind raced. Was this just a chance meeting, or had someone sent Newbery to check up on him? The man did not seem to be more than politely curious. Still, what were the odds of running into an American government official in this backwater town?

"Whereabouts is your *estancia?*" Butch inquired.

"On the shore of Lake Nahuel Huapi, up north quite a ways. I usually don't get this far south, but I'm meeting someone. In fact" — he checked his pocket watch — "I should be going. No time for that drink, I'm afraid. Pleasure to see you again, Gardiner, and to make your acquaintance, Mister Ryan. You and your friends must come for an *asado* soon. Missus Newbery would be delighted to meet another American woman." Nodding to both men, the official took his leave.

Butch watched him go, then turned to Gardiner. "What's a vice-consul do?"

The younger man shrugged. "Not much, probably. He's actually a dentist in Buenos Aires, and a damn' good one. I've been to see him meself. The vice-consul job's mostly honorary, I gather."

A dentist. Christ, what a story that would make if Butch Cassidy and the Sundance Kid were turned in by a god-damned dentist.

Butch drained his drink and stood. "Gotta get to the post office. Thanks for the drinks."

Gardiner threw some coins on the table and followed him out. The sun teetered on the tops of the mountains, turning the thread-like wisps of clouds a glowing

214

salmon color. The village square still teemed with activity — native women sold fruits and vegetables from makeshift carts, and barefoot children darted up to beg for a *centavo* or two. Grinning, Butch handed out all his spare change, turning his pockets inside out to show he had none left.

"Ye're a soft touch, Jim," chided Gardiner.

"That's me, all right," laughed the outlaw.

"Well, speakin' of soft touches, I'm goin' to drop in at *Doña* Quesada's. Last time I was there, she had a wee lass just off the farm, prettiest thing ya ever seen. Let me know if ya hear from Etta."

Butch veered off the square and entered the post office, a small adobe building attached to the general store that smelled of dust and mold. He slapped his letter to Mrs. Davis on the clerk's counter. "How much?" he asked.

The clerk shook his head, not understanding.

"Jesus," sighed Butch. "OK, uh, *cuanto?*"

"*Diez centavos,*" said the clerk.

Butch stuck his hand in his pocket. "Shit," he muttered, realizing he had given all his coins to the kids in the street. He pulled out his money clip and thumbed a bill out, hoping the clerk could make change. The clerk blanched at the size of the bill, but opened his drawer and managed to come up with the correct combination of coins. Butch gathered the money together and dropped it into his pocket. *"Gracias,"* he said, and turned to go.

"Un momento."

Turning back, he saw the clerk examining the letter he had just posted. *"Tu eres Señor* Ryan?" the clerk asked.

"Sí."

The clerk rose from his stool and went into a back room. When he returned, he held a letter in his hand addressed to *James Ryan, Chubut, Argentina Republic, South America.* Butch took it. There was no return address, but he recognized Harry's hand-writing.

"Christ, how long have you had this?" he cried.

The clerk shrugged, signaling either that he did not know, or that he did not under-stand the question.

Shaking his head at the inefficiency of South American mail delivery, Butch stepped outside and ripped open the enve-lope. The letter was dated July 10, 1902. Jim, — it said — *We sail today on the* S.S. Honorius, *arriving Buenos Aires August 11.* That was today! *Will close out bank account as agreed and return to Cholila with all haste.* At the bottom of the page was a note in Etta's hand: *We've missed you. Lots to show and tell!*

With a huge smile on his face, Butch crumpled the letter, and then burned it, grinding the ashes into the rocky soil. They were back! He turned and headed for *Doña* Quesada's to share the news with Gardiner.

Early the next morning, his head a little fuzzy but the rest of his body loose and languid after a night of celebrating, Butch hit the road. It would be several days, he knew, before Harry and Etta made it back to the ranch, but he wanted to make sure the place was in tip-top shape for their arrival. Jock had told him he wanted to ride back with him to Cholila, but, when Butch looked in on him, Gardiner was sacked out, a pretty young whore draped across his body. Butch left him there.

A little way out of town, he ran into a heavy patch of ground fog that obscured the road. But even the return of rain and fog could not dampen his spirits. Hiding in the thick grasses, sparrows communicated back and forth like rapid-fire telegraphers. His horse, a beautiful bay he had purchased over a year ago when they had gotten off the train in Neuquén, kept a steady pace. He was just thinking how this animal would make a good getaway horse with a little training, when he heard noises ahead. Men's voices, sudden and harsh, the jingle of harness and creak of leather.

He pulled up and strained to listen. Whoever was up ahead was not too far away, but the fog prevented him from seeing them . . . or them him.

More loud voices, then a barked command he could hear clearly. *"¡Bajate! ¡Vacia sus bolsillos!"*

The creak of saddle leather as someone dismounted. "Please, don't shoot! Take whatever you want."

Butch started. If he wasn't mistaken, that was George Newbery's voice.

"Down on your hands and knees," a different voice shouted in slurred English. Then the chilling sound of a hammer being drawn back.

"No . . . no, please!"

Without thinking, Butch kicked his horse forward, drawing his .45 as he raced toward the pleading voice of George Newbery. Emerging from the mist, he saw two desperadoes on horseback, one pointing a gun at the terrified vice-consul, kneeling in the road.

Startled, all three turned to see him barreling toward them. Taking advantage of their confusion, he steered his mount between the two thugs, pistol-whipping the gunman as he swept past. The man fell half off his horse, dropping his weapon in the dust.

The other one went for his revolver, swinging around to draw, but Butch shot first, aiming for the bandit's hand. The man screamed as the gun leaped out of his bloody fingers. Butch swung back around to the first man, but both had seen enough. Jabbing their spurs into their mounts, they fled into the fog.

Butch turned back to locate Newbery, finding him cowering in the tall grass by the side of the road. "You all right?" he asked, jumping down from his horse and retrieving Newbery's reins.

Still shaking, the vice-consul came to his feet, patting himself as though making sure he was all there. "Yes . . . yes, all right," he panted. "I had heard there were desperadoes on the road, but I've never had any trouble before." He wiped his face with his handkerchief, and then looked more closely at Butch. "It's James Ryan, isn't it? Gardiner's neighbor?"

Butch nodded.

"Well, sir, I certainly owe you a debt. I dare say you just saved my life."

Butch bent over and picked up Newbery's crumpled hat. "Don't mention it," he said, passing it to the grateful man. "Glad I came by when I did."

"You deserve a reward, Mister Ryan." Newbery crossed to his horse and fumbled with the strap on his saddlebags. "I'd like to pay you something. . . ."

"That ain't necessary." Butch mounted up. "If you're going my way, I'd be happy to ride with you for a spell, make sure those varmints don't come back."

Still looking dazed, Newbery shook his head. "I believe I'll ride back to town. Perhaps hire a bodyguard for the remainder of my trip. I do thank you for your offer."

Butch tipped his hat and rode off. *What luck,* he thought wryly. *I've just made a lifelong friend of the United States vice-consul.*

CHAPTER SIXTEEN

Alone in his large corner office, William Pinkerton gripped the photograph tightly. A man and woman, young and attractive, dressed in their finest, stared back at him, mocking him with their self-assured expressions. He looked at the picture for several minutes, absorbing every detail, before turning it over. Stamped on the back was the photographer's name and address — *DeYoung's Studio, 857 Broadway, New York, New York* — and a handwritten date, *February, 1901.*

Uttering a mild oath, Pinkerton dropped the photo on top of the open file strewn across his desk and stuck his head out the door. "Miss O'Reilly, send for my brother . . . immediately."

He closed the door and went to stand by the window that afforded a view of lower Broadway, mere blocks from DeYoung's Studio. The people of New York had taken to the streets on this fine fall day, enjoying a brief respite between the heat and humidity of August and the coming winter. Two months ago, if he had stood here and looked down on the passers-by, he might have seen Harry Longabaugh and his girlfriend strolling the avenue. But two months was an eternity in the detective business.

Pinkerton swung his big, bulldog head at the sound of the door opening. In walked his younger brother, Robert. No one would take the two men for brothers. William had inherited his mother's broad face and features. With advancing age, the pockets under his bulging eyes puffed out like dumplings. Robert, on the other hand, favored their father, with his high brow, aquiline nose, and deep-set eyes. Allan Pinkerton's famous temper had likewise been handed down to his younger son, a circumstance that had made for quite a rebellious youth. But the old man had been dead for years, and the agency he had built from scratch was now run in partnership by his two sons.

Robert's eyes fell on the open file. "You've seen the updates to the Cassidy file," he said, closing the door behind him.

"Indeed," William replied, his tone acerbic. "You're familiar with this, then?" He pointed to the file with a thick finger.

"I reviewed it earlier today before sending it over. Seems we're always a step behind those two, doesn't it?" Robert pulled up a chair and sat, crossing his legs. He pulled out a cigarette case and lit up.

"Those *three*, it would appear. They've got a woman with them." William retrieved the picture from the top of his desk and studied it again.

"I'd noticed," Robert said, exhaling smoke.

"Damn it all!" William came around his desk and sat heavily. "They were right here, right under our noses, and we let them slip away. Not once, but twice. It just goes to show how daring these men are . . . while we're looking for them in the wilderness and mountains, here they are in the midst of society!"

Robert leaned forward to snuff his cigarette. "There's no doubt they are clever outlaws and that our surveillance has been sloppy. But rather than piss and moan about things" — he shot a look at his brother — "let's review where we are and decide on a course of action."

William's brow lowered. Clearing his throat, he shuffled through the file. "Here we have reports written in the fall of Nineteen Hundred, two years ago almost exactly, detailing the train robbery in Tipton, Wyoming, and the bank hold-up in Winnemucca, Nevada. Both ascribed to Cassidy's gang, although we're not entirely certain who the individual participants were."

Robert nodded. "Evidently the cashier of the Winnemucca bank is having a difficult time making a positive identification, but the circumstantial evidence points to Cassidy."

"Correct." William dropped those reports and picked up another. "No further information until one of our operatives filed this report on May Tenth of this year, describing a visit by Longabaugh and an unknown woman to an unknown medical facility for an unknown ailment."

Robert templed his fingers under his chin. "Which came to our attention via one of our postal informants, as I recall."

"Yes. We finally tracked down Longabaugh's sister and began monitoring her mail . . . too late to have learned about the outlaws' movements up to May of Nineteen-Oh-Two, unfortunately. Lastly, we have a report written in July of this year which belatedly reveals that Longabaugh, the woman, and another man, most likely Cassidy, were in New York early last year, sailed for Argentina, and then returned to New York on the *Soldier Prince* in April. That is, Longabaugh and the woman returned. There is no evidence Cassidy came back with them."

"The photograph taken in February of last year confirms their presence in New York," Robert stated, "or at least that of Longabaugh and the woman. Do we know for a fact that it's the same woman who accompanied Longabaugh to the infirmary in May?"

William shuffled more papers. "The woman with Longabaugh in May is described as in her early twenties, approximately five feet, five inches, one hundred and ten pounds, medium dark hair, blue or gray eyes, regular features, medium complexion with no marks or blemishes." He picked up the DeYoung photograph. "I'd say there's very little doubt it's the same woman."

"I agree," said Robert. "So Longabaugh and this woman return to the States in April, presumably seeking medical care of some sort for Harry. They get that taken care of, visit with his family, and sail back to Argentina on July Tenth. Our operative was hot on their trail, but they eluded us."

"Again," lamented William. "The woman intrigues me. Who the hell is she?"

Robert took the photo and walked with it

to the window. "A real beauty, for one thing. Looks more refined than your average gunfighter's chippy. Why is she mixed up with someone like Longabaugh, I wonder?"

"Don't get sentimental, Brother," cautioned William. "She's probably an illiterate prostitute like all the rest of them."

Robert shrugged his thin shoulders and returned the photo to the file. "Anything else of importance?"

"Not really. A few details about their activities here in New York. The first time they were here they registered at a boarding house on West Twelfth under the names Mister and Missus Harry Place and James Ryan. Evidently Cassidy posed as Missus Place's brother. The landlady recalls hearing the men refer to Missus Place as Ethel or Etta." William closed the file and rested his hands on top of it. "Any recommendations?"

"Of course. Continue to monitor the sister's mail and that of any other relatives we know of. Send copies of this photo to law enforcement out West . . . perhaps someone can identify our mysterious Missus Place." Robert rubbed his chin, thinking. "Who's our man in South America right now?"

"Dimaio," said William. "He's on assignment in Brazil."

"We should contact him. When he's finished with his current assignment, he can do some digging in Buenos Aires. It's a big country down there, but maybe our happy threesome will get sloppy."

William tapped his thumbs together, frowning. "If we do as you suggest, perhaps we can establish their whereabouts without a great deal of expense. But frankly I wonder how enthusiastically our clients will embrace a continued pursuit."

"Don't be ridiculous!" scoffed Robert. "Our clients will spare no expense to capture these marauding thieves."

"Are you sure of that? Cassidy's no threat to them in South America. Perhaps they'd just as soon forget about him rather than risk bringing him back for trial."

Leaning forward, Robert pounded his fist on his brother's desk. "We will find them. And they will be brought to justice."

CHAPTER SEVENTEEN

Harry and Etta arrived back in Cholila, and it was as if they had never left. Now that she was back in his life, Butch's yearning for his best friend's woman receded to a manageable level. In fact, he dismissed as ridiculous the amorous thoughts he had entertained during her absence; it had simply been a bad case of the blues brought on by loneliness.

For her part, Etta seemed delighted to be back. They returned with a wagonload of furnishings for the cabin, and what they did not carry with them they had shipped, including six double-hung windows. On the day Harry and Butch installed them, Etta brought out a precious bottle of champagne, and they merrily toasted their elegant abode.

Most of the shipments only made it as far as the coast, necessitating several lengthy trips across the pampas. They made a holiday of these occasions, staying over at the Hotel del Globo in Trelew where they became friendly with the good-natured Italian owner. This part of the country sported a sizable community of Welsh immigrants as well, with whom the trio enjoyed socializing. Butch especially appreciated conducting business with English-speaking merchants. One man in particular whose acquaintance he made was the local banker who thought nothing of giving the dandy-looking Mr. Ryan a tour of the vault. Butch sized it up with a professional eye, but never did it occur to him to act on his knowledge.

Compared to Trelew's commercial activity, the ranch in Cholila felt like the end of the earth. For their purposes, of course, that was ideal.

Ranch life was more sedate, but not without its distractions. Just like at home, Patagonians loved their horses and cards. As they became less wary of strangers, the Americans expanded their circle of friends, getting to know several of the neighboring ranchers. Jock Gardiner was still a frequent visitor as was Welshman Daniel Gibbon and former Texans Jarred Jones and John Commodore Perry.

Life was defined by the seasons. Calving and shearing in the spring, harvesting in late summer and fall, comparative idleness in winter. Although Etta had her hands full with domestic duties, she often pitched in with the heavier ranch work. On one trip to Trelew, she purchased several pairs of pants; upon her return to Cholila she packed away all her dresses and, thereafter, at least at the ranch, appeared only in pants tucked into the tops of her knee-high boots. Harry and Butch had no complaint — pants showed off her comely figure like no dress ever could.

Although they were settling in, making friends, and becoming more comfortable with their surroundings, Butch never forgot why they were there. It seemed highly unlikely, if not impossible, that anyone would track them to this remote corner of the earth, but the outlaw had not survived this long without being cautious. Thus, he made sure their horses stayed in shape, exercising them daily. He and Harry took regular target practice, and, although Etta never proved much of a shot with a revolver, they made certain she was adept with a rifle. Harry insisted Etta improve her horsemanship as well, which she did willingly.

Incredibly Etta's dream was coming true in a way she could not have foreseen. She had wanted to share a life of adventure with the man she loved, and she was doing just that, times two. Late at night, lying next to the snoring Harry, whose sinus condition had improved but was still troublesome, she worried that she was alone in viewing their current circumstances as adventurous. What if her men became bored with the repetitive, uneventful life they led? How could these daring longriders, who courted danger and thrived on adrenaline, be content with their staid existence? But if either man had second thoughts, he kept them to himself.

Toward the end of harvest time, they received a visit from Dan Gibbon who brought with him the local *comisario*, Edward Humphreys. Butch and Harry had heard of Humphreys, also a Welsh immigrant, who was the equivalent of a county sheriff. By unspoken agreement, they had not gone out of their way to meet the man. But he turned out to be a pleasant sort who had no inkling that the *americanos del norte* living in his district were notorious outlaws. They invited him to sup with them. Over the *empanadas* and *maté* he asked if they would do him a favor. Would Mr. Ryan and Mr. and Mrs. Place be so kind as to host an *asado* for Governor Lezana who would be paying a visit to the district in a few days? Word had gotten around that Mrs. Place's elegant hospitality had no parallel in the territory, and

Humphreys would consider their entertainment of the governor a personal favor.

The three expatriates exchanged quick glances before Etta spoke up to assure their guest they would be pleased to oblige. After all, as they later agreed, to have refused the *comisario*'s request would have raised unwanted suspicions.

On the appointed day, everyone who lived within a three-day ride streamed into the ranch, curious to meet the governor, but even more eager to sample the renowned conviviality of the *Americanos*. Etta served beef, lamb, and chicken as well as a concoction of vegetables from her garden. Wine and punch flowed freely, and, as the evening fell, Harry was prevailed upon to fetch his guitar. Someone else produced *maracas* and a set of *bongos* and soon the gathering was dancing to the soft rhythms and pulsing beats of *sambas* and *merengues*.

Even stately Governor Lezana took a turn, elegantly handing Etta onto the floor. At the end of the dance, the governor bowed and Etta curtsied, her face flushed with heat and excitement. The other women, including the wives of Jarred Jones and John Perry, looked on enviously while the men, led by Jock Gardiner, appeared star struck.

Longabaugh, his chest puffed with jeal-
ousy, laid down his guitar and took Etta by
the elbow to lead her away. But the young
daughter of *Don* Ventura Solís, a refined
Chilean gentleman who ranched nearby,
picked up the instrument, strummed a few
chords, and then sang a lovely native tune,
her voice high and sweet as a meadowlark's.
Smiling, Etta took Harry's hand, and they
listened to the girl's song with the rest of the
enchanted revelers.

Later, after the crowd had exhausted itself
singing and dancing, Butch and Harry led a
delegation of male guests out to the stables
where Butch kept a stash of sour mash. The
nighttime breeze felt refreshing after the stifling heat in the cabin, and the whisky went
down smooth as a lover's caress. The men
complimented their hosts' foresight in
bringing from the States such a fine distilla-
tion. Butch acknowledged their praise by
pouring another generous round. "There's
just some comforts a man shouldn't be
without," he declared.

There were nods all around at the wisdom
of this statement. Young Jock Gardiner
gazed dreamily at the flickering lantern
light. "Wine, women, and song . . . a man's
greatest comforts," he mused. "I envy you
married gents."

"How's that?" growled Jarred Jones from beneath a handlebar mustache that could have doubled as a whiskbroom.

"Well, all of you are lucky enough to enjoy the daily company of your lovely wives. The rest of us poor suckers have to make do with only occasional doses of female companionship."

"You ask me, Jim here's got the best deal," said Dan Gibbon. "He's got the charming Missus Place to do for him, yet he didn't have to marry her for the privilege."

"She don't exactly do for him, though," drawled Harry, already well in his cups. "Not like she does for me, if you get my meaning."

There was laughter all around while Butch mugged a rueful smile.

"I would hope not," commented John Perry. "Ain't you the lady's brother?"

Butch and Harry exchanged glances. When the threesome had first come to Cholila, Butch and Etta were still posing as brother and sister, but, over time, they had let that story slide. Both Gibbon and Gardiner knew the two were unrelated, although no one suspected that Harry and Etta's marriage was a fiction.

Although he knew Perry's inquiry was innocent, Butch chose his words carefully, mindful of the man's former position as a Texas sheriff. "Now how could a fella with an ugly mug like mine be brother to such a pretty gal?" He smiled. "We just cooked up that story so's not to raise eyebrows when we go traveling."

"I hear ya," Perry said, holding out his glass that Butch generously filled to the brim. "Folks'll think the worst these days. How is it the three of you came to travel together, then?"

"Well, it was like this . . . ," began Butch.

"Me and Bu . . . Jim go way back," interrupted Longabaugh, staggering slightly as he grabbed the bottle. "Got ourselves in a little hot water and thought to cool things down here in the jungle. Ain't no fuckin' jungle though . . . more like Wyoming where we's from."

"Wyoming?" Perry seemed interested. "Back when I was the law in Crockett County, Texas, Wyoming had quite a reputation. Home of gunfighters and rustlers, don't ya know."

"Worse than Texas?" quipped Butch, trying to catch Harry's eye to signal him to shut up.

Perry chuckled. "Well, you got a point there. Texas has its share of law-breakers. Musta been some kind of trouble you boys were in to skedaddle all the way to Argentina."

Harry coughed nervously, finally realizing the dangerous tack the conversation had taken. "Wasn't really all that bad. . . ." He looked around the circle at Gardiner, Gibbon, and Jones staring at him in fascination. "Aw, shit," he muttered.

"Look, boys," Butch stepped in. "No need to concern yourselves you got rascals for neighbors. Our noses ain't squeaky clean, but it ain't like you got to lock up your daughters."

"Better tell that to *Don* Solís," grinned Jock Gardiner. "The way you was lookin' at his daughter, he's going to lock her up and throw away the key!"

The others laughed, and Butch gratefully launched into a discussion of the merits of the beautiful *Señorita* Solís. But Perry's lawman memories had been rekindled. At the next opportunity, he brought the talk back around to his days as a sheriff.

"Yes, sir, I handed in my badge back in 'Ninety-Four. No money in it, and the county wanted me to do everything from catching crooks to running the waterworks. But I used to hear plenty about the goings on out West . . . Hole-in-the-Wall, Brown's Hole, and the like. Guess this Wild Bunch gang had the meanest, hell-raisin' sons-of-bitches you ever seen. Bold as you please and too damn' smart to get caught. Hear tell their leader, fella name of Butch Cassidy, insisted on training for months before pulling a job. Musta been some character to keep all those hardcases in line. I been down here so long I kinda lost track of things, but my brother wrote me the Wild Bunch ain't pulled any jobs in the last couple of years. Reckon they decided to quit while they was ahead."

During this speech Harry's head sank lower and lower into his collar. Butch listened with a detached smile on his broad face. At the mention of Butch Cassidy, Jock Gardiner turned to stare at his friend Jim Ryan. The fact that Ryan and the Places had been in Cholila for just about two years was not lost on anyone present.

Butch's blue eyes twinkled as he poured all the way around again. "Reckon that's what I'd do was I in their spot . . . quit while I was ahead."

"Only way for someone like Cassidy to quit would be to drop off the face of the earth," said Perry, holding his host's gaze.

Butch grinned. "Something like that."

A rustling at the door prompted them to look up and see Etta standing there, her eyes wide. "Mister Jones, Mister Perry," she said, "your wives are seeking you. The governor is prepared to retire should anyone wish a final word with him."

All the men but Butch and Harry filed out, thanking Etta for her hospitality and promising to return the favor in due course. Swaying on his feet, Harry put a heavy arm around his lover's shoulders. Etta caught the scent of whisky and raised her eyebrows ever so slightly. "I can see you two have been having a good time," she said lightly.

"Even better now that you're here," answered Harry, nuzzling her ear.

Etta stepped away from his embrace and pointed him in the direction of the house. "Why don't you go see our guests off. I want a word with Butch."

"No, ma'am." Harry shook his head emphatically. "You're looking far too pretty tonight to leave ya alone with another man." He reached for her again, but Etta laughingly evaded his grasp and gave him a small push out the door.

"Don't be silly, it's just Butch. Go on now."

As Harry stumbled across the yard, Etta turned around to see Butch regarding her wryly. "Just Butch, eh? Lady, you sure know how to hurt a fella."

Etta laughed. "Don't play games with me, now. You had your chance."

"If I ask real nice, could I have another one?"

Etta shrugged playfully. "That train's already left the station, darlin'."

Butch poured two whiskys and handed her one. They clinked glasses, smiling into each other's eyes. Etta did look especially beautiful tonight. She had dipped into her trunk for one of her New York frocks, a summer silk the color of pale lemons whose bodice revealed a hint of shadow between her breasts. Her hair was done up, and she had stuck a purple flower over her ear just like one of the native girls. With her dark hair, she could have been mistaken for a native, were it not for the creamy whiteness of her skin.

Butch took a sip and turned away.

"I heard Perry talking just now," Etta said, seating herself on a bale of hay. "Does he know something?"

"Not for sure. Harry let on as how we was on the run from something, but, hell, that's true for a lot of folks down here."

"Oh, dear," — Etta frowned — "I'm afraid that man of mine gets a little careless when he's had one too many."

"No harm done, far as I can tell. Don't matter much anyway if folks know the truth about us. Nobody around here's gonna turn us in." Butch finished his drink and leaned back against one of the horse stalls. In honor of the governor's visit, he had worn his best coat and vest, but the sultry night had dictated the removal of the coat and unbuttoning of the vest. His crisp white shirt was open at the neck, and he had rolled up the sleeves to just below the elbow.

Etta looked at him shrewdly. "You're probably right, but it pays to be cautious, don't you think?"

Butch grinned. "I learned a long time ago to sit with my back to the wall, facing the door. Old habits are hard to break. But there ain't no need to worry, honey. You and me and Harry's gonna live to a ripe old age here on the pampas."

"You haven't called me honey in years," said Etta, a touch of color coming to her cheeks. "Not since that winter at the Roost."

Butch smiled and said nothing. The sound of softly strummed guitar chords reached them on the balmy night air. The musician tried several different keys before segueing into a seductive Latin melody.

"Must be *Señorita* Solís playing," murmured Etta, her ear cocked. "Harry can't pick the strings like that even when he's sober."

They listened for a moment, the sultry melody combining with the warmth of the night and the scent of whisky and horses to create a mood of languorous anticipation. Pushing away from the stall, Butch held out his hand. Etta took it, and he pulled her to her feet. Wrapping one arm around her waist, he enclosed her hand in his and held them both close to his chest. They began to dance, moving slowly back and forth over the straw-covered floor. He gazed down into hazel eyes that looked back with . . . well, not love exactly, perhaps more like devotion.

"Are you happy here, Butch?" Etta whispered. "Do you want to grow old in the pampas like you said?"

He thought of many things: the worn face of his mother, Mary Boyd's flashing dark eyes, Etta brushing her long, thick hair as she sat on his bedroll. He could have answered her question in many different ways but all he said was — "Yes."

Etta smiled and tucked her head under his chin. When the song ended, they stood together, holding each other gently. After a while, he took a half step back and tipped her chin up. They looked long into each other's eyes, knowing what they were to each other, feeling each other's strength. Slowly he bent his head and touched his lips to hers, so tenderly Etta felt her heart swell in her breast. The kiss lingered without deepening. Finally he pulled away, a curious glow lighting his face.

With a sigh, Etta placed her palm on his rough cheek. "Darling Butch," she whispered, "if only you had needed me more."

She turned and walked back to the house.

CHAPTER EIGHTEEN

Pinkerton Agent Frank Dimaio took a seat in the waiting room. Although it was well past the height of the summer season, Buenos Aires was steamy today, so he was gratified when the receptionist got up to turn on the electric fan in the corner. His deceptively sleepy-looking eyes roamed over the magazine selection on the table in front of him. All were in English, he noticed. He picked up a six month old *National Geographic* and opened it on his lap. The fan riffled the pages so that he had to hold it with both hands to keep from losing his place.

After a few minutes, he checked his watch. He had dropped in without an appointment, and the receptionist had said he might have to wait a while. Crossing his legs, he surreptitiously regarded the other people in the waiting room: a well-dressed older gentleman, probably a banker or government official, and a matronly woman who periodically dabbed her sweating brow with a lace-trimmed handkerchief. With a sigh, he returned to his magazine.

It probably would have made more sense to visit the vice-consul in his office at the legation, but, as it happened, the detective was suffering from a sore tooth and had decided to kill two birds with one stone. Newbery had the reputation of being a very fine dentist.

Dimaio had skimmed through half the magazines on the table when, finally, his name was called. Picking up his briefcase, he followed the receptionist to the examination room.

"Mister Dimaio, is it?" said the gangly man seated next to a dentist's chair, flipping through a chart. "I'm Doctor Newbery. What can I do for you today?"

Dimaio set down his briefcase and rubbed his jaw. "Got a molar that's paining me some. But, quite honestly, that's not the only reason for my visit. I wonder if we could speak privately, Doctor."

Newbery looked up in surprise. He took in Dimaio's erect bearing and well-cut suit, the sloe eyes behind wire-framed spectacles. "I've quite a busy schedule today, sir, but I suppose I can give you a few minutes. Please excuse us, Nurse."

His assistant left the room, closing the door behind her.

"Forgive me for barging in with no notice," said Dimaio, reaching into his breast pocket for one of his cards. "I'm with the Pinkerton Detective Agency, and I have a matter to discuss with you in your capacity as vice-consul. In point of fact, I also need the assistance of a good dentist," he added sheepishly.

"Indeed. Well, we'd better get the talking out of the way first. Sometimes my patients aren't terribly communicative when I'm finished with them."

Dimaio blanched. "That's a good one, Doctor. Well, to make a long story short, I've been sent to Buenos Aires to investigate the whereabouts of the famous criminals Butch Cassidy and Harry Longabaugh, also known as the Sundance Kid. No doubt you've heard of them."

"Can't say as I have," admitted Newbery, leaning back on his stool and crossing his arms on his chest.

"Really!" Dimaio appeared nonplused. "Well, sir, Cassidy is the leader and Longabaugh one of the top lieutenants in a gang of thieves known as the Wild Bunch. They've caused untold mayhem throughout the West for the past eight years or so. We have it on good authority that the two of them, along with Longabaugh's female companion, escaped to this country early in Nineteen-Oh-One. As vice-consul you are familiar with the expatriate community in Argentina, are you not?"

"I try to be. That's not to say I know everyone."

"Of course not. Do you, by any chance, know these people?" Dimaio removed two photographs from his satchel and handed them to Newbery, watching him closely for any reaction. The dentist's face remained blank as he regarded the DeYoung photograph of Harry and Etta. But at the next photo, Butch Cassidy's Wyoming State Penitentiary mug shot, Newbery's eyebrows shot up. He glanced quickly to Dimaio, and then back to the picture.

"You know him?" asked the agent.

Newbery hesitated. Of course, he knew him. This was the man who had saved his life on the road from Leleque.

"Well, Doctor?"

"Perhaps . . . that is, well . . . yes, I believe I have met him."

"Under what circumstances?"

"It was some time ago, at least a year or two, I can't quite recall. I was on my way to my *estancia* in the province of Neuquén, and

I ran into an acquaintance who was with this man."

"What name did he use?"

Newbery placed his chin in his hand, affecting to think. "It escapes me at the moment."

"Was it James Ryan?"

"Why, yes, I believe it was," the dentist said as though it had just occurred to him.

"Did you see Longabaugh or the woman?"

"No, but. . . ."

"But what, sir?"

"Well, we discussed her . . . the fact that it was unusual to find a white woman in the province."

"What else did you talk about?"

"Nothing. I had to leave to meet someone so I couldn't stay but a minute."

"And that was the only time you saw him?"

"As I said, I was in a bit of a rush." Newbery crossed to the window and stood with his back to the agent. He did not want to reveal the incident on the road the following day, did not want Dimaio to think he had a reason to cover up for Ryan, or Cassidy, if that's who he really was. He would do his duty as vice-consul, but he'd be damned if he would go out of his way to help them capture a man who had saved his life.

"You said you discussed the fact that there was now another white woman living in the province. I gather that means you know where Cassidy and the others are hiding out."

"I would hardly call it hiding out!" Newbery turned to face Dimaio who looked at him steadily. Too late, the dentist realized he had fallen in a trap. "No, sir," he explained, trying to put the best face on things, "they are not hiding out. They are living quite openly on a sheep ranch at Cholila in the province of Chubut. I understand they are doing quite well, indeed have managed to double their stock since arriving. By all accounts, Ryan and . . . the other fellow . . ."

"He's using the name Place these days."

"Yes, that's right, Mister and Missus Place. Anyway, by all accounts, they're decent folks, well liked by their neighbors, I hear. That's all I can tell you."

"Doctor Newbery," said Dimaio, removing his spectacles, polishing them, and placing them back on his narrow face, "it does not surprise me to hear that Cassidy has decided to lay low for a while. I'm sure he and his cohorts have been building a reputation as model citizens. But I guarantee you this . . . they will strike again. They can't help themselves. It's in their blood. Cassidy is simply waiting for the right opportunity, probably scouting out banks as we speak. I know that you'll want to assist us in apprehending these dangerous outlaws before they rob again, perhaps even a bank in your province."

Newbery's mind raced. "Indeed, I do, Mister Dimaio. That is why I must warn you that it would be virtually impossible to apprehend these criminals at this time."

Dimaio looked puzzled. "Why is that?"

"The rainy season is almost upon us," Newbery improvised, "and that part of the country becomes flooded, the roads impassable. Not only that, we're talking about a fifteen-day trip on horseback through the jungle to get to Cholila. It simply could not be done during the rainy season. Perhaps a man or two on their own could do it, but, if Cassidy is as dangerous as you say, it will take an entire squadron to arrest him. No, it will simply have to wait until spring. Even then, you'll have to hire a *peón* to guide you through the jungle, and, of course, arrangements must be made with the commandant of the garrison in the district to effect an arrest. Proper procedure must be followed, you understand."

With any luck, the Pinkerton agent was

unfamiliar enough with the geography of Patagonia to realize that there was no jungle of any description between the coast and Cholila. Dimaio's confused expression confirmed that the deception had worked. The agent pulled a small notebook from his pocket and jotted down some notes. "Well, sir, you've given me a great deal of information and a lot to think about. I shall pass on your comments to my superiors. In the meantime, how do you suggest we keep an eye on these scoundrels?"

Newbery thought for a moment. "They're as unlikely to go anywhere during the rainy season as are the authorities, so I shouldn't worry about it for now. Come November, I shall be returning to my *estancia,* and I could perhaps think of a ruse to get them to come to Buenos Aires."

"Excellent idea! And I know just the thing. I ran across a petition signed by both Ryan and Place and registered with the land department. You could tell them their petition has been granted, and they need to return to Buenos Aires to sign the title for their land."

"Yes, that would work," Newbery admitted.

"Very good." Dimaio continued to speak as he scribbled more notes. "You must stay in touch, Doctor, but discreetly. These men are quite sophisticated and may well have contacts here in Buenos Aires. If you hear anything at all about their movements, wire the Pinkerton office using this code." He tore off the page and handed it over.

"Citron for Cassidy, lemons for Longabaugh, and peaches for Missus Place?" Newbery sounded amazed.

"Why not?" Dimaio looked pleased with himself. "From what I know of this threesome, those are rather apt descriptions. Now, if you wouldn't mind, Doctor, I've got this awful pain in my tooth. . . ."

Robert Pinkerton allowed himself a satisfied smile as he finished reading Frank Dimaio's report. Good man, Dimaio, thorough and professional. The ease with which the agent had been able to track down Cassidy indicated the outlaw had let down his guard, was no longer being careful to cover his tracks. Foolish, to underestimate his pursuers so recklessly.

To be sure, Dimaio's report concerning the weather conditions down there was disappointing. Now that the thief had been located, further delay in effecting his arrest was nigh to intolerable. Pinkerton re-read that part of the report, frowning dubiously.

Surely the conditions could not be so severe as to prevent all travel for nearly four months. Nevertheless, Dimaio was the man on the scene; his observations must be relied upon. In any event, now there was time to plan carefully, enlist the local authorities' assistance, make sure all the proper channels were followed. When this arrest did go down, it needed to go down perfectly.

How competent were the police down there, Pinkerton wondered. Not very, in all likelihood. He doubted whether there was a *comisario* in all of Argentina who had the experience or fortitude to capture a man like Cassidy. No, it would be far better to lead his own expedition to Cholila rather than chance some South American yokel screwing things up. Sitting back in his chair, Pinkerton calculated what it would cost to mount such an expedition. Surely not more than a few thousand dollars. Chicken feed to the railroad companies and banks who were his clients. With a smug expression on his chiseled face, he reached for the telephone.

But, as his brother, William, had predicted, they would have none of it. Cassidy's victims were perfectly happy to leave him where he was. Why spend all that money to extradite the scoundrel and run the risk that he would escape and start preying on their trains and banks once again? Good riddance, they declared.

Pinkerton was incensed, but there was nothing he could do, short of paying for the expedition himself, something even he realized would be foolhardy. He satisfied himself with sending a letter to the chief of police in Buenos Aires: *It is our firm belief that it is only a question of time until these men commit some desperate robbery in the Argentine Republic. If there are reported to you any bank or train hold-up robberies or any other similar crimes, you will find that they were undoubtedly committed by these men.*

CHAPTER NINETEEN

The two horses clip-clopped along at a leisurely pace, their hoofs raising little clouds of dust that blew sideways across the road. Etta lifted the stray tendrils that had come loose from her bun and let the soft breeze cool the back of her neck. To her right, across the broad expanse of Lake Nahuel Huapi, rose the craggy peaks of the Andes. Tiny, pine-covered islands dotted the lake, like pebbles that had rolled off the sides of the mountains to float on the iridescent surface.

She glanced at Harry who rode a length ahead, his eyes fixed on the road, oblivious to the beauty that surrounded him. They were returning from a trip to Jarred Jones's *estancia* where Harry had bought some bulls. Knowing it would be one of the last opportunities to see the countryside before the rains came, Etta had asked to come along. She had anticipated a pleasant journey, visiting with Mrs. Jones, enjoying the breathtaking scenery of the lake area, but Harry had been so sullen and distracted throughout the trip she was almost sorry she had bothered.

Lifting her shoulders, she let them fall with a heavy sigh. *Remember the first time we rode together,* she wanted to say to him, *through the cañon where we discovered those Indian drawings? Remember the passion of that day, the promise it held?* Ah, well, those kinds of feelings were impossible to sustain, she supposed. What you're left with when the passion dies is caring — caring and loyalty. She still cared deeply for Harry Longabaugh, and was loyal to him as well, although she knew from the way men looked at her she had not lost any of her beauty, her ability to seduce. She could have any man she wanted, most likely, but it was a game to her, this toying with men's affections, nothing more than a game.

As for Harry, she did not doubt his love for her. He still told her he loved her, sometimes even looked at her the way he had that day he laid claim to her, like a man coming home after a long, fruitless quest. But she no longer deluded herself that she was the only source of his comfort. She could tell by the way he touched her that things had changed.

Etta shook her head, ridding herself of

these unhappy thoughts. On a day like today it should be a crime to have anything on one's mind but the joy of being alive. She clucked her horse even with Harry and gave him a sunny smile. He returned it grudgingly and went back to studying the road.

"I think you struck a good bargain for those bulls, don't you?" she said, refusing to give in to his bleak mood.

"Jones is an idiot." He punctuated the remark by leaning over the side of his horse and spitting in the road.

Etta's mouth grew tight. Everybody knew Jarred Jones was one of the sharpest business men in the district. "Well, he certainly has a lovely place," she said, resisting the urge to contradict Harry outright. "Perhaps ours will look like that someday."

Longabaugh turned to stare at her, then shook his head and looked away.

Etta's anger boiled over. "What is it with you today? Did I say something wrong?"

He refused to answer for a time, then pulled up suddenly. "Sounds like you're planning on being here a while."

Etta was taken aback. "Aren't you?"

"I ain't planning a damn' thing," he muttered. "I'm just along for the ride." He moved forward again, leaving Etta to stare at his back.

"Wait a minute!" She caught up with him and grabbed his arm, forcing him to stop. "What's that supposed to mean?"

"You and Butch got big plans," he said, his voice tight. "Gonna have yourselves a regular empire pretty soon, ain't that right? Well, I got news for you, sweetheart. We ain't nothin' but shit-eatin' sheepherders. That's all we'll ever be."

"Harry!"

He looked at her with something like fear in his eyes. "I never wanted to be no sheepman."

"You aren't just a sheepherder! You're a rancher, and a very successful one!"

"Call it what you like. All I know is I'm stuck in this two-bit, backwater shithole where it rains half the year and the other half there ain't nothing to do but tend a bunch of stinking sheep!"

She stared at him, speechless.

"I never thought you'd like this life, Etta," he went on. "That ain't what you told me when we hooked up."

"I said I wanted to be by your side wherever you went."

"But we was talking about the gang, about you being part of the gang, riding with us and helping us pull jobs. You wasn't like other women, all dainty and . . . I don't

257

know . . . needy all the time. That's what drew me to you . . . well, that and the fact you're the most god-damn' beautiful woman I've ever seen. But look at us now, Etta. Look at us! A couple of stinking . . . hell, we ain't even a couple! We're a fuckin' trio! Three old ladies sitting around, nagging each other, getting up early to feed the chickens, and going to bed just because the sun goes down. What the hell happened, Etta?"

Her hand fell from his arm. How long had he felt like this? How could she not have known? "I . . . I know Cholila's not very exciting," she said, "but at least it's safe. You were on the verge of being arrested back home. Surely this life, dull as it is, is better than rotting in jail."

"That's bullshit!" he cried. "Butch is the one they was on to, the one they wanted. They was never that interested in me. Butch made it sound worse'n it was 'cause he wanted someone to go with him to South America. That is, he wanted *you* to go with him, but he knew that meant I had to come, too. So he made it look like a posse was chewing up my god-damn' back trail when no such thing was happening." Harry's horse pulled on the reins fretfully, nervous at the sound of his master's angry voice.

"Harry, we talked about it before agreeing to come here." She shook her head slowly, amazed that he could have forgotten. "We decided that after they identified you at Tipton, after they discovered that photograph you boys foolishly sat for in Fort Worth, it was too dangerous to stay. Butch didn't talk us into anything we hadn't already decided to do." Etta chose to ignore her lover's insinuations about her and his partner.

"You're always taking his side, ain't ya?"

"That's not true!"

He took a deep breath, brought himself under control. "I'm telling you, Etta, I don't like the way things are going down here. I want to go back to the States . . . for good."

"You can't be serious!"

"I'm serious as hell."

"It wouldn't be safe!"

"Jesus, Etta, you don't really believe all of Butch's talk, do ya? When we went back to see Samanna, did the law find us? Hell, no! They ain't even interested in me any more. It's Butch they wanted all along."

Etta suddenly felt sick to her stomach. She slid to the ground and leaned against her horse's neck, wondering how long Harry had felt such resentment. "Even if you're right," she said quietly, "they might use you to get to Butch."

"I've thought of that," he conceded, "but they'd have to find me first. I'm pretty good at getting lost when I want to. And I'd a hell of a lot rather be lost in the U.S. of A. than in this miserable pesthole."

Etta closed her eyes, smelled her horse's animal scent. "Would you want me to go back with you?"

Harry looked at her in surprise. Dismounting, he came around to stand next to her, touching her elbow in concern. "You know I want you with me."

"I'm not sure I know that at all," she said, her voice shaking.

"Etta, I didn't think I needed to tell you you're the only woman for me."

A laugh burst out of her. "Oh, Harry, you must think I'm stupid, or naïve, either one."

He tightened his grip on her arm and made her turn to face him. "What do you mean?"

"You've been sleeping with other women for over a year now! Every time you come back from town you've got that stink all over you. The stink of the whorehouse!" She stared at him, daring him to deny it.

Harry's face turned ugly. "You ought to fuckin' know," he growled.

With a gasp, Etta made to slap him. He caught her wrist in mid-air, squeezing it painfully, his eyes narrowed to a dangerous slit. Finally he shoved her away and climbed on his horse. Knees shaking, she watched him move down the road. After a minute, she mounted up and followed.

When they reached the ranch where they had made arrangements to stay the night, they managed to make pleasant conversation with the proprietors without saying a word to each other. Later, in bed, Etta felt the space between them like a void.

Harry gave in first, rolling over to wrap his arm across her rigid body. "I didn't mean what I said before," he whispered.

She considered how to respond. "Which part?" she said finally.

He sighed. "Don't make me say it again, Etta."

"You mean the part about me being a whore? No need to apologize for speaking the truth."

"Jesus, Etta, don't be like that."

Despite her vow not to, she began to cry, the tears falling silently to her pillow.

"Etta . . . Etta. . . ." He kissed her shoulder, her neck. She let him roll her over, and he brushed her tears away with his lips. They fell asleep holding each other.

★ ★ ★

The next day when they arrived home, Butch met them in the yard. He told them that, while they were gone, the *comisario*, Edward Humphreys, had paid a visit, bearing news. A bank in the town of Rió Gallegos, seven hundred and fifty miles to the south, had been held up by two *gringos*. The police chief in Buenos Aires had notified Humphreys that the prime suspects were two *Americanos* living in his district, Santiago Ryan and Enrique Place.

Butch was already making plans to leave.

CHAPTER TWENTY

Etta was shocked at how quickly four years' worth of hard work could be disposed of. In less than a month's time, Butch and Harry sold their livestock to Dan Gibbon and the rest of their holdings to the local land company. They canceled pending orders of goods and assigned others to their neighbors. What they could not carry with them, which was almost everything, they left, telling their foreman to keep whatever he wanted and parcel out the rest to his friends and family.

Climbing onto the wagon on the day of their departure, Etta refused to look back at all she was leaving behind — her furniture and china, linens and draperies, pictures and knick-knacks . . . her beautiful double-hung windows. Her life had been reduced to what she could pack into one trunk.

Wenceslao Solís, their loyal *peón,* drove them north to Bariloche where they took a steamer across Lake Nahuel Huapi and entered into Chile. Rain fell in sheets, and thick clouds obscured the tops of the mountains — so different from that day only a few weeks ago when Etta and Harry had skirted the lake on their return from the Jones *estancia*. It occurred to Etta that her lover had been granted the wish he had expressed that day — to leave their ranch in Cholila — although she was sure he would not have scripted this particular reason for departure. Indeed, where Butch had been matter-of-fact and methodical in preparing to leave, Harry had reacted with anger and frustration at being forced out of their home. It was one thing, evidently, to want to go, another thing to *have* to go.

Etta tried not to draw comparisons between the two men, but it was hard not to. Harry's ranting and raving about the injustice of being falsely suspected only made her own unhappiness greater while Butch's perpetual optimism, his quiet smiles, understanding nods, and sympathetic winks, bolstered her ability to cope. She forgave Harry — after all, what had happened *was* unfair — but she could not help wishing he would take a more philosophic view. When you thought about it, they had a lot to be grateful for, including their friendships with people like Edward Humphreys, who had risked his job in order to tip them off, and Dan Gibbon, who was well aware of their true identities but would go to his grave covering for them.

Once across the border, the weary threesome headed north to Valparaíso, a good-size city nestled on the narrow, cliff-bound shores of a busy harbor. Winter was coming on, the season of *temporales* — mighty northers that swept in on sea-sprayed gusts of wind. From their rooms, perched precariously on the side of a cliff, they could hear the relentless crashing of the surf against the stone seawalls.

Immediately Harry announced plans to return to the States. He would come back to Chile, he said, when winter was over to conclude wrapping up their affairs. After that ... well, they would just have to see.

Butch protested that a trip to the States was foolish, that the Río Gallegos business proved the authorities had not forgotten about them, but Longabaugh said what difference did it make, they were wanted in South America as well as in the States, so he'd just as soon take his chances in the good old U.S.A. He booked passage for himself and Etta to San Francisco, where his brother lived. Secretly Etta agreed with Butch that returning to the States was fraught with risk, but, fearful of setting off Harry's volatile temper, she kept quiet. At the end of June, they set sail.

Once again, Butch was left to weather a wet, miserable winter on his own. But this time, although he missed Etta, he avoided despair and fought off self-pity. For one thing, he was certain of his friends' return as Harry still needed to attend to unfinished business from the settling of their affairs in Cholila. More importantly he was too busy assessing their options and making plans for their future to waste time moping. He was thirty-nine years old, Harry a year younger, and Etta several years younger than that. They had a lot of life yet to live.

After three months in San Francisco, the outlaw couple, now calling themselves Mr. and Mrs. Frank Boyd, returned to Valparaíso. Their choice of a new alias seemed curious, and Butch momentarily wondered if it had been made to tweak him about his long ago romance with Mary Boyd. But he knew neither one of them had ever heard her name from his lips, and even if they had found out about her from someone else, it seemed unlikely that they would throw her in his face. He decided to assume they had picked the name out of thin air. For his part, he was now known as James, or Santiago, Maxwell.

Butch met them on the wharf, carrying a handful of *copihue* that were just beginning to break into bright red blossoms. Handing them to Etta, he leaned forward to peck her cheek.

"Welcome home," he murmured, appreciating the soft pressure of her hand on his back.

Burying her nose in the crimson blooms, Etta smiled at him sideways. "Where on earth did you find these? It's early yet for flowers."

"I've got ways." He grinned. Stepping back, he planted a good-natured punch on Harry's shoulder. "D'ja stay out of trouble?" he said lightly.

Harry shrugged, brushing off the question. Digging some coins out of his pocket, he tossed them to the boy who had carted their luggage off the boat, and then walked away in search of a wagon.

Embarrassed, Etta slipped her arm through Butch's. "Harry's a little out of sorts," she explained. "He and his brother didn't exactly see eye to eye. Samanna's always been so understanding . . . I think it threw him that his brother was rather disapproving. But anyway, here we are, together again. I did miss you, Butch." She looked up, her cheeks tinged pink.

Butch reached over with his free hand and squeezed her arm, surprised and pleased at Etta's joy in seeing him again. Since the night of their party for Governor Lezana, they had been careful around each other, avoiding opportunities to be alone. Butch told himself their kiss had been nothing more than a friendly show of affection, but it worried him that he found himself wanting to repeat it.

Harry returned with a wagon and supervised the driver in loading their luggage. "Where to?" he asked his partner.

"The train station," replied Butch.

"What?" Harry and Etta spoke in union.

Smiling, Butch instructed the driver to meet them at the depot, then turned to his friends. "We're going to Antofagasta. That's where I've been staying."

"What the hell's in Antofagasta?" asked Harry.

"A lot of desert, mostly. Nitrate mines. It's cold and empty, and nobody in their right mind would want to live there, so I figured it was the perfect place for us."

"Now wait a minute . . . ," Harry protested.

"Hold on! Hear me out." Butch started walking, and motioned for them to follow.

268

"Right after you left, I got the feeling I was being watched. Ain't sure who it was, maybe a Pinkerton, but I figured it was time to move on. You remember Wenceslao told us he has a cousin living in Antofagasta . . . someone we could trust, if we needed help? Well, I looked him up, and he's a good man, all right. Anyway, I've spent a lot of time thinking . . . what are we gonna do now? . . . how're we gonna live?"

"I can answer that," Harry declared. "I'm getting the rest of my money out of Cholila and going back home, back to the States."

Etta gave her lover an exasperated look. "Harry, listen to him, will you?"

"Kid," Butch said, "I'd like to go back home, too. But the only way we can do that, and stay out of prison, is if we keep our noses clean. That means we got to have a stake . . . enough to set us up for the rest of our lives."

Harry furrowed his brow. "That's right. That's why I want my Cholila money."

"But it ain't enough. We never owned the land, and the rest of it, once we split it up, ain't enough to live on forever. The way I see it, we got to pad the ol' nest egg a bit before we can call it quits down here."

"How do you propose to do that?" asked Etta.

Butch spread his hands, grinning broadly. "By doing what we do best, Missus Boyd."

Harry and Etta stopped in their tracks. "You're shittin' me," Harry said, slack-jawed.

"I am not," replied Butch, still grinning. "What have we got to lose? The law's after us anyway because of Río Gallegos, and even if we could prove our innocence, we'd only wind up drawing attention to ourselves so that pretty soon the damn' Pinkertons'd talk them into extraditing us. So I figure if they want us to be bank robbers, hell, we'll just oblige them. We'll pull one job, a big one, lay low for a couple of years, and go back home in style!"

For the first time in months, Harry smiled. "Now you're talking! I reckon I could stand this stinkin' country for a couple more years if it meant being able to go home like you said. You been studying a particular place for the hold-up?"

"If I know Butch," Etta piped up, "he knows where, when, how, and how much."

"Your confidence is greatly appreciated, ma'am," said Butch, doffing his hat. "As it happens, I do have a plan."

On the train to Antofagasta, Butch filled them in. The target was the Banco de la

Nación in Villa Mercedes, a busy cattle-trading town in central Argentina. Monthly livestock fairs attracted ranchers from great distances, and the bank was sure to be brimming with cash during one of these fairs. They would need four men to do the job, and Wenceslao's cousin had agreed to come in.

"That makes three," Harry pointed out. "Who's the fourth?"

Butch turned his gaze on Etta, his blue eyes full of mischief. "What do you say, Missus Boyd? Are you ready to become a *bandida?*"

"Oh, Butch!" Etta clasped her hands together, her face alight with excitement. "You'd really let me join you?"

"Ain't nobody I trust more than you, Etta."

Etta turned to Harry, expecting a protest, but the outlaw merely shrugged. "Guess you might as well," he conceded. "Your riding's as good as any *gaucho* I've seen. Not to mention you're a sight better-looking in the saddle." Wiggling his eyebrows like a play-acting *roué*, he pulled her close, letting his hand slide down to caress the curve of her hip. Laughing, Etta threw her arms around his neck and kissed him.

With a slight smile, Butch turned to watch the treeless, colorless vista roll by.

★ ★ ★

They stayed in Antofagasta long enough to hook up with their fourth robber, José Solís, and purchase some supplies, then slowly made their way back into Argentina, crossing the border at one of the more remote mountain passes. Moving camp every few days, they scouted the area around Villa Mercedes, seeking the fastest escape routes and recruiting *peónes* to hold the relay horses. Butch and Harry made several forays into town, checking the bank from all angles and at different times of day. They struck up conversations with locals and learned that the largest of the livestock fairs would likely be held right before Christmas.

Shortly before the chosen date, the four of them took up residence at a nearby ranch called Estancia de Luna. Posing as wealthy Americans looking to establish a horse ranch in the area, they raised no suspicions on the part of the *estancia*'s owners who were quite charmed by the beautiful, pants-wearing *americana del norte* lady who loved to race her pony.

One afternoon, Harry took José to do a final check on the one of the relay stations. Butch and Etta saddled up and rode into the country for some shooting practice. When they returned to their cabin, hot and dusty,

Etta made a pitcher of lemonade and set it on the table between them. Butch took a long drink and settled back in his chair, eyeing appreciatively the woman across from him. Out on the range, she had tucked her hair up under a hat, and when she had removed it on coming inside, the long, dark tresses had tumbled down around her shoulders. Her color was high, and her brow glowed with the sheen of sweat. He thought to compliment her on her disheveled beauty, but held back, mindful of the danger in being alone with her.

She cocked her head and looked at him quizzically. "You were going to say something," she noted.

He gave her a lop-sided grin, marveling at how well she could read him. "I was, but changed my mind."

"Don't you know you can tell me anything, Butch?" she said, raising the glass to her lips.

He leaned forward and rested his elbows on the table. "I've never known anyone in my life who I could tell anything."

Her eyes flickered with momentary hurt. "Is that the fault of the people you've known, or your own?"

"I don't consider it a fault," he said evenly. "I consider it a virtue."

"Not being able to confide in someone close to you is a virtue? I hope you don't really believe that."

"In my line of work, it's best to keep things close to your vest."

Etta looked him straight in the eye. "Is that why you lost Mary?"

Butch flinched. "What the hell are you talking about?"

"Mary Boyd," Etta went on. "Maude Lay told me all about her. How you lived with her for the better part of a year, how she broke your heart by marrying someone else while you were in prison. . . ."

He stood abruptly. "I told you once I didn't want to talk about that. It's all over with."

"Who are you fooling, Butch?" she said quietly. "Those things are never really over. You don't have to act like a tough guy in front of me. I'm glad to know you loved someone. It makes me feel better about what we're going to do next week."

"How's that?"

Etta rose and came toward him. "If something should happen to you, I'd know who you'd want me to tell. I'd know where to send that cross you wear." Gently she placed her hand on his chest, covering the place where Mary's cross lay beneath his shirt.

"Jesus, Etta," he whispered, "what kind of talk is this? I ain't gonna die next week. No one is."

She dropped her hand from his chest. "I believe you. Still, just thinking about what could happen makes me . . . not scared, but . . . apprehensive."

His eyes softened as he placed a comforting hand on her shoulder. "It's good to be concerned . . . makes a person cautious. I've seen men killed by their own cockiness. But you don't need to worry, Etta . . . you'll be fine."

She nodded at his words, appreciating his confidence in her but unable to shake the feeling of doom that had settled on her. Turning away, she went to stare out the window, hugging her arms as though chilled.

He stood for a moment, wondering what he could say to lighten her mood. Something occurred to him, and he blurted it out without thinking. "Etta, you ain't never said a word about your family. Is there anyone you'd want me to notify if . . . well, you know, if I needed to?"

Looking over her shoulder, a sad smile played on her lips. "Why, Butch darling, I'm with the only two people in the world I love."

The two people she loved. Her words hung in the air, and he knew he should say something to defuse them. But if he did, it would give her an opportunity to explain. Surely she meant that she loved Harry as a woman loves her husband while what she felt for him was a friendly sort of love. But the way she was looking at him now, her eyes gone dark and smoky, put the lie to that theory.

She turned to face him, still clutching her arms. "You heard me right. I love you, Butch, I always have. But I didn't think you needed me, so I found someone who did. And I love him, too." She laughed sadly. "Too bad we can't be Mormons in reverse . . . one woman with two husbands. God knows I'd take you both to my bed."

Something busted loose inside him, and he felt all his reserve, all his caution drain out of him like blood from a wound. He crossed the room in two strides and caught her in his arms, hesitating only long enough to assure himself of her desire. Bending his head, he kissed her, spreading her lips with his tongue to remind himself of the sweet taste of her mouth. She fell against him, her hands pushing hard into the small of his back.

"Jesus God, Etta," he growled, swiping the hair away from her face, "if I take you now, that makes you a whore and me a bastard. Is it worth it?"

She kissed him again while her fingers worked the buttons on his trousers. "Let's repent tomorrow," she suggested, and then led him to her bed.

CHAPTER TWENTY-ONE

On December 19th, Etta awoke from a fitful sleep. She dressed in her customary costume of cotton shirt and pants, added a bulky coat to hide her figure, pinned her hair up under a Montana Peak hat, and rode with Butch, Harry, and José Solís into Villa Mercedes. Everything was in place, the plan well rehearsed. But when Butch told them, just before mounting up, to expect the unexpected, a cold sword of fear sliced through her forced calm. What they were about to do, she had long dreamed of. But in her dreams, all she had felt was sweet intoxication. Now that she was faced with reality, she felt a nervousness that made her almost physically sick.

As they rode silently, side-by-side, Etta was comforted by the noise and commotion in the busy streets. No one took notice of the four horsemen among the hundreds already there for the huge cattle sale. Nevertheless, she kept her hat pulled low and her head down to avoid any curious stares. She had made several visits to town clothed in male attire, so her appearance should not have attracted attention, but she could not help feeling like all eyes were upon her today.

Butch reined up in front of a bar two blocks from the bank. He and Harry stepped down and pushed through the batwing doors, leaving Etta and José with the horses. This was a planned stop, designed with two goals in mind — to cement their appearance as cowboys come to town for a good time at the cattle show and, more importantly, to pick up any last-minute gossip that might be of particular interest. If, for example, the local *comisario* had beefed up his troops to handle the large crowds, that would be handy to know. In keeping with their cover, José lounged on the steps of the saloon, deliberately rolling a smoke while his eyes scanned the street. Etta remained on her horse, wishing she could feel as relaxed as José looked. Taking deep breaths, she tried to control her twitching muscles.

Twenty minutes later, the two outlaws emerged. Butch casually tapped José on the shoulder, and then swung on his horse. Stepping into his stirrups, Harry winked at his girlfriend. "This is it, baby," he said under his breath. "Make me proud."

Following the men down the street, Etta tried to concentrate on the task at hand. Her rôle was relatively simple — she was to hold the horses and keep watch on the outside of the bank. Nothing to it — unless something went wrong. She leaned over and loosened her rifle in its scabbard.

The Banco de la Nación fronted on Ríobamba Street, but, unlike most commercial establishments, it sported a fenced-in garden streetside. The entrance was around the corner on Belgrano Street. Butch turned the corner and pulled up by the gate. Dismounting, he handed his reins to Etta. Harry and José did the same. Looking discreetly, side to side, the men strolled up the walk and into the bank.

Holding the reins tightly in her left hand, Etta unbuttoned her coat and rested her right hand on her thigh, near the holstered revolver at her hip. She had practiced a quick draw from this position but knew she was no match for most gunmen. Her eyes flickered to the rifle attached to her saddle — this was her best bet in case of trouble.

It was still silent inside the bank. What was going on in there? Sour-tasting bile rose in her throat. She forced it down, silently cursing her weak, female nerves.

Suddenly shots rang out, three of them,

followed by shouts of surprise. Etta jumped, nearly losing her grip on the reins. Sounds of a violent scuffle now, like people being thrown against the walls. Passers-by stopped in their tracks, glancing with alarm toward the bank. Etta inched her shaking hand closer to the revolver.

Across the street, a man in shirtsleeves burst out the door, running straight for the bank. Etta's hand twitched. *Shoot him!* a voice inside her said. *No, wait! He's not the law. He's not even armed!* Her hand closed on the butt of the gun, but she hesitated. The man ran past her, leaped the fence, and headed for the door. Etta pulled the revolver and pointed it at his back. There was a second when she could have fired, but she did not.

Amidst the shouting and shoving on the street around her, Etta was having a hard time keeping the horses quiet. She reholstered the revolver and held the reins in both hands. "Come on, come on," she whispered, wondering if one of the outlaws had been shot. *My God, what if Harry or Butch lay bleeding on the floor, unable to move?*

Just then, another shot pierced the air, whistling by her ear. She crouched low over her horse's neck, screaming Butch's name. At that same moment, the man who had run into the bank reappeared, his shirt ripped at the shoulder, and started toward her.

Shoot him! Shoot him! She transferred the reins and grabbed for her rifle. It cleared leather, but as she brought it up to shoot, her horse danced sideways, throwing her off balance. She grasped the horn, trying to keep ahold of the reins and her rifle and at the same time stay aboard her riled mount. The man passed her, ran back across the street, and disappeared through a door.

Panic seized her. What was going on in there? What had the man seen? Had he heard her call Butch's name? He was an eyewitness, and she had let him get away.

The door to the bank slammed open, and Harry leaped down the steps, a bulging canvas bag slung over his shoulder. José followed with a bag of his own, and Butch brought up the rear, shooting behind him as he ran. They cleared the fence and were almost mounted when the man from across the street bolted into the middle of the dusty road, dropped to one knee, and leveled a rifle at them.

"Go! Go! Go!" shouted Butch, turning his horse so sharply the animal nearly lost its footing.

The man fired. Etta kicked at her horse, wishing she had shot the bastard. They raced away, gunfire chasing them. Beside her, she heard a soft exhalation of air, and José grabbed at his arm. Blood sprayed across her leg. Instinctively she started to pull up, but behind her Harry screamed: "Go! Go!"

Glancing back, she saw a group of mounted policemen no more than two blocks away, their weapons blazing. Bending low, she dug her heels into her horse's flanks. North through town the outlaws raced, crossing the Quinto River on a rickety wooden bridge, and then circling around to the south. The police were sticking close. Stealing a glance over her shoulder, Etta was alarmed to see them no more than a few hundred yards behind. Still, the outlaws' horseflesh was clearly superior; they should soon start to pull ahead.

Turning back around, Etta was stunned when Butch veered off into an arroyo and leaped down, reloading as he hit the ground. The rest of them followed suit, all except José who collapsed on the rocky slope.

"Etta!" Butch commanded, "check on José!"

Kneeling beside the injured man, she peeled back his bloody shirt, revealing an ugly wound. The bullet had entered the back of his arm high up, near the shoulder, and come out below his collarbone. His eyes were dilated, and he appeared on the verge of losing consciousness.

"Throw me your handkerchiefs!" Etta shouted.

Butch and Harry paused their shooting long enough to comply. Using the cloths to fashion a bandage, Etta wrapped the wound tightly, knowing it would be only a matter of seconds before it became soaked with blood.

"How's he doing?" Butch rolled over on his back to reload, his face grim.

"Not good," she replied. "I don't think he can ride."

Butch and Harry exchanged glances. Butch rolled over and squeezed off more shots. Etta noticed the returning gunfire seemed to be getting sparse.

"We shoulda kept going," Harry hissed. "If we'd've made it to the first relay, we could've lost them."

"José wouldn't've made it that far," Butch answered.

Longabaugh turned to stare at his fallen comrade with a look that said it was every man for himself. Etta felt chilled to the bone.

Holding up a hand, Butch signaled for quiet. In the distance, where the police had taken cover behind some low-growing conifers, they could hear voices arguing, then boots scraping on rocky soil. With a clattering of hoofs, their pursuers mounted up and fled in retreat.

Sticking his head above the edge of the gully, Butch watched them go. "I knew it!" he crowed, dropping back down. "Could tell they wasn't armed well enough to last for long. Come on, let's get José on his horse and get out of here."

Muscling the woozy man into his saddle, they tied him on so he would not fall off if he lost consciousness.

They rode through the night, stopping frequently to change José's bandages. By dawn, Etta had used up every shred of cloth they could spare, and still the wound bled.

"He's bleeding to death," she announced, wetting the edge of her coat and wiping at José's feverish face. "He's got to see a doctor."

At the next relay, on the banks of the Salado River, they directed the *peón*, holding their horses, to get their friend to shelter and see that he was cared for. Reluctant to be caught harboring a fugitive, the *peón* at first refused, but two hundred *pesos* in his pocket quickly changed his mind. Etta whispered into José's ear to meet them back at Antofagasta when he had recovered.

★ ★ ★

Over the next few weeks, they continued to hide out, moving constantly in zigzag patterns but still heading generally south and west. They were aided in their escape by torrential early season rains that flooded the rivers and turned the pampas to a swamp. Travel was difficult, but equally so for the posses trailing them.

Finally they crossed into Chile — wet, tired, hungry, sore . . . and 12,000 *pesos* richer.

Etta was a true criminal now — a bank robber with, for all she knew, a price on her head. None of that concerned her. What made her blood run cold and brought her wide awake in the middle of the night was the memory of Harry's face when he had turned to look at poor José, lying wounded on the ground, a look that said he cared for nothing and no one but himself.

CHAPTER TWENTY-TWO

Sunshine streamed through the window of Denver's St. Joseph Hospital, illuminating dancing dust motes in the long, narrow corridor. The light seemed out of place in this gloomy hallway where people waited, some to see a doctor themselves, others for news of their loved ones. They sat silently, staring at their shoes, all except for a young mother who cooed to an obviously sick baby cradled on her lap.

Harry watched a ray of light slowly move across the floor, over his foot, up his leg, and onto his lap. When it got too hot, he stood up and ambled down the hallway, stopping to peer out at the broad lawn and busy street. He drummed his fingers impatiently on the sill.

When Etta had announced, shortly after their return to Antofagasta, following the Villa Mercedes job, she wanted to make a visit to the States, he and Butch had been surprised, to say the least. Even Harry had been reconciled to remaining in South America for another couple of years. Both men had argued that such a lengthy trip, coming so soon after the robbery, was reckless. In uncharacteristic fashion, Etta had pleaded to go. She was blue, she said, and needed the distraction of travel to raise her spirits.

Privately Butch and Harry had conferred. Harry was in favor of simply telling her no, but his partner disagreed. "Go ahead and take her," Butch had said. "It'll be worse if we make her stay."

Longabaugh was surprised at his friend's lackadaisical attitude. Butch had always acted lovingly and solicitously toward Etta — not in an improper way, of course, but it was obvious he thought a lot of her. After all, the two had been lovers all those years ago, and, although Harry had no special soft spot for his former girlfriends, he could see where affection might remain in certain cases. Yet here was Cassidy, refusing to prevent Etta, and Harry, too, for that matter, from undertaking a potentially dangerous journey.

He did not understand it, but there was a lot he did not understand these days. Things had changed since Villa Mercedes. The three of them seemed, more often than not, to get on each other's nerves. Long silences marked their conversations, and occasionally tempers flared. Perhaps some time apart would be good for all of them.

Of course, taking Etta on a trip might separate them from Butch, but would wind up throwing the two of them even closer together, a circumstance that did not entirely please Harry. Strange, how at one point in his life, he had mourned every second spent away from his beautiful mistress, and now he sometimes felt as though he were merely enduring her company.

Pulling out his pocket watch, he checked the time, wondering if he could go get a bite to eat and a quick drink before the doctor reported back. He was not particularly worried about Etta's condition. They had started their trip in fine style, taking the train to Buenos Aires and, from there, a steamer to London. After enjoying that historic city, they had crossed the Atlantic, spent a couple of agreeable weeks in New York, and then boarded another train headed west. They had planned to wind up in San Francisco where they would catch a boat bound for Valparaíso. But halfway across the country, Etta had started to complain of a pain in her side, so they had stopped in Denver to have it checked out. Harry was sure it was nothing;

despite this mysterious pain, she looked as healthy as a *peón*.

The door to Etta's room opened, and a white-clad Sister of Charity stepped into the hallway, followed by the doctor. Both were smiling.

Harry approached them. "Well, what is it?" he asked, certain now that everything was all right.

"She can tell you the good news," said the doctor, holding the door for him. "We're keeping her overnight for observation, but she's just fine." The young nurse looked at Harry shyly, her cheeks pink, as he walked past.

Inside the room, Etta lay propped up on the single bed, dressed in a long-sleeved hospital gown, the covers pulled up around her chest, anchored by arms that she held stiffly at her sides. She gave him an apprehensive look, then stared at her toes sticking up under the blanket.

"Must not be appendicitis like you thought," said Harry cheerfully. "The doc didn't seem at all worried."

"No. It's not appendicitis." She continued to stare at her feet.

Harry perched on the edge of the bed, his fingers working the brim of his hat. "Well . . . what then?"

Etta closed her eyes and leaned her head back against the pillows. "I'm pregnant."

His hands, playing with the hat, went still. He blinked and shook his head like someone trying to regain their senses after being knocked silly. "I . . . that's . . . well, Etta . . . that's a surprise." Standing abruptly, he walked away.

Taking a deep breath, Etta gathered her nerve. She had been dreading this conversation ever since she knew of the pregnancy, mere weeks after the Villa Mercedes robbery. The pregnancy, of course, was why she had wanted to come to the States. She desperately wanted this baby, wanted it to be born healthy and strong, and so had wanted to ensure herself of the best medical care available.

But she knew Harry would have a different view of things. So she had manufactured an excuse for this journey, ultimately planning to tell him when they reached San Francisco that she intended to stay there to have her baby. Unfortunately she had started to feel sickly on the train and, erring on the side of caution, had decided to get a doctor's examination. Thus, they were having this conversation in a hospital room instead of over a candlelight dinner or in bed, either of which would have been a better place to break the news.

He turned and looked at her accusingly. "How did it happen?"

She arched an eyebrow. "There's only one way I know of."

"No, I mean . . . we've been together ten years, and you never . . . I figured you couldn't have children."

"Why would you assume it was me and not you?"

Harry snorted. "From what I hear, there's living proof I ain't got any problems in that area."

"Oh, for God's sake, Harry, you should be ashamed of yourself!"

He leaned over her, a nasty look on his face. "Listen, I never claimed to be no saint. I've been with more women than I can count, and, if some of them managed to get theirselves caught, that's their problem. Myself, I was always happy you managed to be smarter than that."

"What makes you think I was?"

He hesitated. "You mean . . . ?"

Etta flung herself out of bed, grabbing her robe from the back of a chair. "God, Harry, didn't you ever wonder, or think to ask?"

"Wonder what?"

Slipping on the robe, Etta poured a drink of water from the carafe by the bed, struggling to stay calm. "Most of the time," she explained patiently, "I took precautions. But sometimes . . . sometimes we just got carried away. Since you and I have been together there have been two times . . . ," she trailed off.

Understanding slowly dawned on Harry, followed by a curious resentment. "You got rid of them?" he asked, his eyes flat.

She nodded. "Both times were in Cholila. I didn't intend for it to happen, but I suppose somewhere in the back of my mind, I thought it wouldn't be so bad if it did. We were happy and together, like normal husbands and wives. It was easy to get careless. But then" — she dropped her eyes — "I remembered who we are . . . outlaws, pirates, thieves. Not exactly parent material. So I went to a native woman, took some herbs she mixed up . . . it worked like a charm. But it made me sick for quite a while. I thought you'd notice."

He had wondered why she had turned away from him in bed for so long, figured it was just normal female trouble. Instead of asking her about it, however, he had chosen to seek relief at the local bordello. At the time, that had seemed a simpler solution.

Now, he was not sure what he thought. He did not want children, never had, but he found himself feeling put out that Etta had destroyed the offspring of his seed without even consulting him. Still, she had been right to do what she had done. Kids were nothing but a nuisance. He really ought to be pleased that his mistress took such a sensible view of things.

"I just didn't know, baby, I'm sorry," he said, affecting a humble attitude. "You're right, we ain't in no situation to be raising kids. From now on, you just tell me, you know, when's a good time and when ain't, and I'll be more careful."

She gave him a funny look. "Maybe you don't understand. I'm going to have this baby."

"*What?*" he shouted, then lowered his voice, mindful of the people just outside the door. "Why wouldn't you just . . . do like you did before?"

Etta crossed her arms defiantly. "I don't want to. This time it's different."

"The hell it is! Nothing's changed except now you're an outlaw as much as me. What if you're caught, Etta, you thought about that? You want to have a baby in prison, want it taken away from you and put in some orphanage, never knowing who its mother is? Or maybe knowing damn' well about you and being ashamed all its life for having a thief and a whore for a mother!"

"Stop it, Harry, stop it! You can say all the awful things you want to, but I am going to have this baby. You can't stop me."

Longabaugh stomped around the room, his frustration rising. "Jesus Christ, Etta, try to look at this sensibly. Now ain't no time to be having a baby! We had a plan . . . lay low for a couple of years and then come back and find some place to settle down. Maybe then . . . just maybe . . . we could, you know . . . talk about, well, kids and all."

Etta looked at him, disgusted. "Listen, I didn't plan to get pregnant, but it happened, and this time I'm going through with it. You can stick around for it or go back to Chile on your own. Either way is fine with me."

"Well, ain't you the tough one," said Harry, grabbing his hat off the bed. "If I show up in the morning, you'll know what I decided." He stormed out the door, slamming it behind him.

Slowly, as though aching from a bone-deep soreness, Etta climbed back into bed. That had not gone well, yet she had only herself to blame. She should never have mentioned the two previous pregnancies. Naturally Harry would wonder what made this one special. And she could never, ever, tell him that this one was special because she was nearly certain the child she carried was Butch Cassidy's.

Steaming mad, Harry left the hospital and detoured into the nearest bar. Several hours later, he stumbled out of that establishment and into another, and so on until he lost track of exactly where he was or what he was doing.

At some point, a semi-pretty woman with chubby cheeks and enormous bosoms joined up with him. He told the woman — he never did ask her name — all about his dilemma: should he stick by his girlfriend even though she had betrayed him, or should he leave her to work things out on her own? His new friend commiserated with him, made him eat some dinner and, when closing time came around, offered to find a cab to take him home.

As they stood on the street, waiting, the woman slipped her hand in his pocket, trying to make off with his wallet. He caught her at it, and, enraged at falling victim to yet another perfidious female, he began dragging her back to his room, intending to teach her a lesson.

The woman shrieked in alarm, but, when he threatened to expose her attempted theft to the police, she quieted down. This was not the first time she had run this game on some unsuspecting drunk, nor the first time she had been caught at it, and she could not afford another trip to the slammer.

Inside his room, he threw the woman on the bed and drew his pistol. Back-pedaling furiously, she cringed against the head-board, clutching a pillow to her ample chest.

"Now, listen, buster," she pleaded, her eyes wide with fear, "you don't want to do nothing you're gonna regret."

Harry chuckled and walked unsteadily toward her. He cocked the pistol and placed the barrel right between her eyes. "I never regret anything I do," he declared, feeling his power over the thieving slut trembling beneath him.

The woman stayed perfectly still. Her breath came out in short little puffs.

Finally he raised the pistol and lowered the hammer with a noisy click. "You're too ugly to fuck reg'lar," he slurred, "so do me the other way."

Crawling off the bed, the woman knelt before him. He sat down, arms extended behind him, still holding the gun. Unbuttoning his trousers, she took him out and went to work. But the liquor had done its job, and after many minutes of energetic effort, the woman sat back on her heels, whimpering: "It ain't no use."

"Bullshit," Harry mumbled, half asleep. "Keep tryin'."

"Listen, lover boy. . . ."

"Shuddup! Keep tryin'!" He roused himself and pointed the gun at her.

With renewed vigor the woman applied herself to the task, with the same results. Finally, exhausted, she sank to the floor. "Go ahead and shoot me," she wailed, "I can't do no more."

"God dammit!" He kicked at the woman, then clumsily pulled himself upright and began stalking the room. "This is all her fault! God damn that bitch! Thinks she can make it on her own . . . let her try, jus' let her try!"

The woman huddled in a corner, watching with frightened eyes as he carried on. "Fuckin' bitch! Only woman I ever . . . only one I ever. . . ." He halted in the middle of the room, wavering on his feet, anger turning into maudlin self-pity. His shoulders started to shake, and the woman realized with a start he was crying.

A sharp rap at the door made her yelp with surprise.

"Mister Boyd? This is the landlord.

What's going on in there? You quiet down now, before you wake the whole house!"

"Shuddup," Harry drawled.

"What was that? You heard me, keep it down!"

"Leave me alone!" Swinging his arm wildly, he unloaded three rounds into the ceiling. "Jus' leave me the fuck alone!"

"That's it!" the landlord called out. "I'm fetching the police."

They could hear his footsteps running down the stairs.

"God dammit!" the outlaw moaned, wiping his tear-streaked face with his coat sleeve.

Reholstering his pistol, he careened around the room, grabbing the few things that had been unpacked and stuffing them into his suitcase. His bleary eyes alighted on what looked to be a pin or brooch lying on the bedside table. Snatching it up, he pocketed it, climbed out the window, and, without a word to the woman still crouching on the floor, disappeared down the fire escape.

Darting to the window, she peeked over the sill and saw him pass through the circle of light from a streetlamp and turn the corner. Letting out a sigh of relief, the woman slumped against the wall, noticing for the first time another suitcase hiding be-hind the chiffarobe door. Scooting over on hands and knees, she opened it . . . and broke into a wide grin. Neatly folded inside was some of the most beautiful women's clothing she had ever seen — blouses, skirts, scarves, lingerie — all of the finest quality.

Down below, she could hear sharp voices — the landlord directing the police up the stairs. Quickly snapping the lid shut, she hauled the case to the window, tipped it on edge, and let it drop over, praying it would be strong enough to survive the fall intact.

"Sorry, honey," she muttered, "but that's what ya get for having such a bastard for a boyfriend."

Throwing her leg over, she followed it out into the night.

CHAPTER TWENTY-THREE

Cassidy waited in Antofagasta, but, after three months had gone by with no word from his globe-trotting companions, he decided it was time to move on. José Solís, recovered from his wounds, showed up to claim his share of the Villa Mercedes money, and Butch told him to tell Longabaugh to look for him, if he was so inclined, somewhere in the high mining country of Bolivia. When José expressed concern for *Doña* Boyd, who had always treated him kindly, Butch shrugged and said not to worry, her husband would look after her. At this, José frowned.

Butch knew something of what José must be thinking. He, too, was troubled by his partner's dark moods that seemed to creep over him like moss on a rock, a little thicker with each occurrence. Although he had never doubted Harry's bedrock devotion to Etta, despite the man's frequent tomcatting, it seemed that Etta's decision to take himself for a lover signified a major shift in her allegiances.

Only once more during the week leading up to the Villa Mercedes job had he and Etta found themselves alone. Still not certain that their previous coupling had not been a sort of accident — just a good-natured toss in the hay for old time's sake — he had waited for her to get things rolling. And boy howdy, had she ever, rolling right over him like a dust devil on the prairie. Now there was a woman who knew how to take charge! No red-blooded male could be expected to withstand such an assault, and, of course, it was doubly sweet because of the true affection he felt for Etta. But, afterward, it bothered him that he had been disloyal to his best friend and partner, and he told her so. Somewhat to his chagrin, she agreed that they had not acted honorably and promised to clear the air after Villa Mercedes.

It was not to be. Things only got more confusing in the weeks following the robbery. Butch had kept to himself, waiting for Etta to say something. Instead, she had come up with the foolish idea of traveling back to the States, which Butch decided was just an excuse to get away from him. Evidently the passion she had shown him was a fleeting thing, probably brought on by nervous anticipation of the robbery. But in the end, it was Harry she wanted, not him.

So the two of them had gone off on their grand tour, undoubtedly made even more titillating, from Etta's perspective, because of her recent unfaithfulness. Nothing to spice up your love life like a little cheating. Why, she had probably told Harry all about her dalliance with his partner, and doubtless they had gotten a good laugh out of it. Either that or now Harry wanted to kill him. Not that he was going to waste time looking over his shoulder — frankly he never expected to see either one of them again.

Leaving sea level, he journeyed by train up into the Andean *altiplano,* a vast, treeless plateau that seemed to mirror the barrenness of his life. Yet in the *altiplano,* upon closer inspection, there were plenty of resources to sustain life. So it was with him, for he soon discovered that, although those closest to him had forsaken him, he could not stay down for long.

Introducing himself as Santiago Maxwell, he hired on at the Concordia tin mine near Tres Cruces, quickly gaining the respect of manager Rolla Glass. Before long, Glass thought enough of his new man to entrust him with carrying the mine's payroll remittances from the main office in La Paz. Butch looked forward to these assignments for the opportunity it gave him to enjoy the colorful capital city with its red-tiled roofs and ancient markets where *cholas* sold everything from fruits and vegetables to alpaca wool ropes. He even developed a taste for *chicha*, the Bolivian version of beer, and found that, after a few mugs of the popular drink, the dark-eyed native girls in their many-layered skirts and curious derby hats lost their comical appearance, becoming almost enticing. Concerned about disease, however, he saved his trade for the high-class houses with their *prostitutas* of European descent.

Many of his co-workers at the mine were expatriates like himself, some from America, but most from various European countries. Despite the hodge-podge of languages, they banded together, each having his own reason for landing at this remote place on the roof of the world, each possessed of a spirit of adventure that made him anything but a typical laborer.

With his ever-ready smile and quick humor, Butch instantly became a favorite with the men, and he found himself once again enjoying the rough camaraderie of the bunkhouse. The smell of sweat and freshly oiled leather, the sound of wind whipping around corners, the feel of gritty blankets, and the taste of strong coffee — there were times when he could close his eyes and imagine himself back in his beloved Wyoming.

But Wyoming was yet a dream. Time was all he needed to make the dream a reality. Time and a plan. Plodding over rocky trails on sure-footed mules, he began to formulate his way back home.

One day, a few months after starting at Concordia, Butch arrived back at the mine carrying a large payroll, over $100,000. He made for the manager's office. Rapping once on the door and identifying himself, he was immediately admitted. Seated at his desk was Rolla Glass, and there, square in the middle of the room, stood Harry Longabaugh. The outlaws exchanged shocked glances.

"You two know each other?" Glass wondered.

Butch thought quickly. "We've crossed paths a time or two, but it's been a while. Reckon you'll have to reintroduce us."

"Gladly. This is Enrique Brown. He's been working for a contractor who supplies our mules, and he just drove up a herd today. Says he'd like to hire on here. Mister

Brown, this is Santiago Maxwell, one of our payroll guards and an occasional livestock dealer."

Brown and Maxwell shook hands, their eyes sparkling with secret pleasure.

"Speaking of payrolls," continued Glass, "did you have any problems?"

"No, sir." Butch dropped the bag of money on Glass's desk. "Every *centavo*'s accounted for."

"I've no doubt of that. You've never once come up short." Glass turned to Harry. "So, Mister Brown, why do you wish to leave Mister Letson's employ? He speaks highly of your abilities."

Harry coughed and dabbed at his nose with a handkerchief. His breath sounded raspy. "Just need a change," he croaked. "I'm good at working with the stock, or guarding payrolls like Maxwell here."

"M-mm." Glass tapped a letter opener on his desk. "Not much need for either at the moment, I'm afraid. Besides, it sounds like you'd be better off working at sea level. Some men never get over the *puna,* you know."

"The *puna?*"

"Mountain sickness. From the altitude. Seems like you'd be rather susceptible to it."

Harry's face darkened. "I'm just getting

306

over a cold, that's all. Hell, I've ridden through mountains all my life. Ain't never had no sickness."

"Yes, well, riding through the mountains isn't exactly the same as living and working at sixteen thousand feet," countered Glass.

"Mister Glass, if you don't mind my saying so, I think we could use another muleskinner," offered Butch. "I know Roy Letson, and, if he says Brown's a good worker, you can bet he is. Besides, you know how it is around here . . . people always coming and going. You may think you don't have need of an extra man today, but tomorrow you might."

"M-mm, perhaps you're right." Glass had opened the payroll bag and was perusing the remittance paperwork, no longer interested in the matter at hand. "Very well, Brown, we'll give you a try. Maxwell, why don't you figure out what to do with him."

Longabaugh took a step forward, intending to give Glass a piece of his mind. His friend grabbed his arm and quickly shepherded him out the door.

"Bastard," Harry muttered when they were safely outside. "Acted like I'm some kind of ninety-pound weakling. I'd've hit him, 'cept he was wearing glasses."

"Forget it," Butch said. "He's actually a decent fella, once you get to know him. Fact is you do look sorta fagged out."

As if to confirm Butch's assessment, Harry broke into a coughing fit, his handkerchief covering his mouth and nose. Bending over, he struggled to regain his breath. As he straightened up, he took away the handkerchief. Bright bloodstains marked the cloth. For a second, Butch feared his friend had coughed up blood, a sure sign of the consumption, but then Harry tilted his head back and wiped at his nose. A bloody nose, that's all it was, quite common at this altitude.

"Come on, let's get you some *maté*," said Butch, turning toward the bunkhouse.

"Shot of whisky sounds better."

At this time of day they had the bunkhouse to themselves. Butch brewed a strong cup of the native tea and sat on the bunk opposite his friend, watching him closely. He did, indeed, look poorly, and not just because of a cold. There were lines at his eyes that had not been there before, and his cheeks were stubbled with a week's growth of graying whiskers. Something had happened to him in the last few months. And, of course, there was the overriding question — where was Etta?

Butch led up to it gently. "Guess José told you where to find me."

Harry shook his head. "Didn't go back to Antofagasta. Never saw José."

"You mean it was just coincidence, you showing up here?"

"That's right." Harry gave him a guilty look. "Oh, I was gonna look you up pretty soon. Just hadn't got around to it yet."

Nodding slowly, Butch took Harry's cup and poured a refill. "Nothing's changed far as I'm concerned. We're still partners . . . we're still in this together." He handed him the cup.

With a shaking hand, Harry started to bring it to his lips, then set it on the floor between his feet, and dropped his head in his hands. "Everything's changed," he said, his voice breaking.

If he didn't ask, Butch thought, maybe he'd never have to know. Was it true that what you didn't know couldn't hurt you? He sat down on the creaky bunk. "Tell me about it."

"I left her," Harry said.

Butch rested his elbows on his knees, clasping his hands tightly. For months now, he had told himself he would likely never see his friends again, but deep in his heart he had not truly believed it. Now the truth

309

hit home — Etta was gone from his life.

"She was feeling poorly," Harry went on, still holding his lowered head. "We stopped in Denver so she could see a doctor. We thought it might be appendicitis, that is, I did. She probably knew better all along. Turns out she was pregnant."

Butch clasped his hands tighter together. Etta was going to have a baby and Harry had left her?

"We got into it, had a few words. It was my fault . . . I shouldn't've got angry with her, but she told me that she'd . . . well, she hadn't always told me the truth about things, you see. I got mad . . . left her there in the hospital, but I wasn't gonna leave for good. Figured I'd blow off some steam and go get her in the morning. Well, I had me a drink or two and headed back to my room, but, I dunno, there was a ruckus of some sort, and the landlord started threatening to call the police." Even in his confessional mood, Harry didn't think it necessary to mention the poor woman he had abused or the shots he had fired in the ceiling. "I had to get out of there fast. A couple days later, I was able to send a message to the hospital, but she'd already checked out . . . hadn't said where she was going. We was on our way to San Francisco, so I figured maybe

310

she'd show up at my brother's, but she didn't. Wired my sister Samanna . . . no luck. I even wrote Miz Davis, thinking Etta might go see Maude Lay for help, but no one's seen her. She's disappeared, Butch." Harry raised his head, his haggard face so full of remorse Butch didn't have the heart to chastise him.

"How long ago was all this?" he asked.

"Six months or so."

"What've you been doing since?"

"When I couldn't find her, I thought about going back to San Antonio or Fort Worth or somewhere else she knew people, in case she showed up. But then I figured if she wanted to find me, she could. She could've checked with my brother or Samanna, and they'd've told her I was looking for her. Well, hell, I figured that meant she was through with me, and I got angry all over again. I come back down here and knocked around, even went back to Cholila to settle up on the stock we left with Gibbon. I meant to track you down, Butch, but I wasn't in no hurry. Reckon I wanted to put off telling you all this."

Butch rose to stoke the fire. At sixteen thousand feet, the bunkhouse was never what you could call warm. "Hardly seems like leaving a pregnant woman's the thing to do," he muttered. "Still, reckon it ain't all your fault. Like you said, she could've found you if she'd wanted. Etta's pretty damn' capable. She can take care of herself. I say we stick to the original plan . . . tough it out here for a while, and then head home. She ain't really disappeared. She'll turn up somewhere . . . her and the baby. We'll find her."

"Reckon we'll find her, all right, but that don't mean she'll want us around no more," Harry lamented. He reached into his coat pocket and absentmindedly pulled out Etta's gold Tiffany watch, the one Butch had bought for her in New York.

"What are you doing with that?" Butch asked sharply.

Harry shrugged. "Grabbed it off the night table when I left. Ain't sure why."

The sight of his knavish partner casually handling one of Etta's prized possessions made him sick to his stomach. "That was a present from me to her," he said tightly. "You shouldn't've taken it."

"You're right. I wasn't thinking."

"Hand it over," Butch demanded.

Harry looked up in surprise. "What for?"

" 'Cause I intend to give it back to her someday."

They stared at each other, Cassidy barely

containing his anger while Longabaugh just seemed puzzled.

"Hell, it's the only thing of hers I've got," Harry sniffed. "It wouldn't kill you to let me keep it. I'd like something to remember her by."

Butch exploded. Grabbing Harry by the lapels, he pinned him against the wall, his ice blue eyes dark with fury. "You ain't got the right to keep it, you piece of shit! You never appreciated her, never treated her like the lady she is! She'd've done anything for you, and what did you do? Walked out on her just when she needed you most. You spineless, cheating bastard!" With an act of will, he released his partner, turned his back, and walked away.

Instantly Harry was on him, spinning him around as he brought up his fists. "You're carrying a torch for her, ain't ya? Well, let's settle it right here, right now!"

"I ain't gonna fight you." Butch waved him off, his anger gone as quickly as it had come. "I'm disappointed in you, Harry, but you and me've been through too much to call it quits now. Besides, I ain't carrying no torch . . . I done give up on hopeless causes."

Lowering his fists, Harry smoothed his lapels, not sure what had come over his partner but secretly glad they had not come to blows. It was bad enough to lose Etta, but life would be bleak, indeed, without Butch's friendship. He reached in his pocket and tossed him Etta's watch. "Here. Reckon this rightly belongs to you now. I'll go get my things."

Alone in the bunkhouse, Butch turned the beautiful timepiece over and over in his rough hand. The three of them together would never have lasted, he saw now, and Etta could not force herself to choose between them. No doubt she had chosen, instead, to be on her own. He could respect that. What had happened was not Harry's fault, or his fault, or anybody's fault. It was just the way the game had played out.

He pocketed the watch and went to help his partner.

CHAPTER TWENTY-FOUR

Mindful of the harsh conditions even in the summer season at 16,000 feet, Rolla Glass frequently treated his crew to outings in La Paz that, at 12,500 feet, was perceptibly milder. In December, the manager traditionally hosted a Christmas party at the Grand Hotel Guibert, a white brick establishment located in the heart of the city on the Plaza Murillo. Recently outfitted with electric lights, the hotel offered its guests every modern convenience, unless one considered a lavatory with running water a convenience. But what it lacked in up-to-date plumbing, it made up in the luxurious elegance of its spacious rooms. Most of the men chose less pricey accommodations, but Maxwell and Brown, evidently possessed of a source of funds in addition to their pay from the mine, took rooms at the Guibert.

The party was well under way when a good-looking chap, small but sturdy, wearing a rumpled suit and loosely knotted tie,

poked his head into the dining room. He was immediately greeted by a number of the men, including Rolla Glass.

"Percy, you've timed your return just right!" exclaimed the mine manager, clapping the smaller man on the back. "Wouldn't want to miss this party, now would you?"

"Would you believe me if I said I had no idea you'd be here today?" laughed Percy, accepting a glass of wine from the passing waiter. "Jeanne and I just arrived a few moments ago . . . that's obvious, perhaps, from my appearance . . . and, as I was checking in, I heard the commotion. Stuck my head in the door, and, by George, if it wasn't the gang from Concordia whooping it up!"

"Well, the men deserve to celebrate . . . we've had a good year. Where is Missus Seibert? I'd like to give her my regards."

"She went on up to the room. It's a long journey from California, and she's quite tired. Although I have to say the trains have improved since I left. And the electric trolley from the depot . . . what a surprise!"

"Yes, progress has reached even this backwater nation, if only in the cities. Of course, things haven't changed much out in the country. You'll see we do things pretty much the same at Concordia."

"My trip home was quite instructive in that regard," Seibert confided. "I've picked up some ideas on ways to improve production."

As they spoke, the sharp crack of billiard balls breaking reached their ears. "Care to watch?" asked Glass, steering his companion into the adjoining game room. A crowd had gathered around the ornately carved billiard table to watch Enrique Brown and another worker by the name of Ingersoll test their skills. Over in the corner, his back to the bar, Santiago Maxwell jokingly advised all those near to place their money on Ingersoll.

The game ended when Brown scratched. Scowling, Harry paid off his wager and retreated to the bar where the whisky flowed freely, courtesy of his employer. Butch grinned at him. "Ain't it nice to know you got other fine qualities, seeing as you can't shoot pool worth a damn?"

"Shuddup." Harry huddled over his drink.

"Like a friendly attitude, outgoing personality . . ." — Cassidy winked at the men gathered around — "always a cheerful loser."

"I said shuddup."

Cassidy chuckled. "Tell you what. I'll play

you a game. Then I can be the cheerful loser."

This caused a great deal of raucous laughter as Maxwell's penchant for losing at billiards was well known.

Penetrating the jovial crowd, Rolla Glass approached Butch and Harry, his arm around the new arrival's shoulders. "Boys, I'd like you to meet Percy Seibert, one of the best mining engineers north or south of the equator. He's just back from an extended trip to the States."

"That right? Whereabouts?" said Butch, extending his hand. Harry greeted the newcomer warily.

"I traveled throughout the West, but spent most of my time in California," replied Seibert. "Your names, gentlemen?"

"James Maxwell, Santiago in these parts."

"Enrique Brown," Harry mumbled.

"I'm guessing from your accents you're Americans, probably from the West. Am I right?"

Harry shot a glance at Butch, but the latter continued affably. "Half right. We're American, but I ain't never been west of the Mississippi, and I believe the same goes for my friend here."

"Come now, Maxwell," said Glass with a twinkle in his eye. "The way you and Brown

handle the stock it's clear you both have had plenty of ranching experience. I've seen you throw a loop and drive a herd. Down here you'd be called *gauchos,* and damn' good ones!"

"Reckon we're quick studies." Butch smiled. "Say Enrique, how about that game of billiards?"

Seibert watched them rack up the balls, a skeptical expression on his face. "If those two are from the East, or even the Midwest, then I'm a Chinaman. Only true Westerners speak that slowly. And look how they walk . . . like they've been on a horse every day of their lives."

Glass drew the engineer to a private corner. "You'd lie about your background, too, if you had as much to hide as they do."

Seibert raised his eyebrows.

"Maxwell and Brown aren't their real names," Glass continued in a low voice. "Ever heard of Butch Cassidy or the Sundance Kid?"

"You're kidding." Seibert stared at the two outlaws casually circling the game table. "What makes you so sure it's them?"

"One of the men saw a Pinkerton flyer in Buenos Aires . . . said there was no doubt it's them. Seems they held up a couple of banks in Argentina, the last one about a year ago."

"And you hired them? I certainly hope you don't let them near the money!"

"Actually, they guard the payroll," said Glass, enjoying Seibert's incredulity.

"Are you mad?"

"On the contrary, I think it's rather clever. Who better to anticipate and guard against thieves than another thief? Besides," — Glass sipped his wine, watching Butch shank an easy shot — "this may sound odd, but I trust them. When I hired Cassidy, he looked me in the eye and told me I wouldn't regret it, and I haven't. I'm not so fond of the other one, the Sundance Kid . . . Longabaugh I guess is his real name . . . he seems to walk around with a chip on his shoulder. But as long as Cassidy keeps him in line, I'm not worried."

"Rolla, you've taken leave of your senses. They're merely biding their time until they steal you blind! That kind never changes."

"I don't expect them to change," Glass insisted. "The thing is, I did some checking and discovered those two have never stolen from an employer. It seems they only rob those against whom they carry a grudge. I figure I'm a lot better off with them on my side."

"Well," Percy shrugged, "I hope you don't live to regret it."

★ ★ ★

In the days that followed, Seibert had ample opportunity to draw his own conclusions about the outlaw pair, and it wasn't long before he adopted Rolla Glass's point of view. Cassidy was unfailingly polite, relentlessly cheerful, and one of the hardest workers the engineer had ever encountered. A bit of a practical joker, he sometimes risked annoying whoever was the butt of his jokes, but he inevitably made up with a quick handshake and a good turn of some sort. Longabaugh was less sociable, even distant at times, but he, too, threw himself into his work with uncommon energy.

Shortly after the new year, the company transferred Glass. Percy Seibert took over as manager of the mine. He and his wife moved into the manager's house and soon fell into the habit of inviting the workers, one or two at a time, to Sunday dinner. Their favorite and, therefore, most frequent, guest was Santiago Maxwell.

On a raw Sunday in June, Maxwell and Brown, shielding their faces from the glacial wind, trudged down the rocky trail and presented themselves at the manager's front door. Jeanne Seibert admitted them, expressing delight with the Indian bracelet James, as she called Butch, had brought back from one of his many trips. She led them to the parlor where they sat in their regular seats, a sofa that afforded an unobstructed view all the way down the valley. Now that she had gotten over the shock of hosting renowned outlaws, it always thrilled her a little to see these two renegades sitting so calmly in her living room, dressed in their Sunday best, their hair combed and fingernails scrubbed. Although nothing had been stated directly, at some point it had been tacitly acknowledged that the Seiberts knew their secret. A true lover of adventure, Percy was dying to draw them out, but so far had not found the right opportunity.

"Mind if we listen to your gramophone?" asked Maxwell, crossing his legs like a gentleman.

"Not at all," said Jeanne. "Percy, play that new recording of Caruso . . . it just arrived in the post this week, and I immediately thought of you, James, and how much you love listening to music. Why, you've practically worn out the grooves in our old recordings!"

While Jeanne excused herself to see to dinner, Percy rose to play the record. "Rotten weather out there, though when is it not, eh? I sometimes wonder how it is I wound up posted to this wretched wasteland when I'd much rather be basking in sunny California. I guess a mining engineer must go where the mines are. Still, Jeanne and I are hoping our next assignment will be somewhere with a more temperate climate. How about you boys? Is South America your home now, or . . . ?" He paused in the act of lowering the needle, cognizant of straying onto treacherous ground.

Butch gave him a playful look. "It ain't necessary to watch what you say around us, Perce. Reckon I've known for quite a while you was on to us. Figured if you was gonna do anything about it, you'd've done it by now."

The first strains of *"Che gelida manina"* wafted through the room. "Indeed." Seibert sat across from his outlaw friends. "You realize that that knowledge puts me in a difficult position. Some would argue I have a duty to turn you in."

Longabaugh sat up straight, a startled look in his eyes. "You wouldn't do that, would you? Hell, we ain't never done nothing to you!"

"Of course not," said Seibert, holding up a calming hand. "But the authorities might not see the distinction. It poses a problem for me, surely you understand that."

"Won't be no problem if we hightail it out

323

of here," Harry exclaimed, reaching for his hat. "I, for one, ain't gonna stick around while you wrestle with your conscience. Come on, Bu . . . Santiago. Sounds to me like we got some packing to do."

Cassidy waved his partner back into his seat. "I, for one, don't intend to miss our lovely hostess's Sunday dinner. Relax, Kid, it appears our boss is finished wrestling with his conscience, and he beat it fair and square."

Leaning forward in his chair, the manager fixed his guests with a serious gaze. "Understand where I am on this, boys. I'm not on your side. I don't condone criminal activity. But you two have always been honest and fair in all your dealings with me, and Rolla before me. I won't betray men whom I trust and who've placed their trust in me. That's not to say I'll help you out in a tight spot, or stand by while you commit more crimes. If the police come looking for you, we'll cooperate with them. If I ever get word you're planning to rob someone else, I'll try to warn your intended victim. We clear on that?"

"Clear as day," Butch said with a slight smile.

During dinner, the three men restricted their conversation to more mundane topics, but later, back in the parlor with port and cigars while Jeanne stayed in the kitchen to help her maid clean up, Cassidy asked his employer how he had tumbled onto their secret. Seibert told them how one of the men had seen a flyer in Buenos Aires that mentioned not only their exploits in the United States, but the two bank robberies in Argentina. He expressed surprise when Butch denied responsibility for the Río Gallegos job.

"That goes with the territory," said Butch, puffing on his cigar philosophically. "Once you excel at something, people start giving you credit for stuff you never did."

Percy wound the gramophone and lowered the needle. "But the flyer said it was thought you'd been in South America since Nineteen-Oh-One. What were you doing all that time?"

"Ranching," Harry said with a nostalgic twinge in his voice, evidently forgetting how much he had disliked Cholila. "Had us a good-size spread in the Chubut province of the Argentine, us and . . . Etta."

"Etta? That must be the woman mentioned in the flyer, the one who was with you at Villa Mercedes."

Harry stood at the window, looking out at the barren hillside. "She was my wife."

The admission hung in the room, riding

on the flow of music. Seibert tapped his ash. "And you simply ranched for all those years?"

"We came to South America intending to put our past behind us," said Cassidy, so sincerely his listener could not doubt him. "But the law wouldn't leave us alone, wouldn't let us go straight. When they pinned Río Gallegos on us, even though we was seven hundred and fifty miles away at the time, we realized there wasn't no use in trying to hide out . . . sooner or later they'd come after us. Once you get started, you just gotta keep going, keep moving all the time. 'Course, it takes money to live on the run . . . that's why we held up the bank in Villa Mercedes. Kind of ironic, don't you think? Long as the law keeps chasing us, we gotta keep robbing people."

Seibert shook his head, amazed at the fantastic story. "You fellas seem so decent . . . how did you get started down the outlaw trail?"

Cassidy sighed and stared at the cigar clutched in his callused fingers. "It's a long story, Perce. It starts with a young boy looking for things he can't find at home. Then the boy turns into a man trying to hold onto a way of life that's slipping away."

Longabaugh snorted. "No such highfalutin' nonsense in my case. Hell, when I was a boy, I ran away from home to be a cowboy just 'cause I'd read some novels made the West sound damn' exciting. Come to find out cowboying was boring as hell most of the time. Outlawing was where the thrills was. Can't say I've changed my mind much . . . it's just the older I get, the less thrills I need. I got to be going." He lifted his coat from the hall tree. "Appreciate the fine meal, Percy. Pass on my thanks to the missus, if you would."

Seibert saw his guest out the door and returned to the parlor where Butch sat smoking, eyes half closed. Caruso's emotion-laden tenor filled the room. They listened silently until the end of the record, then sat a moment longer while the needle scratched rhythmically back and forth. Finally Percy got up to turn it off.

"What happened to the woman?" he said quietly, slipping the record into its jacket. "Did she leave him?"

"Ain't clear to me who left who." Butch blew a smoke ring, watched it expand and dissipate. He told Seibert what had happened in Denver, or, at least, Harry's version of the story. "She's a hell of a woman," he admitted. "I reckon I ain't yet reconciled to her being gone for good."

Percy nodded in understanding. "You must have been very close to her, too."

Cassidy dropped his eyes, then shrugged as if none of it meant anything. "Etta was a great housekeeper with the heart of a whore. Who wouldn't miss her?"

They smoked together for a while. Percy offered to play another record, but his guest said he should be going. At the door, he put a hand on the outlaw's arm. "You told me how your story started. But you didn't say how it would end."

Cassidy flipped the stub of his cigar. "Does any man know how his story ends? I'll tell you this much . . . I aim for there to be many more chapters. But don't be surprised if someday you hear that Butch Cassidy has disappeared. And remember, things ain't always what they seem."

CHAPTER TWENTY-FIVE

Francisco Ingersoll was the product of an American father, who had come to South America to work the nitrate mines, and a Chilean mother. Dark-haired and copper-colored, he took after his mother's side of the family, although he was a bit taller than most Chilean men. As a child, Francisco had been a troublemaker, running wild through the streets of Antofagasta with his gang of young *cholos*. His father put him to work in the mines at an early age, but the restrictions of employment did nothing to curb his rebellious nature. More than once, he had run afoul of the law, generally for petty thievery or disorderly conduct, and been thrown in jail for a night or two.

Despite this sketchy history, he had been hired by Rolla Glass at the Concordia mine, because, it turned out, Frank Ingersoll was gifted at working with machinery. Where others would throw up their hands at the finicky new gas-fueled engines made in

Germany that were used to power the mine's extraction mechanisms, Ingersoll would tinker around, tightening a bolt here, tapping his pliers there, until the engines chugged once again to life. His unique skill made him an invaluable employee, a fact that was not lost on the young man. He thought nothing of taking off whenever the mood struck, confident he would be welcomed back under any circumstances.

For close to a year now, however, he had stuck pretty close to Tres Cruces. The reason for his newfound sense of loyalty was the presence of Santiago Maxwell and Enrique Brown. From the beginning, he had recognized kindred spirits in the two older men, an approach to life that could be summarized as: I'll take what I want and damn the consequences. In them, he saw everything he wanted to be — strong, independent, shrewd, secure in their place in the world — men who commanded the respect of other men.

As for Brown and Maxwell, they were amused by Ingersoll and took him under their wing. Seeing something of himself as a young man in the rowdy youth, Maxwell resolved to teach him a thing or two, aimed to soften the edges a bit.

Over many shared mugs of *chicha,* the

three became well acquainted. The two out-laws entrusted Frank with the secret of their past. He was in awe of them, in awe of being drawn into their confidence. Why, he wanted to know, were they wasting their time, working the mines, when they could be living a much more exciting life?

"Hell, kid, you can't rob a bank every day," Maxwell instructed him. "You pull a job, you hide out for a while. That's the natural order of things."

In October, which in this part of the world marked the beginning of summer, Butch and Harry requested a leave of absence from the mine. They desired to make a visit to the eastern part of Bolivia that they had heard was as different from the *altiplano* as the Sahara Desert was from the North Pole. Seibert reluctantly granted their request, knowing they would go even without his approval. Hearing of their plan, Frank Ingersoll begged to come along, and they agreed.

Their destination was the city of Santa Cruz, a lush, tropical paradise reportedly possessed of every type of game and agricultural product. At this time of year, the sandy roads were dry, the temperatures warm, and the breezes constantly blowing from the *serranías* to the west. They took a room, hired a cook, and set out to discover the attributes of this charming, Spanish-style town.

Santa Cruz had been settled by its residents' Iberian ancestors which was evident in the Mediterranean architecture and spacious plazas shaded by wide-branched palm trees. The people, too, were Castilian in appearance, and the three men were immediately enchanted by the town's dark-eyed, laughing *señoritas* who peered out from their quaint, lace-curtained windows.

While taking the sun in the plaza one afternoon, Butch made the acquaintance of the beautiful *Señorita* Rosita Moreno whose father was a leading manufacturer in town. They met again the next day, and the next, and before he quite knew what was happening, he was engaged in a full-blown romance. Luckily, from his point of view, the young lady was as daring as she was beautiful, and was easily persuaded to meet him in his rented rooms. There, he taught *Señorita* Moreno the glories of love, and she, in turn, gave him the gift of renewed youth and vigor.

Longabaugh and Ingersoll teased him mercilessly about his little "Castilian cutie," to which he replied: "What's that greenish tinge on your face? Are you feeling poorly or could that be envy?" Laughing, they threatened to tell Rosita's father how his precious daughter had been deflowered by a blackguard and villain.

"Fine by me," grinned Butch. "If I have to be done in, it might as well be for love, instead of money."

When they were not enjoying the pleasures of the city, they explored the surrounding countryside, which was largely devoted to the production of sugar cane. The abundance of grass for grazing and cheap land prices made the area a good prospect for cattle ranching. The outlaw partners briefly flirted with the idea, but Cholila had soured Harry on ranching and Butch had other plans.

On a lazy afternoon about three weeks into their vacation, the trio lounged at an outdoor café, drinking *chicha* and watching the pretty *cruceñas* in their white dresses and jangling strings of beads sashay by. A whispering breeze fanned the palm trees in the plaza, and hummingbirds played hide and seek among the perfumed blossoms.

Tipping back his chair, Ingersoll concentrated on the townsfolk passing by. Not a one of them took any notice of the *Americanos*. "Would you be able to sit like this, out in the open, taking no steps to disguise yourselves, back in the United States, and have no fear of being recognized?" he asked in softly accented English.

The outlaws considered this for a minute. "Would depend on where it was," Harry concluded. "A big city in the East, like New York, the likelihood of anybody knowing us there is pretty slim. But out West, I'd be damned careful where I showed myself. Them Pinkertons done papered every sheriff's office from Kansas to California. Plus, in America, your average citizen knows how to read a newspaper, so odds are the man in the street knows damn' well who we are. Down here, can't hardly nobody read. Their ignorance helps keep us safe."

"Would you agree with that, Santiago?" Ingersoll asked, leaning forward to refill his mug. Although he had long ago been told his companions' real names, he still called them by their aliases, at their request. You could never be sure who might be listening, Butch had advised.

To prove his point, Cassidy lowered his voice so that he could barely be heard over the hummingbirds' buzzing. "Only partly. He's right that more people back home know about us, either from reading newspapers or just by reputation. But we've been gone for six years now. People are starting to forget . . .

they figure we're gone for good, and they're gonna let down their guard. And believe it or not, Frank, the two of us have changed in six years' time. 'Specially my friend Enrique here. Why, his own mother couldn't pick him out of a line-up what with all those extra pounds he's carrying around!"

Harry slammed down his mug. "I wouldn't talk, I was you. Look at all that hair on your face. Your mama'd take you for a grizzly bear!"

"You're making my point," said Butch. "Seems like it'd be safe to go back home if our own mothers wouldn't recognize us."

"Surely you have not changed that much," interjected Ingersoll. "Six years is enough to age a man, add a few lines here and there, but not enough to alter him entirely."

"You're right, kid." Butch settled back in his chair, waiting for the serving girl to set another pitcher on the table and leave. "Thing is, going undetected ain't all about changing your looks. What's just as important is acting like you got nothing to hide. Hell, if you go ducking around corners and looking over your shoulder all the time, you're gonna raise suspicions. But if you ain't afraid to hold your head up and walk right down the middle of the street, nobody'll look twice at you."

Longabaugh snorted.

"You disagree? Let's see who's right."

"What are you talking about, you crazy fool?"

"I say we pay a visit to the sheriff, act like we're there on regular business. I'm betting he won't recognize either one of us, even though he's probably heard of the *bandidos yanquis,* maybe even got descriptions of us. What do you say?" He grinned mischievously.

"You're out of your mind," Harry hissed. "What if he does recognize us, then what?"

"Then we're screwed."

Longabaugh stared at him across the table, then slowly broke into a smile. He began to chuckle, and Ingersoll joined in, thoroughly enjoying being a witness to this outlaw one-upmanship. Scraping back their chairs, the three tossed down the remains of their *chicha* and headed for the sheriff's office.

Crossing the plaza, they stepped onto the raised cobblestone walkway and paused in front of the two-story building, its wood-beamed galleries supported by broad columns. High archways topped the doors and windows. Official offices in Bolivia tended to look grander than their counterparts in America, disguising the inefficiency that lurked within.

"Remember now," cautioned Butch, "act like Honest Abe." They entered the office, surprising the local *comisario* and his deputy in the middle of their midday meal.

"Afternoon, gentlemen." Butch tipped his hat while Ingersoll translated his words into Spanish. "My friends and me just came to town and are looking for a place to stay. Thought you might be able to recommend a nice, quiet place . . . some place that don't put up with troublemakers."

"*Sí, señor,*" said the *comisario,* wiping his mouth with a large napkin and coming around the front of his desk. His deputy laid down his half eaten *empanada* and waited respectfully. "There are many first-rate accommodations in town. Are you here only for a few days, or will you be staying longer?"

"Couple of weeks, at least. We're looking for some place clean and quiet, like I said, and, if the cooking was top drawer, that wouldn't hurt none."

While Ingersoll translated, Butch glanced over at Harry who had wandered over to look at several flyers and notices posted on the wall. He stopped before a flyer that read, in Spanish: *Wanted: Yankee Bandits Butch Cassidy and Harry Longabaugh aka The Sundance Kid.* It went on to give details of the robberies in Río Gallegos and Villa Mercedes, and, although there were no pictures, it included descriptions of the notorious criminals. A reward of ten thousand *bolivianos* was offered for their capture.

Harry turned and smiled at the lawmen. "Makes me downright ashamed of my own countrymen that they'd take advantage of the poor folks down here. Hardly seems fair. Why don't they stick to robbing all those rich bankers in America?"

"*Sí, sí.*" The *comisario* nodded rueful agreement. "We have not seen them in this country, but they are said to be very canny. They could be hiding anywhere."

Tired of waiting, the deputy resumed eating his meat pie, wiping his mouth with the back of his hand after each bite.

"In our jobs with the mine, we travel around a good bit. We'll keep an eye out for those rascals," offered Butch.

"Thank you, *señor.* But I would not suggest taking any action against them yourselves . . . they are reputed to be very dangerous."

"Good advice. We'll leave it to experts like you to corral them two."

Puffing his chest at the compliment, the sheriff gave them the name of a reputable boarding house and ushered them out the door, entreating them to enjoy their stay in Santa Cruz. As they returned to the plaza, Ingersoll shook his head in wonderment.

"You were right, Santiago. The *comisario* never suspected a thing, not even when Enrique pointed out the Wanted poster."

"That don't prove much," Harry insisted, propping his boot on a bench and lighting a smoke. "So what if some greaser sheriff is so stupid he can't put two and two together? These beaners is slower than most, no offense, Frank, but ain't all of them that dense."

"Hey, Frank," said Butch, reaching for his wallet, "do me a favor and go buy me some smokes."

Ingersoll looked surprised, unaccustomed to being treated like an errand boy.

"Here, have one of mine." Harry held out his cigarette case.

"Don't care for that brand. You don't mind, do you, kid?"

"No," said Ingersoll, although his expression told a different tale. He took Cassidy's money and sauntered off, determined to take his own sweet time.

Butch sat on the bench and crossed his ankle on his knee. Harry smoked silently, waiting for his friend to speak his mind.

"It's time to go home," Butch said finally,

gazing across the plaza at some children playing with their *niñera.*

Harry finished his smoke and tossed it aside. "And where is that, exactly?"

"Somewhere in the U.S.A. There's a lot of details I gotta work out before I know where. Some time in the next few months I'm gonna make a scouting trip, get all the i's dotted and t's crossed before I make the final move. You see I figure the only way I can go back and not live in fear of getting caught is to change my identity. I'm gonna become a new man."

For a minute, Harry thought this was just another of Butch's jokes, but his friend had never looked so serious. Sighing, he sat down next to him. "How you gonna do that?"

"I got a plan. What about you? You've always been hot to go back home."

"The only reason I got for going back is to find Etta."

"That's a pretty good reason."

Harry leaned forward, tenting his fingers between his knees. "Maybe you could find her," he said, looking down. "Let me know if she still . . . wants to see me."

A cloud blotted out the sun, making the breeze seem suddenly chilly. Cassidy stared at his partner's hunched back, recalling the first time they had met, more than ten years ago. They had been in their prime then, living the best years of their lives, although they had not realized it. Maybe, come to think of it, the best years had been on the ranch in Cholila, just the three of them, Etta so happy playing homemaker. But satisfying as that had seemed, life in Cholila had been too solitary for Butch's taste. True, he loved wide-open spaces, loved getting lost in the wilderness, but he wanted to be able to come home to a place where people knew him. Yes, admit it, he wanted to come home to a wife and family. Butch Cassidy would never be able to do that. Another man could.

"Listen, *amigo*" — he cleared his throat to get rid of the frog in it — "when I leave here, I'm cutting all ties. I ain't gonna look up the people I knew from before, not even my family. I'm starting over. Can't afford to leave a trail in places where folks might know me."

"What about Etta?" Harry addressed the ground. "You said you was gonna take her watch back to her."

"That I did, and it was a damned fool thing to say. I've been meaning to give it back to you." He took it out of his pocket and handed it over. "You were right . . . this belongs to you more than me. Etta was your woman, she never said no different. Maybe someday you'll find her."

The two men sat for a while, side-by-side. Harry did not know what to say, had not wanted to think beyond his present circumstances. Part of him wanted to return home, settle down with Etta. But what if he never found her, or, worse yet, what if he found her only to be rejected?

Shaking off the unthinkable, he veered toward a more practical subject. "Reckon you'll need a stake to get started. You got enough?"

"Figure it'll take at least a year to get on my feet, find myself a new career. Been running through my Villa Mercedes money pretty quick," Butch admitted. "Couldn't hurt to pull one more job, our swan song, so to speak. No banks, though . . . something a mite less conspicuous. A payroll, maybe. Not Concordia, of course, I'd never steal from Percy, not to mention we're the first ones he'd suspect. We could use Frank, he's been dying to get into the outlaw business. You reckon he'd keep his cool in a tight spot?"

Just thinking about pulling another job got his blood pumping. Yet if it all worked out as he planned, he would go back home and never again commit a robbery, never feel that rush of adrenaline, that deep satisfaction that came from sticking it to the establishment right where it hurt. Then again, if he managed to reinvent himself as a model citizen, wouldn't he take some pleasure in knowing that he had won? That he had beaten the system? There was, after all, something to be said for surviving long enough to get the last laugh.

Ingersoll walked up empty-handed. "I could not find your brand, Santiago."

Smiling, Butch wrapped an arm around the young man's shoulders. "That's all right, kid. Listen, Enrique and me was thinking. . . ."

Later that day, in bed with Rosita, he asked the beautiful girl if she would run away with him. She threw back her head and laughed, her small, white teeth glowing in the semi-darkened room. "My father would kill me," she said, slowing her Spanish down so Butch would understand. "And you, too. I do not think we love each other enough to risk getting ourselves killed."

He stroked her rich, black hair, wondering why it was always the raven-haired women who attracted him. "That's why we'd run away, *mi corazón*. He'd never find

343

us. We could get married, raise a passel of kids. We could live anywhere you wanted to, anywhere in the world."

Rosita sobered. She searched his eyes for the twinkle that would tell her he was only joking. He looked serious enough, but he was gazing beyond her, seeing a future that could live only in his imagination.

"But you see, Santiago, I do not wish to live anywhere but Santa Cruz. It is my home." She brushed his shoulder with her lips.

His eyes drew back to her, and he smiled. "You're right. You should never leave your home and family. Once you're gone, there's no going back."

She looked confused, and he thought maybe he had not used the right words in Spanish. But then she rested her head in the crook of his arm and held him even tighter underneath the light blanket. "You cannot go home, *mi amor?* You will never see your family again?"

"I ain't got a home, not like what you mean, anyways. And as for family, well, I probably done burned my bridges there. That's why I want you to marry me. Then you'd be my family." Oddly enough, he meant every word of his proposal even though he knew she would say no. He was not prepared for the tears that fell warmly against his chest.

"Don't cry Rosita." He lifted her face and kissed her wet cheeks. "I know you can't marry me. It's just that I . . . I wanted to honor you by asking."

Raising up on her elbow, she kissed him fiercely. "You are a good man, Santiago Maxwell."

CHAPTER TWENTY-SIX

The threesome returned to Concordia, but, not long after, Butch left on his long-planned scouting trip to the United States. After a good deal of thought, he sought out a place where once he had felt safe and welcome.

Now he stood in the road, regarding the trim little farmhouse with a mixture of nostalgia and misgiving. A blustery March wind blew across the fields that had been recently turned in preparation for planting. What a relief not having always to be reversing the seasons in his brain — here, in Michigan, spring meant plowing and planting, as it should.

The wooden porch swing swayed in the breeze, squeaking like chalk on a blackboard. He stilled it with a touch, remembering the night some eleven years ago when the lady of this house had sat there, a harvest moon making her bold, and told him to confront his fate. He could still see her kind face, still hear the fervency in her words.

You're a strong person, George. You can shape your own fate, with God's help. Buoyed by her confidence, he had returned to Wyoming to claim Mary Boyd, but God must have decided he was not worthy of assistance, because Mary had refused to leave her no-account husband for him. Nevertheless, the simple farm wife's words of encouragement had stayed with him, had brought him back to her door.

He knocked hesitantly. Marie Goodloe answered almost immediately, her plain cotton dress covered by a work apron, a dust rag in one hand. She stared at him as at a stranger until he removed his hat, and then a look of recognition crossed her face.

"Good heavens!" she exclaimed, a hand at her throat. "Is it George? George Maxwell?"

"In the flesh." Butch smiled, responding to the alias he had more or less picked out of thin air when he had first alighted on her doorstep on the run from the law.

She held open the door. "Come in, come in! My, I never dreamed I'd see you again. And you're looking so well! You've prospered, George, just as I predicted."

Indeed he had, thought Butch . . . one way or another. He stepped into the neat sitting room. Nothing had changed except for the addition of some new family photographs. The Goodloe boy, he remembered, had been about eighteen when he had hired on here all those years ago. A typical eighteen-year-old, full of piss and vinegar and ready to bust loose. Now, from the photos gracing the top of the upright piano, it appeared young Jack Goodloe had married and started a family.

"Jack's doing well," said Marie, following Butch's gaze. "A circumstance for which I hold you largely responsible."

"That's kind of you, ma'am, but I can't take no credit. Jack had it in him to be a successful man, he just couldn't see it at the time."

"Not until you pointed it out to him. Jack told me how you advised him to go to the university and make something of himself, and that's just what he did. He's a lawyer now, with a fine practice in Pontiac," she finished proudly.

Butch's ears pricked up at this information. "I'm mighty pleased to hear that, ma'am."

"Look at me, where are my manners? Please have a seat while I rustle up some refreshments."

Butch followed her into the kitchen. "Mind if we sit in here, instead? Seems less formal-like. Maybe you're forgetting I used to be your hired man."

"A hired man, yes, but still a gentleman." When Marie smiled, it lit up her entire face. The years had etched a few more lines, dulled her blonde hair a tad, but her crystal blue eyes still sparkled with intelligence.

She pulled out a chair for him, and he sat, resting his arms on the table. "The farm looks good," he commented. "But then, Mister Goodloe always did run a tight ship."

Marie paused, dishing up a piece of pie. "Everett died two years ago."

"I'm sorry to hear that," murmured Butch.

"Thank you. It was quite sudden. He came down with a fever, and a week later it was all over. Doctor never did figure out what happened." She put pie and coffee in front of him and sat with a cup of coffee for herself. "Jack wanted me to go live with him and Ardis, his wife, in Pontiac, but I couldn't leave this place. It's like my favorite old wrapper that keeps me warm in winter, so familiar and comfortable. Anyway, I lease the land to a neighbor and stay busy enough with the house and my garden. But enough about me! Tell me about yourself, George."

He finished his pie and pushed away the plate, praying he could trust this woman.

349

Eleven years ago she had taken him into her home, even though he had strongly hinted at his shady past. Would she be as understanding today?

"Miz Goodloe. . . ."

"Marie, if you please. You're not the hired man any longer."

"Yes, ma'am." He cleared his throat. "When I came here before, I reckon you and Mister Goodloe had an inkling that I was in trouble with the law, but you were kind enough not to ask questions. I ain't never forgot how you trusted me, and, when I left here, I aimed to change my ways. But . . . well, things didn't quite work out that way."

Marie rose to refill their cups. She looked troubled, but dropped back in her chair to listen.

"I'm ashamed to say I continued to flout the law. I make no excuses, ma'am. What I did was wrong, but you should know I never hurt a hair on one person's head." *Well, not too badly, anyway.* "I may be a rascal, but I ain't a violent man."

"I know that, George. If I thought otherwise, you wouldn't be sitting in my kitchen."

Her faith in him was astonishing. How could he ever live up to it?

"Anyway, it got bad enough I had to leave the country. Won't go into the details 'cause it ain't necessary and you're better off not knowing. Let's just say things weren't no better where I was. So I've decided to come back. But it ain't that cut and dried. There's people out there still looking for me."

Marie laced her fingers around her coffee cup, her brow furrowed. "You don't paint a pretty picture. If you're still a wanted man, George, I'm not sure I can help you with a clear conscience."

"This ain't no small thing I'm asking," he agreed. "I would understand completely if you told me to leave."

She sighed and went to stand at the window over the sink, gazing out at the barn, in need of fresh paint, and the chicken coop, its door hanging on a broken hinge. Somewhere upstairs a board creaked, not an unusual sound, but one that made her jump because even now, two years after his death, it brought back memories of Everett, reminded her of how alone she was.

"You know, George," she said timidly, tucking a stray hair back in her bun, "this place could use a man about. I try to keep up, but it's really too much for me. Perhaps you'd consider staying."

He came up behind and placed his hands lightly on her shoulders. She closed her eyes at the intimacy of his touch. "That's more than I have a right to ask, Marie. I'm mighty grateful to you, but I didn't come here today looking for a job."

She considered telling him it was not a job she'd been offering, but he probably knew that. "Then why did you come?" she asked, turning to face him. "I'm nothing but a farm widow. How can I possibly help you?"

He took a step back, met her searching look with his own earnest one. "One day, back when I was working for you and Mister Goodloe, I came in the house for dinner and heard the two of you talking in the kitchen. Not wanting to interrupt, I took a seat in the parlor, waiting for you to finish your conversation. But the door to the kitchen was open, and I could hear what you said. A better man would've gone outside so as not to eavesdrop, but . . . I ain't a better man." He looked at her apologetically.

"Go on," she said calmly.

"You were saying how you'd just gotten a letter from some relative of yours. Mister Goodloe was having a hard time placing who you meant so you said . . . 'You know, the one who had the baby boy out of wedlock that later died'."

"Cousin Celia," Marie confirmed.

"I recollect that was the name you used. The conversation didn't mean nothing to me at the time, but, for some reason, I tucked it away. One of the reasons I'm back here today is to ask you about it."

Marie did not understand. "What could my cousin's situation possibly have to do with you?"

Butch hesitated, then plunged ahead. "I need a new identity, a new name, new history, new papers to back it all up. If it's OK with you, Marie, I'd like to become your cousin Celia's son."

Marie was at a loss for words. She sank into a chair, thinking how this day had begun so normally, and now here she was, talking to a handsome outlaw in her kitchen about fabricating an identity from the ruins of her family history.

"It might not work," Butch hurried on, "if a death certificate was recorded. But I kind of gathered from the way you talked that everything was kept quiet to, you know, save the family from embarrassment."

"That's right. Celia was just a child herself when she gave birth. The baby only lived a couple of weeks. Her parents kept her confined during her pregnancy, and only a few close family members ever knew about it. I imagine most of them considered it a blessing when the baby died." Marie shook her head sadly. "As to the death certificate, I couldn't say. You'd have to get a lawyer to look into that. Perhaps Jack could help you."

That was exactly what Butch was hoping she would suggest. "Nothing would please me more than to see that boy of yours again."

He stuck around for a couple of days — fixed the chicken coop and did some other chores. When she offered to pay him, he refused, feeling mildly guilty about taking advantage of a widow woman's trust in him. But then, for some reason, she credited him with the success of her son, so maybe they were even.

Armed with a letter from Marie, asking her son to do all he could to assist George Maxwell, Butch went to Pontiac to see Jack Goodloe. The young man remembered him fondly and went about creating the necessary documents. It turned out that not only had a death certificate never been recorded, but the county had not issued birth certificates back when Celia's baby was born, so the lawyer drafted an affidavit that at least looked official, even though it carried no legal weight.

When Butch Cassidy, *née* Robert Leroy Parker, alias George Maxwell, alias Santiago Maxwell, alias Jim Lowe, alias who knew what else, left Goodloe's office, he was a new man: William Thadeus Phillips, born June 22, 1865, in Sandusky, Michigan, to Celia Mudge and Laddie J. Phillips.

Reborn at forty-one years of age.

CHAPTER TWENTY-SEVEN

The next step in Cassidy's plan called for scouting out a place to settle when he returned for the last time from South America. He had in mind somewhere in Arizona as he was determined to live in the West, and Arizona was one of the few Western states that did not have a warrant out for his arrest. When Jack Goodloe asked him about his plans, he confided all this and said he hoped to get a job in a machine shop as his years in the mines had made him adept at this sort of work. He did not bother to mention that he had learned this trade from Frank Ingersoll, a kid half his age. Goodloe mentioned that he had a friend who owned a machine shop in southern Michigan who would be certain to hire him on Jack's recommendation. Although Butch did not intend to make Michigan his permanent home, it seemed like a good idea to take the job. After all, the machinery he had worked on at Concordia was quite different from the small engines and machines he would be called upon to fix in a village shop. It would be good training.

So, with a letter of introduction from Jack Goodloe in hand, he went to tiny Adrian, Michigan, and began working in Herman Jansen's machine shop. It was a quiet life — up early for breakfast at his boarding house, work all day at the shop, supper back at his room, maybe a few hands of gin rummy with the other boarders, early to bed. There was a saloon in town, but it did not see much action except on the weekends when the farmers came to town. Even then, Butch steered clear, playing it cautious. The Jansens, a reserved, Scandinavian couple, had him to dinner once, and he was friendly with his co-workers at the shop, but, by and large, he kept to himself, trying to become comfortable with his new identity.

It seemed odd, but, having slipped into the persona of William T. Phillips, he started to imagine an entire history for himself. Ignoring the facts of his illegitimate birth to a very young girl, he decided that, had her baby lived, Celia would have brought up her son in a loving home, would have seen that he received decent schooling, would have taken him to church, and introduced him to proper young girls. William T. Phillips would have become a respected member of the community, would have married a fine woman, and had several beautiful and well-behaved children. Now that he had resurrected Bill Phillips, wasn't it his responsibility to make this imaginary scenario a reality?

He had been in Adrian for about a month, when one afternoon, on the way home from work, he passed by the Baptist church and heard piano music coming from within. Although the instrument sounded a little tinny, the musician played well, with great feeling. Butch slowed his gait and then stopped completely, harkening back to those Sunday afternoons in the Seibert parlor, listening to recordings on the gramophone. Hardly knowing what he was doing, for he had not set foot in a church for nigh on to thirty years, he ambled up the path and slipped inside. With his back to the wall, he stood in the shadows, letting his eyes adjust to the dim light.

The music was coming from the front of the church; he could make out the piano behind the chancel rail, but whoever was playing was hidden behind the tall upright. On and on the music continued, a lush, romantic piece that sounded like no church music he had ever heard, although his experience was admittedly limited. Still, this person was obviously playing for his or her own pleasure, not practicing hymns for Sunday service.

In the dark coolness of the empty church, he leaned his head against the wall and closed his eyes, letting the music draw him in like a siren's song. Hardly realizing it had ended, he opened his eyes and saw a woman standing at the piano, shuffling sheet music. Leaving his hat on the back pew, he walked slowly up the center aisle.

The woman looked up in alarm. "Oh, my! Who's there? You startled me."

"Beg pardon, miss. I was just walking by and heard you playing. Sounded so pretty I came inside to listen. Hope you don't mind."

By this time he had gotten close enough to get a good look at her. She was of average height but exceedingly thin. Underneath her white shirtwaist her bosom swelled nicely, but he could have encircled her waist with his hands, and her dark skirt fell straight to her ankles unimpeded by curves of any description. Her face featured strong, high cheek bones, almost like an Indian's. Wire-framed glasses perched on a rather large nose, and deep lines on either side of her mouth suggested she was well past the bloom of youth. It was an arresting face, however, and Butch found he could not take his eyes off it.

Unnerved by his stare, the woman snatched off her spectacles and let them fall to her chest, held by a chain around her neck. She gave him a tight smile. "I suppose not. So long as you don't tell the preacher I was playing Rachmaninoff instead of 'A Mighty Fortress'."

Butch turned the full force of his smile on her. The woman's breath caught in her throat, so stunned was she by the warmth in his pale blue eyes and the sense of joy in his broad face. As far as she knew, she had never before in thirty-two years of living uttered words that had caused such a reaction.

"Tell you what," he said, leaning an elbow on the top of the piano. "I'll promise not to tell the preacher, if you'll promise to let me buy you a soda."

Her mouth fell open. "Oh, my! Well . . . I . . . I don't even know who you are."

"William T. Phillips," he said with a slight bow. "Bill to my friends. And you are . . ."

"Gertrude Livesay," she responded automatically.

"Well, Miss Livesay, how about that soda?"

"No, no, I couldn't possibly." She busied herself with gathering her music together.

"My mother is expecting me at home. I promised to help her prepare for tonight's meeting of the garden club." Suddenly she stopped, aware of how pathetic she sounded. For the first time in her life a handsome and charming man had asked her out and here she was turning him down. She took a deep breath and cut her eyes to Butch. His lopsided grin turned the tables. "Oh, all right then. But not for long."

At the soda shop, where they both ordered coffee, he explained that he had come to Adrian to work for Mr. Jansen and left it at that. Gertrude described herself as a farm girl who had moved to town with her mother upon her father's death. She now worked in a millinery store. The conversation turned to music, a topic on which Gertrude spoke passionately. Thanks to Percy Seibert's gramophone, Butch could fake some knowledge. Mostly, though, he kept her talking, making her feel unaccustomedly glib.

Finally there was an awkward pause. Gertrude glanced at the clock on the wall and gasped: "Oh, dear! Mother will be beside herself! It's almost time for the garden club meeting, and here I sit passing the time of day. Thank you for the coffee, Mister Phillips." She looked at him shyly. "I've enjoyed talking with you."

"The pleasure's been mine, Miss Livesay." He escorted her out the door and offered to walk her home, but she declined, wanting to avoid the garden club's gossip.

"Good night, then," he said, holding out his hand. Butch thought hard. *How did one go about courting a proper lady? What would William T. Phillips do?*

"Miss Livesay," he ventured, "could I call on you tomorrow?"

"Well, now, Mister Phillips." Flustered, she pulled her hand from his grasp and patted her hair. "Tomorrow's Sunday. I'll be in church most of the day."

"Oh."

They stood stiffly, neither knowing how to say good night without making it a final good bye. Clutching her music to her chest, she stammered: "Perhaps . . . that is . . . if you're not attending a different service to-morrow . . . you're welcome to come to ours. It starts around nine, and there will be a pot-luck dinner afterwards."

Butch winced. A man had certain limits. "I ain't much of a church-goer, sorry to say. My ma was a true believer" — *what did the Baptists think of Mormons?* he wondered — "but hard as she tried, she couldn't pound it into me. How 'bout we meet at the church on Monday, go for a walk or something?"

Gertrude brightened. "That would be lovely."

"All right, then. I'll meet you there after work." Once again, he turned on his hundred-watt smile. Her heart pounding, Gertrude said good night and fairly skipped down the block.

Back in his room, Butch sat on the edge of his bed and held counsel with himself. Somewhere in the back of his mind, he realized that taking a wife had always been part of his plan. Not only would it enhance his cover, but he was forty-one, no forty-two, years old now and tired of living alone. He didn't suppose he needed to be in any particular rush to wed, but, on the other hand, if the right woman came along, why wait? Was Gertrude Livesay the right woman? Too early to tell, but she had many intriguing qualities. She was old enough, and plain enough, that he might be her last chance. Odds are he could lay on the charm so that by the time he got around to telling her about his outlaw past — for he would not marry anyone under false pretenses — she would be so smitten, and so afraid of losing her ticket out of spinsterhood, she would not refuse him. And, yes, she might be plain, but, somehow, he liked her looks. She looked . . . interesting. There was something solid about her despite her thin frame. This was a woman who would not cut and run at the first sign of trouble. Moreover, he liked the fact there was no father to deal with — that always made things easier. Only an overbearing mother from whom she was probably dying to escape.

Butch undressed and lay back on his bed, hands behind his head, the wheels spinning. Should he employ a full frontal attack, or lure her with the off and on game? Should he attempt to seduce her, or play the perfect gentleman? Should he get the mother on his side, or play off the mother's disapproval? So many nuances to consider, so many details that needed to be gotten just right. By God, getting a woman to marry you was more of a challenge than robbing a bank!

But not too much of a challenge for Butch Cassidy. On May 14, 1908, William T. Phillips and Gertrude Livesay were married in a tiny ceremony performed by the Methodist minister. Gertrude's Baptist preacher had objected to such a speedy courtship and refused to sanction the marriage, a circumstance that dissuaded her not in the least. They spent a month traveling west, and wound up in Globe, Arizona, where Butch deposited Gertrude in a tiny apartment . . .

and then left her. He told her he had some unfinished business and promised to return. If he did not come back in six months, and, if she had not heard from him, she was to look up a lawyer in Wyoming by the name of Douglas Preston, and she would be taken care of. He pecked her on the cheek, swung up onto the train's vestibule, and disappeared into the waves of heat rising from the desert floor.

CHAPTER TWENTY-EIGHT

Back in Bolivia, Cassidy said nothing to Longabaugh and Ingersoll about getting married. Nor did he tell them his new moniker, William T. Phillips. He said only that he had been successful in preparing for his retirement from the outlaw life, which he was still planning to do, after one last big job.

His two comrades had not been idle in his absence. They had quit the Concordia Mine when word got out that Maxwell and Brown were, in reality, the bandits who had robbed two banks in Argentina. Percy Seibert could no longer provide them with cover, so Longabaugh packed up and rode out, Ingersoll at his side. They had hired on with a transportation company that hauled passengers and freight in mule-drawn coaches and wagons.

While waiting for Butch to return, Harry had taken it upon himself to educate his young *compadre* in the intricacies of a hold-up. Once in May and again in August, they had stolen payrolls being transported on the same rail line. Butch was taken aback at the brazenness of their actions, but Harry assured him they had gotten away clean — authorities believed the robberies had been committed by disgruntled rail workers. Moreover, it had served as a test of Ingersoll's mettle, and Harry proudly reported that the young renegade had performed well.

"The first job, I did all the talking . . . Frank was back-up. But the second time, damn if the kid didn't jump right in and run the show. Stuck his piece in the paymaster's ribs and, with this cool looking grin on his face, asked him real nice like to hand over the goods. Kind of reminded me of you, Butch."

Being as they were still partners, Harry cut him in on the take from the two jobs, and Butch began to wonder if they really needed to pull another one before he went home to Gertrude. He had more than enough money to tide him over, enough in fact to build his bride a brand new home with all the latest furniture, including a fancy piano. But Frank was onto another heist that he said would be the biggest yet. The kid was so excited about it, Butch decided what the hell, it'd be sort of fun to go out with a bang. Besides, being well-off was good, but being rich was better.

The job Frank had in mind was robbing the Banco Nacíonal in Tupiza, a small town near the Argentine border that was the headquarters for various mining companies extracting gold, silver, tin, antimony, lead, zinc, and bismuth from the surrounding *cerros*. A picturesque little city, its adobe buildings and dust-covered plaza gave scant indication of the enormous wealth that passed through its financial institutions. Although the town itself was situated in a verdant valley, it was surrounded by rough, forbidding country — red rock hills split by dry cañons where roads were virtually unknown. Perfect for an outlaw making a quick getaway.

But shortly after their arrival in Tupiza, a cavalry regiment moved in, and, worse luck, its officers took quarters in the same square as the bank. Not willing to risk a hold-up directly under the noses of Bolivia's most elite soldiers, the trio withdrew.

As they crossed the river, headed for the hills, they passed by a prosperous-looking *hacienda* built in the style of an Italianate villa. Harry let loose with a low whistle, impressed by the magnificent dwelling.

"That is Chajrahuasi," Ingersoll informed them, a note of envy in his voice.

"Chajra who?" asked Butch.

"Chajrahuasi. The home of the Aramayo family."

"Don't they own most of the mines around here?"

"Many of them, yes. *Señor* Aramayo operates all of the mines on Chorolque." Frank turned to look at the towering mountain looming on the horizon. "I have heard there are men digging for tin and bismuth at eighteen thousand feet on the slopes of that *cerro*."

Longabaugh whistled again. "Mighty tough at that altitude."

"The company has a large establishment for the refining of ores at Quechisla, about twenty-five leagues from here," Ingersoll went on. "My uncle used to work there before he took sick and died."

"They must be running payrolls all over the place," mused Harry. "Wonder what kind of escort they use."

"Most likely none at all," said Frank, half joking. "With a company that large, they figure no one would bother to steal from them because it is like stealing from your brother or your neighbor . . . everybody knows somebody who works for Aramayo, Francke y Compañía."

"Well, I don't know nobody," said Harry.

Frank caught his eye and quickly picked up on the older man's train of thought. "It is possible I have some cousins still working there, but they are not close enough to count."

"Hold on, now," interrupted Butch, leaning over to spit in the road. "Can't argue with your thinking . . . I'd hold up a payroll over a bank any day. But we ain't got much time to put this together, boys. Rainy season's almost here, and these roads, if you can call them that, are gonna be knee-high in mud. Don't see how we got enough time to scout it out proper."

"Hell, we could be ready in a week," Harry said scornfully.

"Enrique's right," said Frank, warming to the idea. "The Aramayo company is so big it has become lazy. It probably sends out its remittances on the same day every month, with little or no guard. I would bet on it."

"That right?" Butch eyed the kid with amusement. "Think you could find out in a week's time what the routine is . . . how much they carry, what routes they take?"

"No problem." Frank tossed a cocky look at his mentors.

"All right then." Butch reined up, and the others followed suit. "Ride back to Tupiza.

Get a room at the Hotel Términus and start scouting. Me and Enrique will hole up somewhere nearby and check in with you from time to time."

With a short nod, Ingersoll turned his horse and trotted back toward town. Harry cast his partner a doubtful look. "One man can't scout a job like that in just a week."

"Thought you said it'd be easy." Butch kneed his horse to a walk. Harry fell in beside him.

"Hell, I was just playing devil's advocate. Seeing if the kid would bite."

Butch smiled. "Took himself a mouthful, didn't he? Reckon it'll take closer to a month, and we'll have to help him out, but might as well see what he can do. Besides, he needs to learn the ropes if he's gonna make outlawing his career. You and me ain't gonna be around after this to call the shots."

Harry frowned and looked away. "You know, Butch, I ain't sure what my plans are from here on out."

Butch pondered that for a moment. After a while he said: "Thought you was gonna go back to the States and look for Etta."

"I just don't know."

Didn't know if he should go back? Didn't know if he should look for Etta? Didn't know if Etta still loved him? Butch supposed his partner probably meant all of those things by his answer. They rode along for a while, the creak of saddle leather and swishing of their horses' tails the only sounds.

Finally Harry confronted him. "Why are you going back, Butch? What can you find back home that you can't find here?"

Butch shrugged. "Reckon you just said it. It's home. It's where things feel right . . . where the seasons ain't backwards, and the people talk so's I can understand them. Where there's dollars and miles instead of *bolivianos* and leagues. Hell, I spend half my time down here just doing figuring in my head so I'll know how much something costs or how far away some place is. It's where. . . ." He sighed. "I'm just tired of feeling out of place." He'd been about to say — "It's where my wife is." — but, even now, he couldn't bring himself to tell his long-time friend about that. Anyway, to be perfectly honest, Gertrude was not any part of the reason he wanted to go home.

Harry shook his head, not satisfied with this response. Butch looked at him with narrowed eyes. "You tell me, then. Why don't you want to go home?"

" 'Cause it ain't home no longer," said Harry sadly. "It ain't like it was ten, fifteen years ago and never will be. There's too damn' many people, too damn' many rules. Suits me fine right here where progress" — he gave the word a nasty shading — "ain't intruded yet."

"Reckon a person's gotta change to keep up with the times, 'cause progress ain't gonna slow down for any man," Butch philosophized.

"I don't want to change," Harry muttered.

"Neither do I, friend. Given my druthers, I'd just as soon live the last forty years of my life pretty much like I lived the first forty. But it ain't gonna happen. Outlawing's for young men, like Frank, not for old codgers like you and me. All in all, I'd rather die in bed than at the point of a gun." Butch studied the scree-covered hills, marveling that such a desolate landscape contained such a lode of wealth.

Harry settled his hat lower on his head. "Me, I'm going out with guns blazing."

Butch smiled at his partner's theatrics. "Shit, you'll probably live to a hundred and die in the old folks' home."

Back in Tupiza, they had heard that the transportation company that employed them, when they weren't off on one of their jaunts, had the contract to move a gold dredge from one nearby mining outpost to another. Introducing themselves with yet another pair of aliases — Frank Smith for Longabaugh and George Lowe for Cassidy — they offered their assistance to the friendly British engineer in charge of the operation. Only too happy to gain the company of two able white men, several steps above the rest of his crew of criminals and half-castes, the engineer, A. G. Francis by name, welcomed them. For the next few weeks — Butch had been correct in his prediction that the scouting of the Aramayo company's payroll practices would take longer than seven days — the two of them helped Francis oversee the transporting of the huge dredge while one or the other, usually Butch, made frequent trips to Tupiza to check on Ingersoll's progress.

In the last week of October, very nearly the end of the dry season, Francis asked Longabaugh to accompany him to Tomahuaico, a small Spanish-built settlement a short distance away, to check on a stone dike that would prevent the coming rains from washing out their work site. A few days later, Cassidy, who had been in Tupiza, found them there. He and Longabaugh conferred late into the night.

The next morning, Cassidy asked Francis if he could borrow his big gray horse. Without asking why, the engineer said yes. To his dismay, both Smith and Lowe mounted up and rode away. Francis wondered if he'd ever see them, or his horse, again.

CHAPTER TWENTY-NINE

Carlos Peró, Aramayo's manager, squinted into the distance, trying to bring into focus two black dots on top of the far hillside. At first, he thought they were nothing more than clumps of cactus or yareta bushes. But then it seemed they moved.

"Mariano," he called to his teen-aged son, riding ahead of him. "Do you see anything at the top of the hill . . . up there?" He pointed north, in the direction that he, his son, and his servant were traveling.

Mariano followed the angle of his father's outstretched arm. "I do not see . . . wait! Something just moved."

"*Sí*. Did you see it, Gil?" Peró asked the servant.

"No, *señor*," replied Gil, after inspecting carefully the crest of the hill. "Only boulders and cactus."

Peró frowned. Surely he had seen two figures up there, although it was unlikely anybody else would be on this isolated trail, which was why, if there were people watching them, it was cause for concern. "Could you tell if they were mounted or on foot?" he said to his son.

"No, *papá*. It is too far away."

Peró grunted. "Keep an eye out. We do not want any trouble."

The trio plodded on, Mariano and Gil leading several pack mules, Peró walking in the rear. The early morning sun began to dissipate the chill in the air, and Peró was soon sweating under its warmth. Before long he would call a halt and switch places with Mariano — let the boy's strong young legs navigate these twisting gullies that snaked over and around the mountainside. Huaca Huañusca it was called. Dead cow hill. Looking up to the ridgeline, Peró understood how it got its name, for it resembled nothing so much as the spine and haunches of a cow's skeleton.

Yawning despite his exertions, the Aramayo manager slipped his canteen off one of the mule packs, swished water in his mouth, and spat into the dust. They had left Tupiza with the payroll yesterday morning, and had spent the night at the company's *hacienda* in Salo. He should have rested well in such relative comfort, but he never slept satisfactorily on one of these trips. For months now, he had been urging his superiors to take extra precautions when transporting cash shipments. He had pleaded for an armed guard, at the very least, to protect against all the unemployed *americanos del norte* with all their fancy weaponry who roamed the area. The small pistol he kept tucked in his waistband would do nothing to deter a well-armed bandit. They were sitting ducks. Sitting ducks on a dead cow.

Sighing tiredly, Peró took a final swig of water and hung the canteen back on the mule. Just up ahead, the trail curved around the hill. Time to rest the animals and switch with Mariano. Ahead of him, Mariano and Gil rounded the bend. He heard a shout of surprise. Seconds later, right on their heels, he saw the reason. Blocking the path were two *bandoleros,* aiming small-caliber Mauser carbines. At their hips hung Colt revolvers, and both carried small Browning revolvers tucked into their fully loaded cartridge belts. Peró jerked his hands into the air, not even considering going for his tiny pistol.

" 'Mornin'," said the smaller *bandolero* affably. "Appreciate it if you two would hop down."

Mariano and Gil dismounted and stood, shaking, by their mules.

"Step away," the thief ordered. Bandannas covered both of the outlaws' faces, and their hat brims were pulled down low so only their eyes were visible. The one who spoke had blue eyes, Peró noted. And he spoke English. Yankees. Just as he had predicted.

"That's it. Now, if you don't mind, we're gonna requisition some of your load."

Peró knew it was hopeless. "You may search us and take whatever you want, *señor*. We are at your mercy."

The gunman stuck his weapon in his pants and untied the straps on the manager's saddlebags. His companion moved forward to cover him, and Peró thought he heard a gun cock behind some rocks that formed a natural cave at the foot of the hill.

Finding nothing in Peró's bags, the thief moved on to Gil's and then Mariano's. "All right, friends," he said, his voice for the first time carrying a touch of menace, "it's here somewhere. Unload all this baggage. We ain't interested in your own money, nor your watches or jewelry. Just the payroll. Eighty thousand *bolivianos,* if I ain't mistaken."

Peró nodded to the others who began upacking the mules. As the canvas and leather bags were dropped to the ground, the outlaw searched them quickly, not bothering to unwrap all the packages. It appeared he knew exactly what he was looking for.

"*Señor*," Peró said carefully, "I am afraid you are mistaken. We are carrying only a small payroll today. Next week we are scheduled to carry a larger amount, something around eighty thousand *bolivianos*. But on this trip . . . only fifteen thousand."

The robber looked up sharply, his eyes, the only feature visible to Peró, dark with anger. Uttering an oath, he swung his glance to his partner standing guard. The gunman shook his head in dismay. Silently the leader turned back to his work, coming across a thick packet wrapped in homespun cloth. Without unwrapping it, he tossed it to his partner and pulled the gun out of his waistband.

"Unsaddle that mule," he ordered, gesturing to the dark brown animal that was Gil's mount. The servant leaped to obey.

Taking the mule and a brand new hemp rope, the pair of outlaws backed away, still pointing their weapons. "Don't try anything funny. We don't want no one to get hurt," said the leader. His three victims stood mute, no threat to anyone.

In the flash of an eye, the robbers disappeared deeper into the ravine from whence

Peró had earlier heard a gun cock. Now the sound of packs being refitted reached their ears, and then hoofs clattering on rocky soil. The noises receded and soon were gone.

"What should we do?" Mariano asked, his eyes wide with excitement.

His father removed his hat and wiped the sweat from his brow. From here, trails led in all directions. Impossible to tell exactly where the bandits had fled. "Repack the mules," he commanded. "We will continue toward Guadalupe. With any luck, we will meet someone on the road who can alert the authorities."

Cassidy led his outfit far enough away from the hold-up site to be out of earshot, then dismounted. Motioning Longabaugh and Ingersoll to stay with the mules, he scrambled up a cactus-studded slope and watched as the payroll party restowed their gear and continued on their way. Sliding back down the hill, he climbed aboard Francis's gray horse and headed south, his mouth set in a thin line of anger. Rage boiled within him, but now was not the time or place to give in to it. Right now, they must put miles between themselves and Huaca Huañusca.

Ingersoll hung back, eyes cast down. From

his hiding place within the ravine, where he had been holding the animals, he had heard everything — the manager confessing the payroll amounted to only fifteen thousand *bolivianos*, Santiago's muttered curse. His face burned with shame, for he was the one who had picked this date for the hold-up. His only hope was that the manager had been lying, and that, when the package was unwrapped, they would find the eighty thousand *bolivianos* that had been promised.

They rode for hours without speaking. According to plan, they halted as they approached the more populated outskirts of Tupiza, holing up in a well-hidden spot that Butch had scouted days before. Loosening their cinches, the men rested in the shade of a rare cottonwood and ate a cold meal. Ingersoll tried to act indifferent, but he was conscious of Santiago's cool blue gaze sizing him up.

Finally Cassidy retrieved the packet of money and folded back the layers of cloth. There was no need to count it — the small stack of bills told the story — but he picked up each bundle in turn and riffled through them with his thumb. He tossed the last batch of bills on the pile and sat back in disgust. "Fifteen thousand, just like the man said. How do you explain that, Frank?"

Ingersoll shrugged, trying to hide his embarrassment. "I cannot. My information was that this remittance would be in the amount of eighty thousand *bolivianos*. Everything else my source told me was correct . . . the route they would take, who would escort it, even how the money would be packaged. I do not know what happened."

"That won't wash, kid," Harry threatened.

Frank held out his hands. "I do not know what else to say."

"An apology might be a good place to start," said Cassidy, smooth as steel.

Frank bristled. "I will not apologize for what is not my fault. The man told me yesterday, November Third, was the day of the largest transport. It is his mistake, not mine."

"We trusted you, kid. This was the money we was gonna retire on. Now look what we got." Cassidy kicked at the pile of money. "Five thousand apiece. That ain't hardly enough to pay my bar bill for a year."

Ingersoll came to his feet, his black eyes snapping with injured pride. "Without me you would have nothing. Granted, it is not as much as I was told, but it is still a goodly sum."

Cassidy snorted. "It ain't enough to make it worth the risk involved. I don't see as we've got a damned thing to thank you for, kid. First off, you brought us to a town that was crawling with soldiers, then you got the wrong day for the robbery. I've got a mind to shoot you just to put you out of your ignorant misery!"

Ingersoll grabbed for his gun even though Butch had made no move for his own weapon. He found himself staring down the barrel of Longabaugh's six-shooter.

"Don't be stupid," Harry warned.

"Too late," Cassidy grumbled.

Such insults from men who he thought were his *compadres* were too much for Ingersoll to bear. He jammed his gun back in its holster and stalked over to his horse, yanking roughly on the cinch strap. "Keep the god-damned money. I want no part of it, or you." Swinging into the saddle, he turned his horse sharply and rode away, following the dry riverbed back the way they had come.

"Looks like he's headed for trouble," said Harry dryly. "Reckon we should let him go?"

"He'll be back. He ain't gonna walk away from his five thousand fuckin' *bolivianos*." Adjusting his saddlebags, Butch leaned back and closed his eyes, struggling to get over his bitterness at this turn of events. It wasn't so bad, he told himself. Sure, he had wanted to score big on his last job, but he didn't really need the money. Still, it stuck in his craw because he knew he had no one to blame but himself. He had trusted an inexperienced kid with too many important details. Now, instead of going out with a bang, he was leaving the outlaw life with a whimper.

The two men rested until nightfall, then continued on to Tomahuaico, arriving shortly after midnight. They circled the small white house that was A. G. Francis's quarters to make certain it was not being watched. The little outpost was quiet, its adobe shacks reflecting the bright starlight of high altitude. Their approach, quiet as it was, alerted Francis's dog whose barking roused its master from where he had been sleeping in a hammock on the verandah.

"¿Quiénes son?" came a whispered query.

Butch rode up to the porch and dropped to the ground. "Don't you know your old horse in the dark, kid?"

"Lowe! You gave me a fright, sneaking up like that. What are you doing here at this hour? Is that Smith with you?"

"Keep it down, kid," shushed Harry. "Yeah, it's me. Come help us unload and we'll tell you all about it."

The two men unsaddled and hobbled the

horses, then carried some of the bags into the house. Longabaugh went directly to the cupboard where the whisky was kept. Cassidy, uncharacteristically silent, entered the single bedroom and closed the door behind him.

"Something wrong with George?" asked Francis.

"He ain't feeling too good. What've you got to eat around here?"

While Francis set out a meal of sorts, the outlaw told him what they'd been up to since arriving in Tupiza. The young engineer turned pale, and his eyes went wide as the story progressed. Finally Longabaugh ran out of words, about the same time the whisky bottle came up dry. He got to his feet, groaning. "Reckon I oughta turn in. Got a full day in the saddle tomorrow." He rested his hand suggestively on the gun at his hip. "Don't even think of turning us in, kid. Somebody'll keep watch all night long. You go anywhere, you'll be asking for trouble. G'night now." He closed the bedroom door behind him.

Stunned and scared, Francis stumbled back to the hammock. Were there other members of the outlaw gang out there watching as Smith had implied? For a long time, the engineer lay awake, straining his ears for any suspicious sound, but all he heard was the occasional sighs and tail twitchings of his dog on the floor beside him. Around dawn, he fell into a restless sleep.

The two bandits were up first the next morning. Seemingly in no hurry, they washed themselves and tended to their animals. Cassidy appeared less tense than he had the previous night, but he still had little to say. They sent Francis out into the neighborhood to see if news of the robbery had spread. He reported back that all was quiet.

Mid-morning the three men were seated on the verandah, taking a break from chores, when a man they recognized as one of Francis's workers rode up, his horse lathered. The engineer bolted to his feet. Smith and Lowe regarded the newcomer with interest but not alarm.

"You better get out of here, boys . . . they're saddling up a hundred men to come after you!" the half-breed cried.

Longabaugh slowly lowered his chair legs to the floor. "Tell us what you know."

The informant dismounted and accepted a cup of water from Francis. "I've just come from Tupiza," he explained, still breathing hard. "News of the hold-up is all over town. Parties of soldiers using Indian trackers have been out all night, searching. Early this morning, I heard that tracks had been found, and the soldiers began mustering in the plaza. I borrowed the fastest horse I could find to come warn you."

"How did you know we was here?" asked Longabaugh. Neither outlaw had moved, but the man couldn't help noticing the proximity of their hands to the guns at their waists.

"I saw you ride in last night," he said, his voice trembling. "It seemed strange, you getting here so late, and . . . well, there have been rumors about you two ever since you came here." He stole a glance at Francis who appeared dumbfounded. "I decided to go to Tupiza to find out what happened. I will admit the thought occurred to me that I could turn you in if there was a reward offered. But when I found out the crime was having relieved Carlos Peró of a payroll headed for Quechisla" — a sly smile played on the man's face — "then I knew I could not turn you in. I have no sympathy for the Aramayo company. They have not been good to my family. So I have galloped all the way here to warn you. You must hurry, *señores* . . . the soldiers cannot be very far away."

The outlaws thanked the man for bringing

them this information, paid him a small reward, and sent him away. Longabaugh stood and stretched. "You might tell that boy of yours to get breakfast ready quickly, will you, kid?" he said to Francis. "I suppose we had better be moving."

While his guests repacked their gear, Francis helped the kitchen boy scramble eggs and fry sausages. When the food was ready, Cassidy and Longabaugh filled their plates and ate heartily. The engineer picked at his meal, expecting to hear a regiment of soldiers ride into the yard at any moment. Would they accuse him of harboring dangerous criminals? Would he even get a chance to explain his position? Time dragged as he waited for the bandits to finish eating and be on their way.

"Say, kid," said Longabaugh, stuffing the last bite of biscuit into his mouth, "you better saddle up and come with us."

Francis's fork clattered to his plate. "Come with you?"

"That's right. We're feeling the need for some company."

It was not an invitation that could be refused. Francis prepared his mount, and shortly the three of them headed up the riverbed, Cassidy astride the gray horse leading the stolen pack mule, Longabaugh and the engineer bringing up the rear.

Francis kept stealing looks over his shoulder, scanning the hilltops for any sign of the army. He rightly figured the two men with whom he rode posed no threat; the danger would come from enthusiastic soldiers descending upon them with guns afire. Likely they would shoot first, ask questions later. He gave Longabaugh a nervous glance. "Suppose the soldiers arrive. What are you going to do about it?"

Longabaugh grinned. "Why, we'll just sit down behind a rock and get to work."

Francis shuddered inwardly. They rode on, the sun high overhead. The engineer wondered where they were taking him and inquired whether Argentina was their destination.

"Not any more," said the outlaw. "We didn't expect the news to get out this quickly. Likely the border patrols have been notified. You're gonna guide us to Estarca, and, from there, we're gonna make for Uyuni and up north again. There's a place there we can lie low for a while."

"I think you're foolish," said Francis primly.

Longabaugh chuckled. "Oh, they won't get us."

Very soon, they turned off the main bed of

the river, and Francis led them through narrow, twisting cañons to the small Indian pueblo of Estarca. On the outskirts of the village, they sent the engineer ahead to scout for danger. He returned promptly and reported that no news of the hold-up had yet reached the tiny settlement. They next asked him to make arrangements for a place to stay the night, which he did at the home of a widow lady where he had previously lodged on many occasions. All three men slept in the same room, the two robbers sharing a bed, and Francis on a mattress on the floor.

At daybreak, Cassidy shook the young man awake and sent him into town for provisions. When he returned, the horses were saddled and the stolen mule packed and ready to go. The trio rode out, making a U-turn and heading back north toward Uyuni.

After an hour or so, Cassidy pulled up and dismounted. "This is where we part," he said, walking back toward the others. "Looks like the trail's pretty easy to follow from here on out."

Francis looked down in surprise. "You mean, I can go now?"

"That's right, kid," said Longabaugh. "Reckon you don't want to come no farther with us. If you meet those soldiers, tell them you passed us on the road to the Argentine."

"Good luck," said Francis, surprising himself.

Shaking hands all around, the bandits departed, kicking up dust in their wake. The young engineer watched them until they rounded a bend in the valley and were out of sight. With a sigh of regret or relief, he wasn't sure which, he turned his horse and headed back to Tomahuaico.

Cassidy and Longabaugh continued on, stopping briefly in the town of Cucho to refresh themselves and then, turning slightly west, headed toward a little village called San Vicente where they intended to stop for the night.

Butch was still not himself, still upset with the way things were playing out. If they'd kept to the original plan, they'd be in Argentina by now, but Carlos Peró had managed to get the word out quicker than they'd anticipated. Now, it was too dangerous to attempt a border crossing. Not only that, by now they had expected to be safely in their warm hide-out, not still on the road. They had not, therefore, brought cold weather gear with them, which made camping at fourteen thousand feet impossible. So far, they had been able to find shelter in small, out-of-the-way villages, but even those places would soon be on the look-out for the daring *gringos bandoleros*. These would all be acceptable risks if they had made off with the larger payroll, but Butch couldn't help agreeing with Francis that they were foolish for having placed their lives in danger for a measly fifteen thousand *bolivianos*.

The two partners rode silently, commenting only when necessary about the various twists and turns in the trail. Longabaugh sensed his friend's turmoil, guessed that the blame for bringing Frank Ingersoll into their midst was being laid at his feet. Pointless to remind him that Butch had been the one to send the kid off to Tupiza alone to scout the Aramayo job.

Sunk in their individual thoughts, they nevertheless remained alert, constantly scanning the horizon for signs of pursuit. They had just paused to rest their horses when Butch caught the sound of a rider coming up behind them. Cover was slim along the barren trail — the best they could do was crouch beside their mounts, guns drawn. The rider stopped well out of range and waved his hat.

"It's Ingersoll," said Harry.

They straightened up as their erstwhile partner trotted forward.

"Howdy, boys! How's tricks?" Grinning atop his prancing horse, Ingersoll appeared to have put aside the hard feelings of the previous day.

Cassidy jammed his gun back in his holster and eyed him coldly. "Figured you'd be back. Five thousand *bolivianos* is a lot of money to small fry like you. Cash is in that bag on the Aramayo mule. Take your share and get out of here."

"I did not come back just for the money," protested Frank, his grin fading. "I want to join up with you again . . . make amends for my mistake."

"Thanks, but you already done enough. Here's your money." Butch pulled out the packet and tossed it on the ground. "Now get."

"Wait a minute," Harry broke in. "Ain't you being a mite hasty, Butch? The kid admitted he was wrong . . . wants to make it up. What more can he do?"

"Quit tracking us, for starters. Shit, he's such a greenhorn, he's probably got the entire Bolivian army on his tail. There's probably a thousand soldiers right over the hill yonder, taking a bead on us as we speak. Am I right, kid? Or did it possibly occur to you to hide your sign along the way to make sure you wasn't followed?" Cassidy was nearly shouting now, his anger reeling out of control.

"No one followed me," Ingersoll insisted, although his voice lacked certainty.

"We're wasting time here," growled Harry, picking up the money and stuffing it in his saddlebag. "Let's go." He swung up and looked down at his partner expectantly.

Butch closed his eyes and rubbed his forehead, trying to think. Everything had felt wrong from the get-go, and the kid's showing up only made things worse. Even if the youngster was right that he had not been followed, odds were Francis had alerted authorities to their whereabouts. Harry had vouched for the engineer's loyalty, but the fear and nervousness on the man's face had been obvious. If they had counted him as a friend before, likely that had changed once they kidnapped him.

He perused the landscape once more, and then turned to the two mounted men. "I think we should split up."

Harry frowned, losing his patience. "Ain't no need. Once the army reaches Tomahuaico, Francis'll point them towards the border."

"So you say." His mind made up, Butch

snagged a stirrup and settled aboard the big gray.

"We've been partners for over ten years," Harry pointed out, "and you ain't never doubted me yet."

"It ain't you I'm doubting. It's everything else about this god-damned job. Things ain't going down right. We got a better chance of slipping by them soldiers if we split up."

Resentment flared from Harry's deep-set eyes. "Ain't that just like you? Always got to call the shots. Always know better than everybody else. Well, I ain't buying it this time. I say we're better off sticking together."

"Suit yourself." Butch touched the reins to his horse's neck and trotted off, headed due west.

"Son-of-a-bitch."

Ingersoll watched the retreating outlaw with a small smile of satisfaction. "He did not take his share of the money."

Harry glared at Ingersoll, then grabbed the lead rope of the Aramayo mule and started forward.

"Where are we going?" asked Ingersoll.

"San Vicente."

CHAPTER THIRTY

When Butch left Gertrude in Arizona, he had promised to return within six months. That deadline was rapidly approaching. The fastest route home was to cross over into Chile and pick up a steamer headed north. Instead, he circled around Uyuni and rode into Santa Cruz.

Taking a cheap room well off the main thoroughfares, he spent his days in bed with Rosita and his nights in bars with a bottle of booze. He aimed for numbness, and, thanks to those two palliatives, he largely achieved it.

One afternoon, he struggled out of a dream-filled sleep to find himself soaked in sweat and breathing hard. Rosita brought a cool cloth and bathed his forehead, crooning words of comfort. He closed his eyes and let her minister to him. "Bad dream, I guess."

The girl's face filled with concern. "It is like this always when you sleep. You twist and turn, utter words I cannot understand. It is as though the devil was bargaining for your soul."

He caught her wrist and looked into her black eyes, so wise for one so young. "The devil won my soul the day I was born," he whispered. Kissing the palm of her hand, he drew her close, staring beyond her at the light filtering through the slatted shutters.

That night, he ate alone in a small café. At the table next to him, a well-dressed gentleman finished his meal, paid his bill, and left. Butch noticed the man had left behind a newspaper. Up to now, the outlaw had purposely avoided reading the papers, not really caring if the law found him or not. But it was time to pull his head out of the sand.

The paper was from Oruro, a large mining center situated on the high plateaus to the west. Although his Spanish was still not terribly good, the following headline caught and held his attention: *Aramayo Bandidos Asesinados en una Balacera.*

He looked away, his face twisted in pain. "Etta," he breathed.

After a moment, he read on, translating enough Spanish to get the gist of the story.

A posse of policemen tracked the bandits to San Vicente where they were resting for the night. Upon seeing the patrol approaching, the thieves went for their guns, resolved to battle heroically for the stolen money. And without further notice, the bandits unleashed a veritable hail of bullets at their pursuers, who answered with a blaze of fire as if hunting wild animals. The fight was intense; a tremendous din and the furious shouting of the bandits and the police were all that could be heard. In the end, after a battle of more than an hour, the bandits fell lifeless, their bodies riddled with bullets. One policeman died, and two others were wounded. The stolen shipment was found beside the bodies of the bandits, whose faces were frozen in rage, and whose lips formed a last grimace of hate. The names and nationalities of these two birds so fiercely bound together are not yet known.

Butch folded the paper carefully and laid it on the table. He rose and walked out into the starlit night. At the livery stable, he left a note instructing the proprietor to contact A. G. Francis in Tomahuaico and tell him his horse was in Santa Cruz. Then he walked to the train station and bought a ticket for home.

EPILOGUE

1957

The smell of freshly baked bread still filled Mary Harris's kitchen although it had long ago gone dark outside. Louisa lifted her head from her arms folded on the table and looked at her grandmother with curiosity. "Is that the end of the story?"

Smiling sadly, the old woman reached across and brushed the hair from Louisa's forehead. "Yes, dear. That's the end of the story."

"But what happened to Butch? Did he go back to Gertrude? Did they have any children? Did he ever find Etta?"

Mary sighed, tired with the telling of a tale in which there were no happy endings. "Butch and Gertrude stayed together for many years. They adopted a son. But by his own admission, he wasn't a very good husband or father. He tried to be, and there were some good times, or so he told my mother. But he was never truly content in his new life."

"So he saw your mother again?"

"Yes, when they were both very old, they met by a lake up in the Wind River mountains. That's where he told her everything I've just told you. He wanted them to spend the rest of their days together . . . try to redeem the years they had lost. But my mother said no. She had built her own life, perhaps one as unhappy as his, but a life that was not dependent on others, and she said she was too old to start over. So they parted. They exchanged a few letters, but that was it. Shortly after that, he got cancer, and his wife couldn't care for him, so she put him in the county sanitarium. He died at seventy-one, all alone."

"How sad," murmured Louisa, a tear trickling down her smooth cheek.

Mary shrugged. "Some would say you reap what you sow. Though I like to think when he reached those pearly gates, he was let in without too much fuss. Butch Cassidy committed many a sin in his lifetime, but he was not an evil man."

"What about Etta?"

"He tried for a while to find her to tell her about Harry and to see if she needed money or help of any kind. But he never did. She disappeared as though she'd never existed. He told my mother he wasn't too worried about her, though. Said if there was ever a woman who could make it on her own, it was Etta Place." The old woman smiled. "Said it was his curse in life to fall in love with women who could live without him easier than they could live with him."

"So Butch Cassidy was my great-grandfather," sighed the little girl, her face cupped in her hands. "I wish I could have known him."

Mary rose and began to cut thick slices of warm bread. "Now you know the legend, anyway. Let that be enough. I guess the real man will always be unknown."

ACKNOWLEDGMENTS

Many thanks to Soraya Mansour for her assistance with the Spanish words and phrases used in this book. Thanks also to the staff at the Utah History Information Center for its prompt and helpful replies to my somewhat obscure queries. Finally I am grateful to all the Butch Cassidy historians, particularly Anne Meadows and Dan Buck, Richard Patterson, and Larry Pointer. Without their dedication to rooting out the facts, the writer of historical fiction would not have a story to tell.

Venezuela

Colombia

Guianas

Ecua-
dor

Peru

Brazil

* La Paz
Bolivia
* Concordia   * Santa Cruz
Mine
* San Vicente
* Huaca Huañusca
Chile   Para-
* Antofagasta   guay

Uru-
guay

* Valparaiso   * Villa   Buenos
Mercedes   Aires
Argentina

* Lake Nahuel
Huapi
* Cholila

About the Author

Raised in the Midwest, Suzanne Lyon moved to Colorado at seventeen to attend The Colorado College. She worked as a lawyer for, among others, the National Park Service before turning her talents to writing. Lured by the landscapes and legends of the West, Lyon's interest is in Western historical fiction. She began the story of Butch Cassidy in her first novel, *Bandit Invincible: Butch Cassidy* (Five Star Westerns, 1999). With *Lady Buckaroo* (Five Star Westerns, 2000) she re-created the world of rodeo riders from the woman's point of view. She resides near Denver with her husband and two children.

The employees of Thorndike Press hope you have enjoyed this Large Print book. All our Thorndike and Wheeler Large Print titles are designed for easy reading, and all our books are made to last. Other Thorndike Press Large Print books are available at your library, through selected bookstores, or directly from us.

For information about titles, please call:

(800) 223-1244

or visit our Web site at:

www.gale.com/thorndike
www.gale.com/wheeler

To share your comments, please write:

Publisher
Thorndike Press
295 Kennedy Memorial Drive
Waterville, ME 04901